Shradha Ghale lives in Kathmandu. She has reported widely on contemporary social and political issues of Nepal. This is her first novel.

The
Wayward
Daughter

A Kathmandu Story

SHRADHA GHALE

SPEAKING
TIGER

SPEAKING TIGER PUBLISHING PVT. LTD
4381/4, Ansari Road, Daryaganj
New Delhi 110002

Copyright © Shradha Ghale 2018
Frst published in India by Speaking Tiger 2018

ISBN: 978-93-88326-08-7
eISBN: 978-93-88070-59-1

10 9 8 7 6 5 4 3 2 1

Printed at Sanat Printers, Kundli

Prologue

A neighbour returned from Kathmandu with happy news for Gajey's mother: her youngest son Gajey was going to become a father soon. Next day she picked up his birth chart and went to see Mangal Bajey, the astrologer-priest and moneylender whose words were regarded as heavenly commands in Lungla. She sat in the front-yard of his house, at a respectful distance from the threshold, careful not to touch the masyaura balls spread out to dry in the sun (even though as a Tamule, she was technically allowed to touch them). After poring over the birth chart and doing several rounds of esoteric calculations, Mangal Bajey recommended doing a special puja for the baby's mother. "If you do it within the next month," he said, "she will almost certainly bring you a grandson." At hearing this Gajey's mother nearly fainted from joy.

It was monsoon. The heavy rains had made the trails steep and slippery. The Arun had swollen over its banks and devoured a boy who'd gone fishing in the neighbouring village. Landslides had destroyed fields and uprooted trees, and cascades of mud and rocks appeared like wounds on the green hillsides. Higher up on the arid slopes, a hut belonging to a Sarki family had caved in, killing mother and child. But this did not deter Gajey's mother. "I must go," she said, ignoring the pleas of her oldest son Tikaram. "Even if I die, it will have been for the sake of my grandson."

A young porter was hired to transport her in a carrier fashioned out of a coarsely woven bamboo doko. When all was ready, the doko was placed on the boy's back, supported by a jute namlo that ran across his forehead. Gajey's mother squeezed herself into the doko and sat facing backwards. The boy bent over, clutched the namlo with both hands and said, "Amai, hold on tight, off we go!" Gajey's mother's heart gave a leap.

Not that she had ever liked Kathmandu, that drab and distant city without a heart. She loved Gajey, the blessed boy whose success had rubbed off on his entire community, but having lived in her own homestead all her life, she could never feel completely at ease in his rented flat. The place was ill-suited for a strict vegetarian like her, one who had forsaken even garlic and onion. That lingering smell of eggs and meat, filthy hen cooked in pungent spices—the stink assaulted her senses even in her sleep, giving her nightmares. As if that was not enough, his kitchen was right opposite the bathroom. The very thought of eating, praying and defecating under the same roof turned her stomach. To crown it all, her daughter-in-law was a pig-eating Limbuni. Try as she might, Gajey's mother could never suppress that queasy feeling while swallowing the food cooked by her. Forget giving up pork, that Limbuni would not even bother using a separate ladle to stir her dal, or a separate knife to chop her vegetables. Even the purest-looking meal she served was no doubt contaminated.

But let her bring us a little baby boy this time and I shall forgive her all her flaws, she thought as she sat doubled up in the doko, gazing towards the fields and forests they had left behind. The bamboo splits poked her back and her shrivelled frame rocked painfully as the porter rushed onwards. Despite Tikaram's warnings, the boy moved recklessly, choosing the shorter, vertical trails over the longer, winding paths. One false step would have sent him and his human cargo hurtling down the hillside. "Amai, hold tight," he said, adjusting the namlo on his sweaty forehead. Gajey's mother braced herself for the jolt as he leapt from one mossy rock to another, bending his rubber slippers to gain a foothold. "Amai, watch out," he warned as he approached an overhanging branch that she'd quickly have to duck. On the treeless slopes down which rocks came tumbling, the boy ran so fast she shut her eyes and called upon her gods. He carried her through the wet forests ringing with the sounds of cicadas, through still, waterlogged paddy fields that mirrored the skies like enormous sheets of glass, through quiet settlements where toddlers played in the dirt and babies slept unattended in cloth cradles, their parents and siblings away at the fields. Several times they crossed paths with porters going uphill, their bodies bent under their loads, their dokos filled with salt, sugar, oil, flour, pots and pans, clothing and footwear brought all the way from Dharan. At sundown they reached the great green valley of Tumlingtar and stayed at a relative's house. Next morning when she went to the airport—a grassy strip with a two-room concrete shed—Gajey's mother found out that her seat on the plane had been given, with no warning, explanation or apology, to the nephew of the chief district officer. For the next two days, flights were cancelled due to rain. She flew on the fourth day on a wobbly Twin Otter of Royal Nepal Airlines, vomiting two bagsful on the half-hour flight.

~

Premkala, pale, thin and nauseous, welcomed her mother-in-law with a stiff smile. Not only was the old lady's head full of superstitious claptrap, she also had an annoying habit of throwing petty tantrums through her son. "Listen, did you put onions in Ama's dal? She said she could smell them," Tamule ji would gently admonish Premkala after closing the door at night. "Couldn't you heat the water properly? Ama said she had to bathe in cold water."

A week after she arrived in Kathmandu, Premkala's mother-in-law organized an elaborate puja for her. Tamule ji bought all the necessary paraphernalia and invited a Bahun priest to officiate the ceremony. The pointless frenzy exasperated Premkala but she did not complain. After all her mother-in-law had risked her life and limb for the occasion. At her request Premkala wore a red sari even though she associated red saris with high-caste women steeped in oppressive traditions. She sat facing east on her designated spot

viii | THE WAYWARD DAUGHTER

with her husband beside her, enduring the din of the conch shell and smoke from the holy fire. With difficulty she swallowed the sanctified curds that her husband was made to feed her. The ordeal was almost over when her mother-in-law knelt down before her and started putting tika on her forehead. "My dear buhari," she said, "may you give birth to a ruddy, healthy little boy. A son is a son after all. He'll gather his father's ashes when the time comes, he'll carry on the lineage, he'll free his ancestors from sins." Premkala clenched her jaws.

During her trip to Lungla soon after her marriage, Premkala had seen elderly Tamule women offer blessings to Sita bhauju, her older sister-in-law. "Buhari, may you learn to look after the house. May you gain the strength to lift a full pail without moaning. May you bring luck and happiness to your husband, in-laws, children. May you learn to tolerate and forgive those who wrong you." To Premkala's dismay, Sita bhauju had bowed her head and accepted their 'blessings' without a murmur of protest.

"What else can I wish for, buhari," her mother-in-law went on, filling up Premkala's entire forehead with the rice and vermilion mixture. "I'm a setting sun. I'll glance at my grandson's face and leave this world, then my soul will rest in peace." Premkala looked at her husband and expressed her displeasure with a slight movement of her eyebrow. "Mother, that's enough," Tamule ji said in a jesting tone, but the old woman carried on. "Buhari, our village priest said you should fast on Mondays. Shiva Bhagwan is the giver of male progeny."

Premkala's patience gave out. "Ama, I don't care if I have a son or a daughter," she said. "Please spare me such blessings, I'm not Sita bhauju." She got up from the consecrated rug and stalked out of the room, leaving her mother-in-law's mouth hanging wide open. The corner of her lower lip twitched uncontrollably. Her wrinkled, red-smeared hand shook as though she had a nerve disorder. "Hey Bhagwan," she whimpered, "what have I done to deserve this?"

"Don't feel bad, Ama," Tamule ji said. "She's unwell. The doctor said mood swings are normal in this state."

Seven months later, when news reached Lungla that Gajey's wife had given birth to a baby girl, the entire Tamule family knew who was to blame. As if to add insult to injury, that Limbuni's mother had named the baby after a Limbu goddess—Sumnima, the wife of the legendary king Paruhang.

1

It was just another Monday morning. Sumnima searched the cupboards, ransacked the drawers and overturned the laundry pile. She could not find her socks. They had been hanging on the verandah until Boju, her maternal grandmother, removed them and strung fresh corncobs. Boju's harvests took up every last space in the house. She hung onion and garlic across the verandah, displayed pumpkins on the roof, and spread grains and fermented vegetables out in the yard, making their two-storey concrete house look like a farmstead all year around.

'Boju, you better find them,' Sumnima fumed. Numa, her younger sister, had already left for the bus stop. Boju rummaged through the piles of scrap that jostled for space in her room. Empty bottles and cans, expired medicines, blunt knives, dead batteries, leftover wool and fabrics, packaging boxes, old invitation cards, frayed toothbrushes, birthday candles, and used wrapping papers salvaged from her granddaughters' wasteful hands. From among these odds and ends she fished out a pair of socks she had saved for a day like this. They were worn, overstretched and had holes in the toes, but Sumnima had no choice. The bus would arrive any minute. She clamped the holes between her toes and buckled her shoes. 'Come eat quickly,' her mother called from the kitchen, but Sumnima picked up her bag, threw the door open and broke into a run. She didn't even say bye to her father, who stood in the front yard washing his motorcycle. He opened his mouth to offer her a ride but stopped. The bike was drenched with water and soapsuds. Besides Sumnima wouldn't want her friends to know her father drove a motorcycle. 'So you want a car, haina?' he often teased her. 'It won't fit into our lane. Why don't we get you a helicopter?'

Bhaisichaur had yet to get a motor road. Located outside the ring road, on the fringe of the city, the neighbourhood had a distant, rural feel. The vast farmlands turned from green to gold to brown as the seasons changed, and on rainy days the air smelled of grass, earth and cowdung. Bramble thickets lined the narrow dirt paths. All morning birds chirped and the bell chimed at the nearby temple. The lowing of a cow, the crowing of a rooster, or the trilling of a bicycle bell broke the afternoon silence. Children played among grazing cows on the open fields that stretched all the way to the ring road. Their shouts and laughter rang through the air and reminded Sumnima of a poem in her fifth-grade textbook.

Such, such were the joys
When we all girls and boys
In our youth time were seen
On the Echoing Green

Sumnima did not know the children who played on those fields, those shabby little kids who rarely changed out of their school uniforms. Every year on the day of Lakshmi Puja they came to sing bhailo at the Tamule house. Sumnima and Numa would watch from the window as they stood on their brightly lit front yard and chanted the festival chorus at the top of their lungs: *Eh yo ghar katro/ Bhaili ram/ eh Singha Durbar jatro/ Bhaili ram.* These lines always made Sumnima smile. Although unremarkable compared to the homes of her classmates, their yellow, two-storey dwelling stood out prominently among the small, cement-grey houses in Bhaisichaur. It boasted an entrance door carved with images of Hindu deities, ornamental railings on the terrace and verandah, and a sloping side-roof with a T-shaped television antenna, the only one in Bhaisichaur. A hodgepodge of flowers and vegetables grew in the small front garden. On the remaining land Boju grew corn, soybeans and mustard with the help of neighbours and relatives, much to the displeasure of Sumnima, who would have preferred a trimmed lawn or a clean, concrete yard. But it was the rear of the house that most offended Sumnima's eye—the washing area layered with green slime, the old buckets and tubs around the hand-pump, the wire-mesh coop that stank of chicken shit, and the tin shed filled with junk. The squalid picture was completed by a tin-roofed latrine meant for hired workers, servants and village relatives to whom the indoor bathroom was off-limits.

'If you don't like it, go build your own,' Tamule ji would scold his daughter. To him, the two-storey house was a dream cast in concrete, a testament to his status as a self-made man, a mark of his arrival—or perhaps his beginning—in a city that had goaded him on since he landed there as a penniless boy from Lungla. Throughout his college years, he had lived in a dank little room of a mud-brick house in Kasai Tol, a butcher-caste quarter in the old part of Kathmandu. After he married Premkala, his landlady's daughter, the couple had moved house many times, progressing from a single room to double rooms to a multiple-room flat as their family grew and relatives from Lungla began seeking shelter under their roof. The last place they rented was near the airport. The roar of aeroplanes shook their walls and cut off their conversations. The landlord rationed water and electricity and monitored their comings and goings.

Now, with a house of his own and a brand-new motorcycle, Tamule ji stood on different ground. He was the only man in Bhaisichaur who went on daily morning walks in a tracksuit and sneakers, news blaring from a handheld transistor. His wife had a B.Ed degree and his daughters went to a school famous for teaching 'good English'. His neighbours paid him the respect warranted to an informed and established man, seeking his advice on finding the right doctor or choosing a course of study for their children. If a pipe leaked or a piece of furniture had to be moved in his house, he only had to look out of the window and holler, and they'd roll up their sleeves and come running through the fields.

~

Across the cornfields and the open playground, on the ring road lined with purple jacaranda trees, the bus stood honking like a maddened beast. Sumnima jumped over a barbed wire fence and raced along the fields. Long wet grass tickled her calves; mud spattered her skirt; her tiffin carrier rattled in her bag. In the distance she could see the conductor flailing his arm, motioning her to run faster. She ran across the open playground, jumping over puddles and cowdung, and arrived at the stop sweating and panting. 'Can't you come on time?' the conductor barked. 'You kept the whole bus waiting.' Sumnima blushed. She wiped her shoes on the grass and hopped on board. 'Sorry I'm late,' she said to no one in particular. Two senior girls glared at her. In the seat behind them sat Numa, looking annoyed and worried. She removed her bag from the seat and gestured Sumnima to sit beside her, but Sumnima huffily walked past her and stood near a window.

The bus rolled along. Outside, raindrops hung on the power lines. Raindrops studded the rusty spikes of a barbed wire fence along the cornfield. The rain had stripped the jacaranda trees and paved the roadsides purple. The limp, wet flowers were still falling, in ones and twos. They fell on the head of a passerby, on the hood of a parked taxi, on the tarpaulin roof of a tea shack where men sat drinking tea. The bus turned and drove past houses and low-rise buildings, steel water tanks glinting on the rooftops. At the army barracks, soldiers stood on a shimmering wet field ready for their exercise. The rain had washed the grimy bus park where Sumnima's mother daily boarded a tempo to work. Today she would be taking a taxi because she had a job interview at a travel agency. Sumnima hoped she would get the job and stop teaching at the obscure little primary school.

A sudden shriek of laughter made her turn around. The two senior girls came scrambling towards the window, elbowed her aside and waved at a group of boys near the gates of St Francis School. The smell of their sweat and body spray enveloped Sumnima. 'Excuse me,' she said, to no avail. She felt like screaming out the Nepali expletives she had picked up from Boju, but all she did was frown and roll her eyes.

~

Rhododendron Girls High School had an unrivalled reputation in town. The high, creeper-covered walls guarded a property that made a lasting impression on first-time visitors. Tall buildings freshly painted each year, spacious classrooms, a grand auditorium with life-size portraits of royal family members, and a sports field with a large grass pitch and an athletics track. Trimmed hedgerows bordered the paths where girls strolled during lunch break, chatting in broken English. Those found speaking in Nepali were subject to a five-rupee fine. Every year during admission season, ambitious parents in Kathmandu arranged coaching classes to drill their six-year-olds for the entrance exam. The queue for admission forms snaked around the main building and spilled out onto the street. But passing the exam alone did not guarantee admission. One also needed *source-force*, or extreme good luck.

The students belonged to three broad categories. The first set, those who gave the school an air of exclusiveness, consisted of a few royal highnesses and their close and distant relatives, most of them associated with the Royal Nepal Army. The second set came from families of royalist politicians and bureaucrats as well as prominent doctors, businessmen and bankers. Between the two sets of families they owned all five-star hotels, private hospitals, private schools, banks and distilleries in Kathmandu. The rest of the students came from middling families and had made it through sheer persistence and dumb luck. The Tamule sisters fell into this category. Their father may have been the pride of his birth village and a well-known figure in Bhaisichaur, but he was an everyman compared to the valued patrons of Rhododendron. An assistant manager at the electricity corporation, he could neither pull strings nor push the authorities. Their mother taught at a primary school that Sumnima was hesitant to mention in her 'My Mother' essays. Often during his morning puja, their father thanked his pitri for their good fortune.

~

At the sound of the first bell, the girls gathered in the auditorium for morning assembly, the blank faces of the royal family members staring at them from the walls. The national anthem, a dull panegyric to the King, roused not even those who endlessly claimed blood ties to royalty. The girls stood limp and droned it out, swallowing half the words. It was time for uniform inspection. Sumnima braced herself as Sangita Miss approached her. But to her utter relief, she walked past her without even glancing at her drooping socks, and pounced on the girl behind her. The assembly shuffled and murmured in anticipation.

Prerana, the daughter of a famed doctor, could never impress Sangita Miss despite her immaculate uniform—a crisp white shirt buttoned to the collar, a sharply pleated navy-blue skirt, fine cotton socks that encased her lotioned calves, and shiny foreign-brand shoes. Most teachers handled Prerana with care in return for the free and expedited services they received at Dr Pandey's clinic. Not Sangita Miss. 'Ask your daddy to open your head and put some brains there,' she said when Prerana failed to answer a question in class. The 'I hate' section of Prerana's auto-book read: 'lijard, caterpilar and a witch called Miss S'.

'What is this?' Sangita Miss said, taking Prerana's left hand. It was covered in a dark-brown henna pattern.

'Miss,' Prerana said tearfully, 'my brother had a wedding yesterday.'

'This is school,' said Sangita Miss. 'You can't come with hands painted like Sridevi's.'

The assembly burst into laughter. A fat teardrop dripped off Prerana's chin and rolled down the tip of her waxed shoe. She took a handkerchief out of her pocket and wiped her nose, shaking with repressed sobs. 'Drama queen,' Sangita Miss said, and then released her with a warning, a modest punishment considering that Prerana had excluded her from the wedding reception.

The first class in the morning was dance. The girls took off their shoes and socks and got ready for audition. 'The lead dancer should have three qualities,' Hemanta Sir repeated. 'Grace, talent and beauty.' Sumnima was thin and dark. She had narrow eyes and a stubby nose pierced with a gold nose-pin, which made her look like her village cousin Ganga. Forget lead dancer, she could not even dream of joining the group of panchakanya who wore the national fariya-cholo and offered dignitaries garlands at special events. Sumnima was eliminated in the first round. She sat in a corner and watched her best friends, Tejaswi and Reshma, prancing on stage. Their chances of becoming lead dancer were nearly as slim. Tejaswi had an aristocratic surname with a string of middle names that were printed in bold letters on all her belongings. Her older sister Anushka had recently married a Rajput prince and moved to Rajasthan, India. Yet Tejaswi's appearance offered no hint of her illustrious lineage. Her small eyes and short nose suggested Matwali rather than Thakuri origin, and to her quiet consternation, people sometimes mistook her for Sumnima's sister. Reshma had unfortunately taken after her father, a portly and shortsighted member of the National Panchayat, instead of

Rajani aunty, her elegant mother and newly elected president of Rhododendron Alumnae Society.

Hemanta Sir shook his head as the girls stamped around on the stage floor. 'Here, let me show you,' he said to Tejaswi. He gripped her waist from behind and swayed to and fro, his hands sliding over her hips, his crotch pressed against her bum. 'One-two, one-two-three, one-two, one-two-three.' Tejaswi followed along with an awkward smile. Sumnima was bored and starting to feel hungry. She thought of the plate of dalbhat she had refused in the morning: the steaming mound of soft white rice, jimbu-flavoured dal, potato-and-cauliflower tarkari, and fresh tomato-chilli achar. She ate dalbhat twice a day, every day, all year round. She never got sick of it. It was only in her friends' auto-books that she declared 'pizza' her favourite food.

In the next class, Sumnima had to bang her desk-cover and move her chair to drown out the rumbling in her stomach. Saraswati Miss rambled on in her soporific voice, holding a book in one hand and gesticulating with the other. *After King Rana Bahadur Shah came back to power, he made Bhimsen Thapa a minister and...* Her armpit sweat soaked through her pink blouse and formed dark-pink circles. The wall clock that hung between the portraits of the King and Queen showed only half past ten. Sumnima fumbled around in her bag and dug out a long-forgotten candy. Keeping her eyes fixed on Saraswati Miss, she tore the wrapper and tossed the candy into her mouth. It tasted a little musty but sweet and fruity.

Maybe Boju was right, she thought, hunger taught respect for all sorts of food. But then, respect did not mean hoarding food till it began to rot, did it? Boju stockpiled food under her bed. Pickles, ghiu and dried fish from Lungla, fruit and biscuits that visitors brought her, leftover raksi and beer from family gatherings, and duty-free Red Labels gifted by Gurkha relatives based in Hong Kong, Singapore or Brunei. Only when the biscuits turned soggy, bananas black and the pickles gained a layer of velvety mould would Boju start doling them out. In her view, anything softer than a rock and harder than a turd qualified as food. And should one thing go missing from her piles, she'd explode into a torrent of abuse that echoed throughout Bhaisichaur.

If only Boju was like Tejaswi's grandmother, thought Sumnima, while Saraswati Miss launched into the heroic conquests of Kaji Amar Singh Thapa. Afumuwa had short silver hair and wore earth-toned saris that made her resemble Indira Gandhi. She had been taking care of Tejaswi since her mother died in an accident when she was two. On report card day, Afumuwa would march into the school with a servant in tow and argue with the teachers over Tejaswi's poor marks. On Parents Day, she would sit in the front row beside the chief guest and watch Tejaswi holding the stage trees or opening the heavy red curtains. On Sports Day, while the rest of the audience cheered the athletes in the field, Afumuwa would lean over the belt barrier and take pictures of Tejaswi holding the finish line ribbon, or carrying the victory stand back and forth.

'You, are you listening me?' Saraswati Miss was staring at Sumnima over her glasses. 'Always dreaming of what-what things. What is the name of Amar Singh Thapa's father?'

Sumnima stood up, trying to hold back a giggle.

'Um...Bhimsen Thapa?'

'Stop smiling.'

'Bhakti Thapa?'

'I said stop smiling,' said Saraswati Miss. Her crumpled blouse had slipped off her shoulder, showing a twisted bra strap. 'Next time if you can't answer to my question I will out you from class!'

Sumnima choked back a laugh and sat down. Reshma and Tejaswi, seated at opposite corners of the classroom, smiled at her. The three of them had been placed in three different corners because they talked too much. Best friends, they shared secrets, swapped pencils and hairbands, and called themselves 'the three musketeers', having seen (though never read) the beautiful hardcover book in the school library.

~

The clock struck noon and a shrill ringing pierced the air, scaring birds away. The girls sprang to life. Chairs scraped, desks banged, and sounds of hurried footsteps filled the corridors and stairways. As usual Sumnima and her friends sat on the wide steps that led to the auditorium. Sumnima began unpacking her lunch, trying to cover her tiffin carrier with a plastic bag. She hated the plain round steel container and the food her mother packed in it. Jam sandwiches with jam spread so thinly the slices didn't even stick together, rice fried with cumin and turmeric that stained her tongue yellow, biscuits made in Nepal, and worst of all, makai-bhatmas grown in their own backyard. Whenever Sumnima complained about her lunch, her mother threatened to put her in a hostel, and her father boasted about his deprived childhood, inspiring her to pen mocking ditties.

Poor Baba went about with bare feet
Slogged like a beast to make ends meet
Ate dhindo and gundruk, never meat
Stuffed his belly with lumps of buckwheat

Tejaswi had a double-decker lunchbox in which she brought rolls and patties wrapped in aluminium foil, or sandwiches pressed in an electric sandwich-maker. Reshma's warm, scrumptious meals were delivered at lunchtime by one of her servants, or 'household staff', as her mother liked to call them. Often it was a thin black boy from her father's home district in west Nepal. Reshma addressed him as 'Chaudhary'.

Today Chaudhary had brought macaroni cooked with cheese, sausage and oregano. 'Mmm, delicious,' Tejaswi said, putting a large spoonful into her mouth. 'I wish my mom could cook like yours.' Reshma darted a quizzical glance at Sumnima, but Sumnima did not notice. She was busy trying to pull the lid off her tiffin carrier. The smell of the macaroni made her mouth water, but there was an unwritten rule that she could only eat her friends' lunch after offering hers. 'It's stuck!' she cried. Her nails and fingertips hurt. She raised the tiffin carrier high above her head and banged it hard on the concrete floor. The lid came off at once. The tiffin carrier slipped from her hand and rolled down the steps, spilling congealed lumps of halua all over the floor. It hit the flagpole and spun a few times with a tinny sound. Reshma and Tejaswi burst out laughing.

Sumnima was mortified. Halua? This was worse than homegrown makai-bhatmas. Halua was meant to be prasad, an offering for her grandma's gods, not a school snack! She associated it with Boju's multi-limbed gods, antiquated rituals, bhajans, and the riotous sounds of bells and drums that emanated from the puja room each morning. How could her mother be so thoughtless? With great effort Sumnima climbed down the steps, picked up the litter and reassembled her tiffin carrier. Then she strode to the garbage bin and threw away everything, including the tiffin carrier.

'You threw it?' her friends asked in unison.

'Yes, I'll get a new one,' she said with a strained smile.

~

Premkala gripped the pestle with both hands and began pounding spices. Her interview at the travel agency hadn't gone well. 'Thirty-two? Impossible,' the manager's voice rang in her ears. 'I swear if you wear a school skirt, you could pass as a ninth grader.' It was precisely to avoid such comments that she had worn a sari and high heels that morning. She had painted her lips, blackened her eyes and dabbed rouge on her cheeks although she preferred herself without makeup. Yet the manager addressed her as 'timi' as if she were his wife. 'Are you in a bad mood? You'll have to smile more often if you get this job.' Those leering eyes, that superior tone. He looked like a horse. A heavy hand had swiped over his long face and pulled his eyes, mouth and chin downward.

Premkala's gullible Matwali face and her small, five-foot frame had become the bane of her life. No one seemed to realize she was a thirty-plus, B.Ed-passed, full-time working mother of two. Co-workers, job interviewers, bank tellers, receptionists, government office staff, shopkeepers, even bus and tempo drivers talked down to her. They called her 'timi' and 'bahini', whereas anyone with that thing hanging between their legs was 'sir' and 'hajur'. Schoolboys clucked their tongues at her. She could never forget how fifth graders had run roughshod over her during her first week at Sunshine Primary. 'Arey, Miss looks like a kid,' a ringleader had announced to his classmates, raising a gale of laughter. They ignored her commands and called her Phuchi Miss behind her back. Over the months she had stopped smiling and stiffened her posture. She spoke little and brandished a ruler at all times. Now they called her Scary Miss, and she didn't mind it as much.

Premkala tossed some garlic in the mortar and crushed it to paste, releasing its pungent smell. The sturdy granite mortar set from Hong Kong had made the task ten times easier than in the past. The set was a gift from her sister-in-law Parvati, who had married a lahure and moved to Hong Kong a year ago. Everyone wondered how Parvati, so plain and past her prime, had caught such a handsome lahure fish. Lucky woman, they said, she had jumped straight from the hills of Lungla into the high-rise flats of Hong Kong—why wouldn't it go to her head? But Premkala rejoiced in her sister-in-law's good fortune. Parvati's newfound prosperity meant one less poor relative depending on her husband. The few Tamules who had escaped destitution, who had earned some money and built a house in the city, were all lahures, or married to lahures. Except my husband, Premkala often thought with pride. Although her father had fought in the Second World War and many of her relatives still served in the Gurkha Regiment, she had never wanted to marry a soldier. She saw her lahure relatives as a moneyed but simple-minded lot, more brawn than brains, and only occasionally envied their late acquired wealth. Her husband stood in a different league from them. Through a combination of great luck and diligence, he had veered away from the preordained path and made himself an educated office-goer. We may not be rich, Premkala would remind herself, but we are educated and cultured folk, well versed in the ways of the world.

Such consolations were far from her mind at this moment. It was better to be a loaded housewife than suffer humiliation at the hands of outsiders. She placed a pot of water on the three-legged stove and pumped the fuel-tank. The loud hum filled her ears. No, she would not get that job. 'Sir, I'll please the customers with my work, not my smile,' she had said, at which the horseface gave her such a look she knew at once she'd blown her chance. It was a flourishing travel agency. She would have received a good salary, a well-furnished workspace, and maybe a free air ticket once in a while. Thailand, Malaysia, Singapore—places where she had travelled only in her dreams. Perhaps she should have controlled herself. She added tea powder, milk and sugar to the boiling water. The mixture frothed up and turned milky brown. The wily headmaster would never give her a raise. In less than two years of opening the school, he had graduated from a motorcycle to a second-hand Maruti car. She wished she could storm into his office and throw her resignation at his face. Alas, life was not a Hindi movie full of heroic rejections. Even to get that loathsome job, she had relied on one of her husband's colleagues, who never lost an opportunity to remind her of his favour.

She poured out tea in two stainless steel mugs and put them on the table along with a few slices of bread. One couldn't move ahead in Kathmandu without connections. Who knew, if it hadn't been for Neeru badi, she might never have got a job in the first place. Neeru badi, a distant relative originally from Tehrathum, worked at the Kathmandu district education office back in the day. When Premkala was in her first year of college, Neeru badi had signed her up for the government's teacher-training course. Every morning for the next ten months, Premkala would ride to Kirtipur on a bus packed with men, hugging a bag to her chest, wary of the hands and crotches around her. The training stipend of hundred rupees a month was the first income of her life. Later, Neeru badi had used her contacts to find her a job at a government school. Premkala hadn't had to beg anyone for money ever since. Neeru badi's single favour had lasted her a lifetime. The good woman had helped many fellow Limbus from her village get small jobs in the city. What a difference it made to have your own people in government. With one word they could clear all bureaucratic hurdles, with one signature set you on a career path. Unfortunately, as a female civil servant of a Matwali tribe, Neeru badi was an exception not the rule, an anomaly in a system dominated by Bahun men.

The sound of footsteps in the corridor broke Premkala's train of thought. Sumnima appeared in the kitchen, her face twisted into a scowl.

'Mummy, why did you pack me halua for lunch?'

Premkala shot her a look and started washing potatoes in the sink. Sumnima dumped her bag on the floor and sat down at the table. Numa, already in her pajamas, came in, glanced at her mother, and quietly took one of the mugs of lukewarm tea. She dunked a piece of bread in the tea and ate carefully, dropping not a single crumb.

'Can't we have a nicer snack?' Sumnima shoved a slice into her mug. 'I haven't eaten anything all day. That halua you sent spilled all over the floor!'

Premkala watched a long strip of potato skin spiralling out of the peeler.

'Mummy!' cried Sumnima. 'You never listen to me. That's why I threw that ugly tiffin carrier.'

'Threw?' Premkala said, finally looking at her.

'I meant I dropped...I lost it,' Sumnima stammered. 'It's right there in the dustbin so I can...'

Premkala leapt up and slapped her hard, cutting her off in mid-sentence. 'You think money grows on trees?' Numa jumped up and fled, leaving her slippers behind. Premkala picked up a slipper, caught Sumnima by the arm and hit her with its dense rubber sole. Sumnima screamed for mercy as blows rained on her with pitiless fury. Her shirt came untucked and a button popped off and skittered across the floor. Stinging red patches appeared on her arms and calves. Premkala did not stop until her husband rushed into the kitchen, shouting, 'Stop, Premkala, I said stop!'

Tamule ji could hardly believe that the woman prone to such violent outbursts had once inspired him to pen poems in his diary. Those were days when he thought of himself not as Tamule ji but as Gajendra Bahadur Tamule of Lungla, ward seven, Bhojpur district. A quiet young man with a tan, fine-boned face, he lived in an old mud-brick house in Kasai Tol. The house stood on a narrow street, with an open courtyard in the back. Beyond the courtyard was an overgrown field that sloped down towards the Tukucha River. People referred to it as 'Jemadar Limbu's house' even though the Jemadar's widow had reigned over the house for more than a decade. Gajendra lived in a ground-floor room with a bed made of wooden planks, two tin trunks, a kerosene wick stove and a few pots and pans. On the niche next to his bed stood the idols of Hindu deities his father had given him before he left the village. A money-plant stem grew in a bottle by the lone window, for luck and prosperity.

Every morning after finishing his puja, Gajendra would wait near this window, his eyes fixed on the stairs that led to the landlady's floor. Sometime between six and six-thirty, Premkala would come running down the stairs, frowning, sticking pins in her hair, fussing over her coarse and bulky uniform sari. The minute she reached the last step, Gajendra would start watering the money plant, hoping for a smile or at least a glance from her. But clacking her platforms on the stone courtyard, she would rush past like a breath of wind. Except on those rare mornings when the stars seemed aligned in his favour. No frowns, no rush. She stepped out of the door looking calm and cheerful, her hair pinned up, her sari starched and ironed stiff. She would stop to greet Gajendra and linger for some small talk. Did you hear the dog wail last night? The sun's out early today. Did you drink your tea? She had a clean, guileless face and an easy, unaffected manner that set Gajendra's heart at rest. Her smile reduced her eyes to twinkling slivers. All day as he went about his business, this scene kept playing in his head like a song.

It was for Premkala that he groomed himself into a city boy. He spoke carefully, making sure not to lapse into village idiom, and was quick to say please, thank you, excuse me. Afraid Premkala might think him a god-fearing hick, he beat his prayer bell as softly as possible, and soon stopped marking his forehead with sandalwood paste. He ate dalbhat with a spoon. He emptied his bowels only after she left for college, for it involved filling water in a bucket and carrying it to the scummy latrine near the banks of the Tukucha.

Premkala remained out of his reach. To get closer to her, he tried to befriend her younger brother Rajan, a good-natured fellow who laughed even when his mother called him a jackass and loafer. But although unemployed, Rajan was always rushing off somewhere, and Gajendra seldom got hold of him except for brief, passing conversations in the courtyard. On Saturday afternoons when Premkala was home, Gajendra imagined climbing those stairs and knocking on her door on some pretext, but his courage failed him at the thought of his landlady. Although Boju loved gossip and bawdy tales, she guarded her territory like a tigress. In her presence the student-lodgers wouldn't dare glance at her daughter. During the festival of Bhai Tika, she had made all the boys line up in the courtyard and receive a tika offering from Premkala, converting her potential suitors into ritual brothers. Luckily Gajendra had gone home for the festival.

Even amid such barriers and uncertainties, Gajendra did not lose hope. He knew Boju wanted both her children to marry someone from a Matwali tribe. She hoped to throw them a big Limbu wedding, alive with drumbeat and dancing and abundant liquor and pork. Although Boju worshipped Hindu deities and celebrated Dasain and Tihar, she felt removed from the ways of upper-caste Hindus and regarded them with a hint of disdain. There was a rumour that she only offered lodgings to chimse-nepte boys from the hills. As a matter of fact, only chimse-nepte men ever came knocking at her door. Jemadar Limbu's house, one of the few Matwali-owned establishments in Kathmandu, was a safe port of arrival for these men who had left behind their ancestral villages to begin a life in an alien city. Despite its dingy rooms and the cranky landlady, the house offered them a community and a home away from home.

Sumnima leaned against a pile of old mattresses and flipped through her auto-book. 'Look, her room is so nice.' Numa looked up from her homework. 'Khai, let me see.'

The photo showed Reshma sitting on her bed with a furry white dog in her arms. In the background was a wall-to-wall closet with mirrors, a wide desk with a pink reading lamp, and a shelf filled with stuffed toys, cassettes and books.

'She's a minister's daughter, what do you expect?' Numa said. 'The dog's cuter than her.' She handed the auto-book back to Sumnima, picked up her exercise book and read out loud: *Why did the great king Prithvi Narayan Shah describe Nepal as a common garden? The great king Prithvi Narayan Shah described Nepal as a common garden because Nepal has four varnas and thirty-six jaats living together in peace and harmony. In a common garden also many different flowers bloom in peace and harmony. That is why the great king described Nepal as a common garden.*

Sumnima closed her auto-book, looked around her and sighed. Their small, shapeless room served more as a depot for things that had outlived their purpose. Used textbooks, old school uniforms, clothes that were discoloured, buttonless, or out of fashion but wholly intact, faded curtains made of durable fabric, and old calendars made of glossy high-quality paper. Everything in the room looked improvised, makeshift, temporary. Their 'desk' was a heavy-duty shipping crate from Hong Kong covered with a crochet tablecloth, their wall hanging a winnowing tray with the word 'Namaste' embroidered on it with colourful yarn. They had no closet, only an overloaded clothes-stand that tipped over at the slightest touch. Their mirror showed their lower half only if they climbed on a stool. There were ink stains on the wall, on the curtain and on the floor—for Sumnima had reached sixth grade and had started using a fountain pen.

At the sound of footsteps, Sumnima shoved the auto-book aside and grabbed a textbook. Their mother appeared at the door, her petite frame wrapped in a dragon-print lungi from Singapore. 'Girls,' she said. 'Will you go get kerosene from Bhairey's shop?'

'Keroseeene?' Numa said. 'We don't know how to buy kerosene.'

'Just tell Bhairey you're Tamule dai's daughters,' said Premkala. 'He's saved a few litres for us. It won't be heavy.'

'We're doing our homework,' Sumnima said. 'Can't Baba go?'

'He isn't home,' said Premkala. 'His uncle and aunt are coming today, so he went to look for mutton.'

Sumnima and Numa frowned at the prospect of meeting new relatives.

Relatives from Lungla fell into two broad categories. The first included young men who came to Kathmandu for work and study and needed a place to stay until they got their initial bearings in the city. Those quiet and uncomplaining lads put little pressure on their hosts. All Premkala had to do was double the amount of rice she normally cooked and spread out an old mattress in the living room at night. During the day if they were not hustling in the city, they would hang around the house and apply themselves to outdoor tasks in the most unobtrusive manner. Silently and voluntarily they would draw water with the hand pump and fill the drums and buckets, weed out the garden, dig up stumps from the farm plot, rearrange the junk in the storage shed, and slash the bramble bushes around the compound with a khukuri. They never used the indoor bathroom and always did the dishes after meals. Even Boju, who abhorred visitors from Lungla and grumbled about the mountains of rice they ate, did not completely mind having them around.

The second category included older folk who came to Kathmandu on pleasure visits or for medical treatment. Tamule ji made every effort to please them, for the stories they told the villagers shaped his reputation in Lungla. In addition to providing food and shelter, Premkala had to treat them with deference and keep track of their complicated dietary restrictions. Among the vegetarians, some ate no meat and eggs, others ate only duck eggs, and a few had forsaken even onion and garlic as impure foods. The non-vegetarians ate only duck and pigeon among birds, and among quadrupeds, only sheep. Premkala had heard that during Dasain, even the most indigent Tamule in Lungla would trek to the high pastures in search of sheep that fed on fragrant wild herbs. The Tamules claimed they could tell the quality of mutton by its smell. 'No wonder your entire flock is as clever as sheep,' Premkala would tease her husband.

Sumnima and Numa followed their mother to the kitchen. She crouched under the counter and reached inside a dark, cluttered, unplastered space meant for a future base cabinet. From among a confusing pile of objects—a sack of potatoes, low wooden seats, rolled-up straw mats, a round winnowing tray—she pulled out a grimy ten-litre jerry can and thrust it in Sumnina's hand. 'Just take this, I can't find the smaller one.'

Sumnima sighed. Kathmandu had been suffering from a shortage of fuel and essential supplies. The exact reason for the shortage was beyond her, but she knew that it was India's fault. She had heard people cursing India. According to Reshma, whose father always knew the inside story, India was punishing Nepal for not dancing to its tune. Outraged, Sumnima had demanded an explanation from her father, but couldn't make head or tail of his lecture. What did Chinese weapons have to do with the shortage? Though her father read every newspaper and never missed the radio news, the fervour of his views outstripped his ability to articulate them. On weekend evenings he and Rajan

Mama talked politics over whisky on the terrace. They would rail against Panche politicians, debate every problem and solution, and exhaust their trove of rumour and speculation about the royal family. On certain matters they disagreed completely. Baba regarded the King as the rightful sovereign and refrained from bad-mouthing him. Rajan Mama held the King every bit as culpable as the Panches and denounced the entire monarchy. With each drink their voices grew louder and their sparring more impassioned, till Rajan Mama cracked a sudden joke and they burst out laughing. Rajan Mama held his opinions lightly. His sense of humour loosened up the atmosphere and lent even grave matters a comic touch.

But a few nights ago, Sumnima had seen Rajan Mama bang his fist on the table. 'Dai, it's plain as day,' he said to Baba. 'Those dhotis just want to control us. They want to steal our name, fame, everything. You tell me, was the Buddha born in India? I hear they're claiming even Mount Everest is in India!'

~

'I hate Indians,' said Sumnima, as she walked towards Bhairey's shop carrying the oversized jerry can.

'Me too,' Numa said. 'Except Aamir Khan, he's too cute.'

It was a still afternoon. Under the quiet sky, the flowering mustard field looked placid as a postcard. The little stone temple always looked sad and godless at this hour. Near the temple stood a large peepal tree, gnarled branches entwined around its trunk like sleeping serpents. A boy came riding on a rickety bicycle, a bag of groceries swinging from the handlebar. He hunched over and blushed as he rode past the girls. A faint smile twitched the corner of his lips.

'Poor boy,' Numa said. 'He's making good use of the bike.'

'Was he the older or the younger one?' Sumnima asked.

'The older one, Rishiram,' Numa said, then pulled up her lips to mimic his expression. Sumnima laughed. Her parents had gifted her the second-hand bicycle on her last birthday. Thrilled beyond words, she had made her father click photos of her posing with her new steed. After the photos came out, she had meticulously cropped out all the unwanted elements in the background—the dirty chicken coop, the garlic bunches strung across the verandah, the tin-roofed toilet, and the mops made out of torn vests hanging on the clothesline. Next day she had posted the photos to her auto-book and passed them among her friends. But after a few falls and a bruised knee, she had lost all motivation and dumped the bike in the storage shed, where it had been lying for months. Her mother had recently handed it down to the boys next door. Their mother, Devi didi, delivered cow milk to the Tamule house every morning. She helped Boju with her farm work and filled her in on neighbourhood gossip. Some evenings the boys came to watch TV at the Tamule house. They would remove their slippers outside the front door, quietly slip into the living room and sit on the floor, staring at the colour bar screen until the broadcast began with the high-pitched national anthem. On windy days one of them would be sent up to the roof to adjust the antenna. Boju allowed them their entertainment as long as they didn't stray into the other rooms, sit on the sofas, or use the indoor bathroom.

~

The girls returned with the jerry can empty.

'Cunning rascal,' Premkala said. 'I'm sure he's selling it on the black market.' The girls nodded vaguely, 'black market' being one of those familiar adult phrases that had no bearing on their universe. Premkala lifted the stove from the countertop and shook it, her ear close to the brass tank. 'Uff, it's almost empty.' She lit a match near the burner. The spark flared up, casting a brief glow on her face. She hastily pumped into the tank. Sweat broke out on her nose and a vein on her temple swelled. 'I'm sick of this blockade,' she said. 'And who suffers the most? Always simple folk like us. The rich and thula bada manage to hoard everything. One colonel's wife in Naxal, I hear she's selling kerosene from her kitchen, at double the price!' The flame sputtered and hissed and died out. 'Ohooo,' she groaned. 'I'm so sick of this blockade! We'll have to use the sawdust chula, that piece of junk.' She looked at the girls. 'It's in the storage shed, will you go dig it out? Your relatives will be here any minute, I have to make tea.'

Sumnima and Numa fled the kitchen at once. When their mother was angry, one never knew where her blows might land.

~

The living room was permeated with that musty, fishy odour which the girls recognized as 'the smell of Lungla'. An elderly man stood gaping at the objects in the display cabinet—a souvenir plate showing the Hong Kong skyline, a miniature replica of Pashupatinath Temple, porcelain dinnerware meant for special occasions, a blond-haired blue-eyed pink-faced doll in lace and frills. A woman in a faded lungi sat on the floor rummaging in a grimy backpack. Her head was wrapped in cloth, her breathing loud and heavy. 'Oi Kuley's father,' she said. 'I can't find the letter.' Her husband didn't seem to hear her. He was looking at a pair of photos hung on the wall. They showed a younger Tamule ji and Premkala, each in a graduation cap and gown, a rolled-up degree certificate in hand. The woman removed the contents of the backpack one by one. Dried river fish in a flat bamboo basket, a bottle of ghiu swathed in greasy cloth, a large packet of kinema and small packets of local condiments such as philinge and silam. 'It's not here either,' she sighed.

Sumnima and Numa appeared at the door. 'Namaste,' they said, joining their hands. The woman's face lit up at once. 'O Kuley's father!' she shouted to her husband. 'Look who's here, our Gajey's daughters.' The man finally turned around. 'Ah, Thuli and Kanchi,' he said with a wide grin.

Everyone from Lungla addressed Sumnima as Thuli, first-born, and Numa as Kanchi, last-born. Sumnima looked at their sunburnt hands and faces, at the sacred threads and amulets hanging from their necks, at the pouches and bundles scattered on the floor. Her heart oscillated between pity and shame. The woman stood up and came towards her, baring her rusty teeth. A faint whistling sound came from her chest. A long strip of off-white cloth was tied around her waist in multiple layers, making an unsightly bulge. 'Dark but pretty, eh?' she said, stroking Sumnima's cheek with her coarse fingers. 'Just like Ganga.' Ganga was the village cousin that Sumnima famously resembled but had never met. Sumnima forced a smile. 'You may not recognize us,' the woman said, speaking in her crude but familiar accent. 'We're Kul Bahadur's parents. Kuley dai, he came here last Dasain, remember?'

The girls looked at each other.

'Kuley dai, oh, yes,' Sumnima lied. She could seldom distinguish between her village cousins or remember their names.

The man nodded blankly, his eyes still feasting on the objects around him. The sofas with floral slipcovers, the television locked inside the slide-door steel cabinet, the fake crystal chandelier that glowed even in daytime.

'O Kuley's father!' the woman said loudly. 'Bajey said the third one will be a boy, didn't he?'

'Huh?'

She moved closer and screamed into his ear, 'Mangal Bajey said our Gajey's third child will be a son, didn't he?'

The man's eyes lit up with sudden comprehension. 'Yes, yes, he did!' he said with a vigorous nod. 'Third child will most certainly be a boy.'

His wife smiled and turned to the girls. 'See,' she said, 'our priest said you'll be blessed with a brother in the future. A brother is a brother. He will carry you when you become brides. He will look after Mummy-Baba when they grow old. You should ask your Mummy for a little brother, shouldn't you?'

Numa kept quiet. Sumnima gave a short, non-committal laugh.

The Tamules' obsession with sons was a running joke on their mother's side of the family, a city-bred crop who only had tenuous links with their ancestral village of Tehrathum. 'You know what your grandmother used to say as she cuddled you?' her aunts would remind Sumnima. 'O my little one, how lovely you are. If only you had something dangling between your legs.' Numa would never forget the first riddle she was asked as a child: 'Why are the Tamules so dim?' Answer: 'Because they only eat sheep. Miaaa!' At family gatherings, stories about the Tamule clan were told and retold amid storms of laughter. The Tamule were a slothful and superstitious people, dupes of high-caste Bahuns and Chhetris, copycats who aped high-caste manners down to the cadence of their sugary speech, self-abasing fools who looked down on fellow Matwali tribes and called them 'Bhote', a catch-all term of insult for all Matwalis including the Tamule.

To dissociate from such a lumpen tribe, Numa had once proposed adopting her mother's surname, an idea Tamule ji found so ridiculous he had simply dismissed it with a laugh. He felt he had already conceded much by allowing his mother-in-law to give his daughters Limbu names. A thoroughbred Tamule, he wanted them to hold onto their roots. Every year, as soon as their school closed for winter, he tried to lure them into making a trip to Lungla. 'Imagine, you'll get to climb trees laden with oranges. You'll get to catch fish in the river, breathe the fresh mountain air!' But Sumnima and Numa would not be carried away. They knew Lungla was no bucolic village with flowing milk and honey. It looked nothing like the English countryside in illustrated storybooks, with spotted cows and white lambs grazing on rolling meadows. Lungla was a hard and inhospitable land, a place of lack and adversity, just another 'remote village' in the hinterland that began outside Kathmandu and grew less and less relevant the further you went from it. They would rather spend their vacation watching Hindi movies on a VCR rented from a video shop in town.

~

'Namaste Thulkaka, Namaste Thulkaki!' Tamule ji said, putting his helmet aside. He looked at his daughters and smiled, glad to see them keeping the visitors company. 'Sorry I'm late. The protestors had blocked the main road, so I had to take a detour.'

Thulkaki touched his head and mumbled a blessing between rasping breaths. 'We saw them too,' she said. 'Lots of red flags. All shouting Panchayat murdabad, bahudal jindabad.'

'Let's hope they'll bring down the Panches this time,' Tamule ji said.

Thulkaki handed him the letter she had at last found under the tattered lining of her bag. Tamule ji discreetly put it inside his pocket. 'Premkala, are you making tea?' He leaned out of the door, his voice edgy but imploring, torn between the desire to please the guests and the fear of irking his wife. There was no response from the kitchen. He turned to Numa. 'Go tell Mummy to bring tea.' Both the girls leapt at this chance to extricate themselves from the guests.

Just then Boju appeared at the door, holding a broken umbrella retrieved from the garbage pit. Her lungi was hitched up to her knees, showing pale calves with knotty, purple veins. 'What tea?' she hissed. 'There's no kerosene.' The guests joined their hands and offered her an effusive greeting. She responded with a jerk of her head. Her eyes wandered over the food pouches on the floor and her face mellowed a bit. As much as she despised Lungla folk, their rare and rustic fare never failed to excite her. 'Is that ghiu?' she said, pointing the umbrella tip at the bottle.

'Yes, Ama, it's made from fresh buffalo milk,' said Thulkaki. 'Chandrey's mother sent it especially for you.' She untied the greasy cloth, wiped off the leaked ghiu with her fingers and offered the bottle to Boju. Then she rubbed the grease all over her chapped hands like lotion. Boju opened the bottle and smelled the ghiu. A hint of a smile appeared on her face. 'Poor Sita,' she said. 'Always remembers to send a little something.' Thulkaki handed Boju the remaining pouches, panting for breath as she relayed a stream of messages and compliments from her relatives. Back in the village they had nicknamed Boju 'boksi budi', old witch. They said she had shamelessly foisted herself on her daughter's home and lived off their Gajey's bounty. But while in Kathmandu, they couldn't get away without appeasing her in every manner possible.

'Nothing special,' Thulkaki said with a smile, 'just little tokens of remembrance.'

Boju bundled up the gifts, took them to her room and carefully stowed them in a corner piled with mouldering foodstuff.

4

As she was tidying the bed next morning, Premkala found a letter under her husband's pillow. It was from his brother Tikaram. The crude scrawl, inky scratches and incomprehensible regional expressions made the letter a tedious read, but she had no difficulty in grasping two major points. First, Tamule ji had made a donation to buy corrugated tin roofs for the village school. Day and night he whined about household expenses, whereas behind her back he had been doling out cash like a lord. Second, his brother wished to send his teenage daughter Ganga to live with them in Kathmandu. Not the poor man's fault; it was her husband who gave the impression that they were rolling in money. She sat on the rumpled bed and waited. Her husband was beating the hand-bell in the puja room. The din rose and grated on her nerves, the cacophony whipping up her anger.

Premkala didn't know whether to applaud or lament her husband's celebrity status in his village. He was the only one in his community to have earned a university degree and built a house in Kathmandu. Among his four siblings, the oldest Tikaram still lived in Lungla, slogging day and night to support an ailing mother, a sickly wife who looked twice her age, and three grown children. Tamule ji often sent him small amounts of cash, medicines and clothes through visitors returning to Lungla. Maila, the second brother, seemed even worse off. As a young man he had married a lowborn Tamangni widow from a neighbouring village and run off to Assam in India. A debt-ridden worker on a tea estate, he had half a dozen daughters he could barely feed. His youngest was living with his wife's relatives in Dharan, a town two days' journey away from Lungla. The Tamule community had reached an unspoken consensus that Maila deserved his suffering and his sonless existence. Perhaps for this reason, his plight did not weigh too heavily on Tamule ji's conscience. As for his youngest sister Nirmala, she had eloped with a good-for-nothing loafer while still a schoolgirl. Within a couple of years the quick-eyed local beauty had metamorphosed into a tired and flabby mother of two, and would doubtless spend her remaining years in grinding toil. Only Parvati had escaped such a fate thanks to the Hong Kong lahure. The good man had set his heart on marrying her despite knowing everyone called her a dried-up spinster.

The clanging in the puja room stopped. Premkala picked up a nail-cutter and spread a newspaper on the floor, hoping to provoke her husband, who believed that cutting nails inside the house brought bad luck. Bits of nails jumped onto the carpet as she clipped away. The bedroom door opened, and in came Tamule ji, carrying lustral water in a small copper pot. He frowned at his wife and turned round to face a framed picture hung on the wall. It showed an old man sitting bolt upright on a studio chair, his solemn gaze fixed on the camera. Tamule ji only drank his morning tea after paying obeisance to the image of his departed father. The old man had always believed that having his photo taken would shorten his life. But on his final trip to Kathmandu, Tamule ji had somehow convinced him to visit a studio. 'I don't care anymore,' he had said, 'I'll be gone soon anyway.' He had passed away a month after he returned to the village, earning himself posthumous fame as a clairvoyant.

Tamule ji sprinkled lustral water at the picture with a tiny copper spoon.

'Buda, how much did you donate to the school?' Premkala asked without a preamble. Tamule ji's face tensed up. He bowed his head and intoned a Sanskrit mantra. Premkala glared at him. 'Mimic Bahun,' she muttered.

~

Although she visited temples and observed the major Hindu

festivals on the calendar, Premkala could not understand her husband's enthusiasm for religious formalities. His fixation with Hindu rituals had been revealed to her during her first trip to Lungla soon after their marriage. The long and strenuous uphill trek, the hordes of relatives and the stifling customs of his household had given her a fever. For several days she lay listless on a floor mattress, drinking strange herbal concoctions. Her aunts-in-law taunted her. 'Our poor Gajey's wife,' one of them said, 'so delicate *hau*, flattened by a single day's walk.'

As newly married guests from Kathmandu, they were offered a makeshift bedroom made with bamboo partitions, but the villagers seemed unaccustomed to privacy, and wandered in and out of the room as if it were a public garden. Aunts, uncles, nieces, nephews and neighbours descended on her from morning to night. They went through her belongings and deluged her with questions, advice and long-winded stories with no beginning or end. Her husband had made the mistake of carrying his brand-new camera. His nephews and nieces wanted their photos taken at every interval and wouldn't let him rest until he used up his very last roll of film. It didn't matter that they might never see the photos. They were thrilled just to strike a pose, hear the shutter click and watch the flash go off.

Until then, Premkala had never thought a woman could resent anyone praising her husband. But her mother-in-law harped on about her son as though a nobler man had never walked the face of the earth. My Gajey did this, my Gajey did that. My Gajey likes this, my Gajey likes that. Premkala got tired of eating their Gajey's favourite foods (no one asked her what she liked), of hearing stories about his childhood antics. His aunts chimed in, recalling how they had nursed and pampered him, made him into the big man he now was. It was as if Premkala should kneel down and thank them for awarding her such a marvellous husband, as if her entire worth lay in being their Gajey's wife, sitting at his side lapping up compliments showered on him. Do you know who I am? She felt like saying to them. I am Premkala Limbu, the daughter of Jemadar Sher Bahadur and Dhan Kumari Limbu. My father fought in the Second World War and built the house where your Gajey took refuge as a penniless upstart. My mother raised me single-handedly and let me marry your son only because he came begging on his knees. From the age of sixteen I worked hard to earn my keep. I am made up of stuff that precedes your Gajey, so stop treating me like his shadow.

But the army of relatives overwhelmed her, and all she could muster was a frosty silence.

To crown it all, her mother-in-law had organized a Satyanarayan puja in honour of the newlyweds. It was a big, confused ceremony. Her in-laws dithered over whether to include her, a pig-eating Limbuni, in their Bahun-style rituals. Only then did she realize that the Tamules ranked themselves higher than other Matwali tribes. The knowledge vexed and amused her at the same time. One moment they would place her beside her husband in a consecrated area, and the next shunt her to a corner like an Untouchable. What shocked her most was her husband's servile devotion to the Bahun priest. After receiving a tika from the priest, he went down on all fours, clasped the priest's legs like a humble supplicant and touched his forehead to his feet. Premkala watched mortified. The scene hadn't fully registered in her mind when her mother-in-law turned to her and said tersely, 'Buhari, your turn now.' Her blood rose to her head but words failed her. At any other time she would have silenced the old woman with a sharp retort, but she was in *their* territory. All eyes seemed to have settled on her. She looked askance at her husband, but his eyes too directed her towards the feet of the priest. Cornered and helpless, she knelt down and did the deed. The memory of those clean, well-pared toenails still made her cringe.

~

At their father's request Sumnima and Numa lent the guests their room and slept in the living room, which was cooler and more spacious. That night as they lay on the floor mattress staring at the fake crystal chandelier glowing in the dark, they heard their parents arguing in the next room. What began as a muffled dialogue grew louder and louder and turned into a heated row. Soon they heard objects being flung around and the Godrej steel almirah, a year older than Sumnima, being opened and slammed shut. A moment later their father erupted in a tirade that reached them in fragments: '...says who? Why can't you...? Haven't I...?' They strained their ears but could not catch the rest of his words, just their mother screaming, 'I never asked you to build this house!' A dog started barking, then another, and another, until all the dogs in the neighbourhood had thrown themselves into a barking frenzy. 'And who watches TV all evening while I slave away?' their mother raged. It was almost midnight but she sounded dreadfully awake. Numa clutched the sheet and turned to her sister, eyeballs alert and gleaming. Then all of a sudden everything seemed to calm down. The dogs stopped barking, a neighbour's window was gently closed, and the angry voices began to fade, leaving behind soft, conciliatory murmurs that gradually merged with the sounds of frogs and insects. Only then could Sumnima and Numa let down their guard and fall sleep.

~

'You were so quick,' Thulkaki said, lighting a bidi. 'You'd jump two miles before your mother could come at you.'

Tamule ji chuckled. The aunt and nephew sat in the kitchen garden soaking up the morning sunshine. String beans, cucumbers, squash, pumpkins, tomatoes and lady's fingers were all ripe and ready for harvest. Chickens roamed the yard pecking and chirping. Dense, sparkling cornfields stretched around them all the way to the ring road.

'As for Maila,' Thulkaki said. 'He wouldn't budge even when she knocked a ladle on his head. Just sat there like a lump of dhindo.' She puffed on her bidi and laughed. 'Idiot. No wonder he fell into that Bhoteni's trap, that husband-eater, you know those Tamang people...ah, here comes buhari.'

Premkala came with a tray bearing three glasses of steaming tea. She gave them their tea, then pulled up a muda and sat down. Her husband was listening to his aunt with a wistful expression on his face. Premkala had only met Thulkaki once, during her first trip to Lungla. She remembered her as a fussy and overbearing woman, eager to instruct her in the error of her ways. With every gesture she seemed to say to Premkala, 'Tch, that's not how we do it here.' People in the village recalled how Thulkaki had spit on the face of Maila's bride when he first brought her home. The incident had sealed her reputation as a blunt, no-nonsense, audacious woman. It seemed Thulkaki sometimes offended people just to live up to the image.

But this was Kathmandu not Lungla, and Premkala would tolerate none of her bullying tricks.

'Poor Thuldaju,' Thulkaki said, turning to Premkala. 'What all he didn't do for our Gajey.' She slurped her tea, puffed on her bidi and blew out a wisp of sweet-smelling smoke. 'I remember one day Gajey fell and cut his toe on the way to school. He only wore slippers back then, sometimes he even went barefoot. You know what Thuldaju did the next day?'

Yes, I do, Premkala felt like saying, your Thuldaju walked all the way to Dharan just to buy him shoes. I've heard the story only a dozen times.

'No one can rise all by himself,' Thulkaki said, her breathing loud and heavy. 'We need family, relatives, neighbours. And they need us.' She turned to her nephew. 'You know Resham?'

'Resham?' Tamule ji said. 'Sammare kaka's eldest son, the quiet one, no?'

'Yes,' Thulkaki said. 'Quiet and timid from outside but smarter than a Bahun. Already found a job in Biratnagar, put his sister in a boarding school. Now he's sending money to rebuild their house. Sammare kaka's troubles are over it seems.' She sucked on the end of her bidi and flicked it away. 'By the way, did you read Tikaram's letter?

'Yes,' Tamule ji said. 'He's asked for medicines. I'll send them with you.'

'Didn't he also write about Ganga?' Thulkaki said.

'He did.'

Thulkaki waited for him to continue, but Tamule ji kept quiet. A rooster scratched the ground, pecked a few times and ran off to mount a hen. The hen's screech rose in the air.

'So will you bring her here?' Thulkaki said after a while.

Tamule ji looked at Premkala. 'Um…we're still wondering,' he said. 'We'd love to bring her here but...'

Premkala sighed. They had already made the decision last night. Why was he mincing his words now?

'She's a good girl, our Ganga,' said Thulkaki. 'A little slow maybe, but very obedient. Talks about her Gajey kaka all the time. Remember the family photos you sent last year? She's put them up on her bedside wall, alongside postcards of Hindi heroes and heronis.' She looked at Premkala. 'She could also help with housework.'

Premkala sipped her tea and glared at her husband over the rim of her glass. Tamule ji met her eyes and looked away. 'But Kaki,' he said. 'It's tough right now…two kids is too many…'

'From two to three, that can't make a difference, can it?' Thulkaki grinned and showed her yellow-brown teeth. 'Not if your heart is big enough. After all what is family for? We must open our hearts, the rest will fall into place.'

Premkala waited for her husband to speak up but all he did was nod his head.

'It's not about heart-shart, Kaki,' she blurted out. 'We have no means to support another child, that's all. We have house loans to pay off. The children's school fees go up every year. Your nephew's salary is hardly enough to cover daily expenses. You tell us, in such a situation how can we have another mouth to feed?'

There was a long silence. A new crease appeared on Thulkaki's forehead. Her breathing grew laboured and a wheezing came from deep within her chest. She fingered the amulet on her neck and glanced at her nephew, who was staring at the ground with a troubled expression. 'Do what you want,' she said. 'Ganga has us, she won't starve and die.' She rose and walked away. 'Out, you cursed thing!' she yelled at a hen that had strayed into the garlic patch. Premkala fixed her accusing eyes on her husband. How he loved being the nice one.

5

Whenever his infirm and elderly relatives visited Kathmandu, Tamule ji took them to the large government-run hospital in the centre of the city. Grimy, crowded and underequipped, it was the only place where the poor from the across the country could afford to get treatment. But this time, in an effort to make up with Thulkaki, he had booked an appointment with Dr Pandey. It would be his first visit to his clinic. He put on a clean, ironed shirt and was combing his hair when Numa came darting into the room.

'Baba, guess what?' she said, her face flushed with excitement. 'No school today!'

'What?'

'Yes, our bus didn't come,' Numa said. 'We heard the protesters have blocked the road near our school.' She clapped her hands and did a little twist dance. 'Aha, I'm so happy. I don't have to see Hemanta Sir's face today. He's such a—'

'Stop blathering and go study,' Tamule ji said.

'Go study go study,' Numa mimicked him. 'Today is chutti so no study!'

~

Kathmandu had been seething with mutinous energy since the blockade. Anger over the fuel shortage had flared up into collective rage against the royalist regime. Every day members of the banned political parties came out to the streets and raised their party flags. They pelted stones at the police and screamed slogans with their fists in the air. 'Death to the Panchayat system!' 'Victory to the multi-party system!' Party activists were being rounded up and arrested across the country. Every day clashes broke out between the police and the protesters. In the latest incident, the police had shot dead four young men in Bhaktapur, the old city in the eastern part of the valley.

Tamule ji had no petrol left in his motorbike. The lone auto-rickshaw he found on the ring road charged him double fare for having to drive through the turbulent streets. Thulkaki's feeble body shook as the auto hurtled along the bumpy roads. 'He's a famous doctor,' Tamule ji told her. 'It's lucky we got an appointment for today.'

'Ah, you know best, my son,' Thulkaki said with a forgiving smile.

They drove past the government buildings guarded by policemen in riot gear. Groups of students stood outside Lalitpur Multiple Campus, waving the starry red flags of the Democratic Party and the hammer-and-sickle flags of the Leftist parties. The boundary walls and buildings along the main road carried freshly painted slogans. 'Death to the Panchayat system', 'Victory to the multi-party system', 'Scoundrel king, leave the country.' A small procession of men in daura suruwal, the official attire of government employees, was passing through the road near the Tundikhel parade ground. 'Jaya desh, jaya naresh!' they chanted. Tamule ji leaned forward to get a better view. A group of ministers sat in a ceremonial horse-drawn carriage bearing larger-than-life portraits of the King and the Queen. Among them was the royal cabinet member whose daughter was Sumnima's best friend.

The auto-rickshaw driver, who'd been silent all along, spoke all of a sudden: 'What a bunch of jokers.'

Tamule ji laughed. Pancha rallies had become a daily phenomenon since anti-Panchayat protests gained momentum across the country. Members of the National Panchayat, willing and unwilling civil servants, and supporters bussed in from neighbouring districts would parade around town carrying Panchayat banners, and the next morning photos of the parade would be splashed across the front pages of national newspapers. Jaya desh, jaya naresh!

~

Despite the tense atmosphere outside, the clinic waiting room was filled with visitors. The doctor had not arrived yet. Tamule ji helped Thulkaki squeeze herself into a bench crammed with patients. She looked spruced up in a clean sari and a new pair of sandals, but her heavy nose ornament of hand-beaten gold, the patuka tied around her waist, and her cloth headgear marked her out as an outsider from a rural hinterland. She sat still and quiet, like an obedient child, and kept glancing at Tamule ji for a cue. Tamule ji felt a wave of pity for her. Watching her now, no one would believe the command she wielded over people back home, and how she cajoled and bullied everyone. The city diminished his kinfolk, reduced even the hardiest among them to helpless nobodies. Day in and day out they braved the adversities of mountain life, carried loads on their backs and mastered the steep, rugged trails, yet the minute they landed in Kathmandu, they needed his help even to cross a busy street.

A full hour passed before an excited murmur ran through the crowd. 'Doctor Saab is here!' Dr Pandey appeared at the door, his grave, bespectacled face exuding a godlike aura. His assistant leapt to his side and briefed him as he strode to his cabin nodding and looking straight ahead. Some of the patients half rose and greeted him with a namaste. Tamule ji gazed at him in awe. Once when Sumnima was a toddler, just beginning to comprehend words, he had asked her, 'You'll become a big person when you grow up, a doctor, won't you?' And to his utter delight, she had nodded and said, 'Yes!'

Tamule ji and Thulkaki waited for another half an hour before the assistant led them inside. Dr Pandey sat behind his desk, looking dignified in his white coat and silver-rimmed glasses, a stethoscope slung around his neck. In a clipped, matter-of-fact tone he asked Thulkaki to describe her symptoms. Thulkaki answered in a weak, breathy voice, bowing her head and clasping her hands like a supplicant. 'Don't be afraid, Kaki,' said Tamule ji. 'You must explain all your problems to Doctor Saab.' Dr Pandey waved a hand to indicate she'd said enough. He tucked his stethoscope into his ears and checked her breathing, then measured her pulse, blood pressure and temperature. He told her to open her mouth, pushed her tongue down with a flat wooden stick, then lit a torch and peered into the glistening cavern of her throat. He put down the tools and took out a prescription pad. The thick silence in the room was starting to make Tamule ji uncomfortable.

'Dr Saab,' he said with a deferential smile. 'Do you know our daughters are classmates? My daughter goes to Rhododendron too.'

'Really?' the doctor said in a nonchalant tone. 'It's just a post-viral cough. Did you consult anyone earlier?'

Tamule ji gave him a blank stare. It took him a moment to register the question. 'No, Doctor Saab,' he answered hurriedly. 'I haven't consulted anyone.' He was glad he hadn't, for Dr Pandey was known to be ill disposed to those who consulted other doctors before paying him a visit.

'Hm.' The doctor wrote something on the prescription pad with a few swift strokes of his pen.

'Doctor Saab,' Tamule ji gently interrupted him. 'She has trouble breathing. Her chest makes this *swaa-swaa* sound all the time, so I was suspecting asthma…'

The doctor looked up from his note-pad and said in a perfectly calm voice, 'If you already diagnosed her, you shouldn't have brought her here in the first place.' He tore off the prescription, handed it to Tamule ji and turned to the door. 'Next!'

~

That evening the Tamule family stood on the roof terrace and watched a torch rally passing through the ring road. People marched in the dark, holding up flaming torches that lit up the jacaranda trees. Their slogans reverberated far and wide. 'Panchayat vyawastha murdabad!' 'Bahudaliya vyawastha jindabad!' All over the city people had turned off the lights in solidarity with the protesters. Only a few dots flickered here and there over the black expanse. 'Those are the houses of Panches and royalists,' said Tamule ji. Sumnima and Numa did not fully comprehend the situation but could sense something momentous happening. A drama was unfolding in the streets, there was a buzz of expectancy in the air. The chaos had upset people's humdrum routines and brought normal life to a halt. They wished the strike would last forever and that the holiday would never come to an end.

6

During his third year at Jemadar Limbu's house, Gajendra had unexpectedly struck up a friendship with Rajan. One evening when he was packing to go home for Dasain, he heard a light knock on his door. It took him a moment to recognize the stocky form that stood outside in the dark. 'Gajendra dai,' Rajan said, furiously puffing on a cigarette, 'can we talk for a minute?' He took one last drag and flicked the stub away. Gajendra let him in, surprised by this unannounced visit.

While Gajendra made preparations for tea, Rajan sat on a muda and gazed around the room in the dim light of a naked bulb that hung from the ceiling. The room smelled of incense and fried onions and spices. The money-plant on the windowsill was thriving. The glossy, heart-shaped leaves trailed up the wall, adding a touch of life and colour to the bare room. One corner of the floor was the cooking area. Gajendra sat on a low wooden pirka, bent over a pot of boiling tea. A few steel utensils were arranged on a raised wooden plank in a neat, shining row. Only the floor around the bed looked cluttered. Half-stuffed bags, clothes of various sizes, a plastic doll, a toy car, pouches of tea, sugar and spices, strings, scissors.

'So you're going home tomorrow,' Rajan said, accepting a glass of tea from his host. Gajendra pulled up a muda and sat down. 'Is everything all right, bhai?' he asked, peering at Rajan's distraught face.

Rajan sipped his tea. 'Actually,' he said, 'I came to ask for a favour.'

He hemmed and hawed for a while before revealing his predicament. As it turned out, he was courting an upper-caste Chhetri girl whose parents would never let her marry him. In their eyes he was a Bhote, a member of one of those jungly tribes only good at drinking, dancing and frittering their lives away. Not until long ago, a Matwali like him would have been punished by law for daring to court a high-caste woman. Besides, he lacked a stable job or any real prospect of success. They had recently found an ideal match for their daughter—a police officer of the same caste who had amassed several ropanis of land in the plains during his young career. For months the girl had been tormented by indecision. In the end, amid many doubts and fears, she had decided to follow her heart and elope with Rajan. They planned to tie the knot at a temple on the main day of Dasain, which was only a week away.

'But then,' Rajan said, 'I need a place to hide her for a night before confronting my mother.' He paused and added with some hesitation, 'You think she could stay in this room while you're away? It's just for one night, she will leave in the morning before the first light.'

Gajendra was at a loss. Letting a strange young woman sleep in his room for a night might tarnish his image beyond repair. His landlady would throw him out if she found out. And what would Premkala think? But then he would never be able to face Rajan again if he turned him down now. He steeled himself and gave him the key.

By the time Gajendra returned from Lungla, Rajan had already brought his bride home. Boju had grudgingly accepted the union after the repeated entreaties of her daughter and relatives. Rajan believed his mother would gradually come around and all would be well. He thanked Gajendra for his help and invited him upstairs for a small celebration.

It was a perfect evening. Gajendra sat on the floormat with Rajan and Boju while Premkala floated in and out of the room, bringing them extra helpings of food, adding hot water in their tongba and joining their conversation every now and then. Her face, adorned by nothing save a pair of thin gold hoops, looked warm and open as usual. Yet there was something different about her today, thought Gajendra, watching her from the corner of his eye. A touch of shyness in her manner, a new spark in her eyes that seemed kindled by his presence. A wave of joy washed over him, muddling up his thoughts as he sat listening to his host. Rajan was in equally high spirits. Not only had he become a man with a wife, he was also planning to start his own business, a momo restaurant on the ground floor of a friend's house. 'Everyone's crazy about buff momo these days,' he said, 'there's no risk at all.' His mother sounded skeptical but pleased. 'Idiot,' she said, slurping tongba through a bamboo straw, 'don't speak too soon or you'll ruin it.'

During a brief interlude Rajan went to his room and came back with a young woman dressed in an all-red ensemble—a red sari, red bangles, a red bead necklace, and red vermillion in the parting of her hair. He introduced her as Shanti. She had a pale face with big, alert eyes and a chiselled nose pierced with a diamond stud. Her little red mouth stretched in a perfunctory smile as she joined her hands and greeted Gajendra. She sat beside her husband in sullen silence while Boju drank one round after another, regaling them with rambunctious stories from her youth. Every once in a while Rajan would aim his straw at Shanti and offer her a sip, and she would crease up her nose and shake her head in mock disgust.

'Oho, look at these lovebirds,' Boju said with fake jocularity. 'Don't force her if she doesn't want to drink. Too much love is not good.'

Shanti's face dropped. A flash of anger lit up her eyes. She opened her mouth to speak but stopped, then stood up and left the room. In the ensuing silence Rajan glared at Boju, who glared back as if challenging him to question her. Gajendra kept his eyes focused on his tongba, bracing himself for the imminent flare-up. But the spark of anger did not last long. The warm, sour-sweet, full-bodied millet tongba quickly eased the tension and restored the merry mood.

After her third round of drink, Boju began heaping praise on her guest. 'What a wonderful man he is, our Gajendra babu, I wonder which fortunate woman will marry him. No matter who you choose, make sure she's a Matwali. Best to stick to your own kind.'

Gajendra gave Rajan an awkward smile.

'Don't get me wrong,' Boju said. 'It's his life, he can do what he wants.' She thought for a moment and added in a self-consoling tone, 'At least he didn't become a lahure.'

'Did you plan to become one?' Gajendra asked Rajan.

'Yes, I'd always wanted to join the army, like our father and uncles,' Rajan said, 'but Ama threatened to disown me if I did.'

'Threatened?' Boju hit him on his shoulder. 'Gadha, I saved you from ending up like that cranky old fogey.'

~

After eighteen years of service in the British Indian Army, Jemadar Sher Bahadur Limbu had returned to his country and bought an old mud-brick house in Kathmandu. One of the first Limbus to own property in the capital city, he had no wish to return to his home village in the far-flung district of Tehrathum. During his long absence, his wife had eloped with a man she had met at a paddy dance in the weekly haat bazaar. There was nothing left of their kipat, the shared land that his ancestors had worked from generation to generation. Plot by plot, gradually and lawfully, the land had gone into the hands of high-caste settlers, like a slow-spreading natural calamity. Many of his relatives had migrated to Sikkim and Burma in search of a better life. Besides, the bullet wound on his knee would no longer allow him to master the steep, hilly terrain. He would rather find a new wife and settle down in his new home in Kathmandu.

For months his relatives tried to find him a suitable Limbu woman from the hills, to no avail. No one wanted to marry a limping and battle-hardened forty-year-old man. Jemadar soon lost hope and had almost given up when a distant relative came up with a promising prospect. There was a young Limbuni in Gwangkhel, a village south of Patan, orphaned as a child and raised by relatives who were eager to marry her off. Why not go see her once?

And this was how Jemadar Limbu and his relatives had come to Dhan Kumari's uncle's house to ask for her hand. They arrived on a spring morning soon after harvest. The fields of Gwangkhel glowed green with young corn, and sheaves of golden wheat lay across their front-yard, ready for threshing. Dhan Kumari sat before Jemadar on the verandah surrounded by relatives from both sides. He was a dour-looking man not much younger than her uncle, his mouth pulled up in an odd grin. The sleeves of his black coat had identical oval patches on the elbows. Was he so frugal that he would make do with a patched coat on a day like this? she wondered. Or was it some kind of curious fashion? On his wrist he sported a gold-rimmed watch with a leather band. Their eyes met once, but he looked away as if he'd been caught stealing.

An elderly relative of his had been assigned the role of intermediary. The old man put a jar of millet liquor, some dried river fish and a one-rupee coin on a brass tray and placed it before Dhan Kumari. Then he began to explain the purpose of their visit in a singsong tone. 'What a special day it is, please accept our greetings. After a long search we've arrived at your door, hoping to gain your hearty consent…' Dhan Kumari and her cousins stifled their giggles. The elder introduced Jemadar and described his family tree. 'We have gladly confirmed that our families are not related, no trace of blood kinship in the past three generations.' Once the proposal was made, Dhan Kumari's aunt turned to Jemadar and plied him with questions. Are you sure you want to marry our niece? Will you promise you'll keep her happy? You won't hurt her if she makes mistakes, will you? Her playful, hectoring tone caused great hilarity among all those gathered. Jemadar nodded or shook his head in response. 'Now you tell us,' the aunt turned to Dhan Kumari, 'are you happy with the arrangement?' Dhan Kumari dutifully nodded her head. 'Arey, our chatterbox has gone silent today,' her uncle broke in, provoking more laughter. 'Say it out loud for everyone to hear.' Dhan Kumari frowned in mock anger. 'All right, I'm happy,' she said. Jemadar got up and placed a coin in his bride-to-be's hand, sealing the deal.

'Thank your stars, my dear,' her relatives said after the guests left. 'You are getting a lahure husband with a lifelong pension.'

The wedding took place a month later. The main ceremony was held at the ancient Kirat temple in Sano Hattiban, the sacred forest where the Rai and Limbu people celebrated their Udhauli and Ubhauli festivals each year. During festival time Dhan Kumari and her friends would spend hours dancing to the music of drums and cymbals that resounded through the forest. Today the ritual kept her fixed to one spot. She sat on a floormat beside Jemadar, her lokanti maids at her side, while the phedangma recited stories from the Mundhum. She looked dazzling in her red mekhli and complete set of Limbu jewellery. An enormous gold disc shone like the sun on top of her head and a crescent moon sat at the centre of her forehead. Her neck was adorned with a red-and-gold kantha and a long necklace made of silver coins. Jemadar, clean-shaven and dressed in a white taga, looked younger than usual. Yet some of the guests were heard whispering that he could easily pass as the bride's father. The phedangma slaughtered a pair of hens before the couple's eyes and drained the blood. Still chanting the Mundhum, he dipped a stick in millet liquor, touched it to the couple's heads and made the groom tie a coin to the end of the bride's shawl. Afterwards, relatives took turns offering tika and blessings to the couple. Dhan Kumari felt restless throughout the ceremony. Her legs ached from sitting in the same position for too long. Jemadar sat like a rock, without a frown or a whimper. In the evening all the guests gathered in the courtyard of Jemadar's house in Kasai Tol. His relatives had made a makeshift stove in the back field and cooked a feast in gigantic pots coated with mud. A pig was slaughtered and a hindquarter put aside to be sent to the bride's family. The rest of the flesh was transformed into a variety of delicacies for the guests. Millet liquor and tongba flowed like water, and a few drunks had to be dragged home even before the meal was served. After the meal, men and women danced hand in hand to the slow beat of drums and the clash of cymbals that echoed through the night.

~

Dhan Kumari had heard many stories of lahures who had fought in foreign battlefields during the two world wars. There was one uncle who had told her how, amid the hail of enemy fire, he had carried his wounded comrade on his shoulders and run for his life. Another relative had, so the story went, boiled his leather boots to prevent himself from starving in the deep forests of Malaya. But Jemadar, who had commanded an entire platoon while fighting in Burma, never mentioned his past. Dhan Kumari found him as impenetrable as a wall. Stiff and taciturn, he spent most of his time digging, fixing, pounding or hacking things in the yard. Within two years of buying the house, he had paved the courtyard with stone slabs and installed a hand-pump for drawing water from the well. He had cleared the overgrown backyard and built a pit latrine with sand and clay extracted from the banks of the nearby Tukucha. Not for him the idle chatter that occupied Dhan Kumari's free time. She had noticed how his eyes narrowed in disapproval when he saw her sitting in the sun hunting for lice in her sisters' hair, or playing gatta and hopscotch with the neighbourhood kids. In his presence she felt compelled to hold her garrulous tongue. She restrained her immodest laughter. If he caught her admiring herself in the mirror or gazing out of the window, her hand would involuntarily reach for the slate on which he sometimes taught her to write. There was no other time when she feared him more. He would make her sit by the window with a slate and a piece of chalk, then plant himself beside her and dictate the alphabet. Her shaky hand scrawled one deformed letter after another on the squeaky board. Her nerves on edge, she would stay braced for the moment when his patience might snap and his hard hand would land on her back. But although she remained a hopeless pupil till the end, Jemadar never once raised his hand on her.

Behind his back Dhan Kumari called him sanki buda and joked with her sisters about his odd habits. He kept, for instance, a small jar filled with black pellets that resembled goat excreta on their bedroom shelf. At night before blowing out the lantern, he would open the jar and swallow two pellets with water. He had told her it was ayurvedic medicine, but when she asked him what it was for, he had given her no answer. 'It must be for constipation,' she told her laughing sisters, 'he always has that look, doesn't he?' Some nights she could hear him muttering and grinding his teeth in his sleep. Once, in the middle of the night she awoke to the sound of him sniffling against his pillow. It sounded like he was crying. She lay listening for a long while, completely at a loss, before asking him warily, 'Jemadar Saab, what's wrong?'

'Nothing,' he said in a hard, clear voice. 'Just go back to sleep.'

Even after they had two children, a son and a daughter, Jemadar remained aloof and unreachable. People in Kasai Tol complained that he always went limping past them without so much as a smile but did not mind greeting stray dogs on the road. They said they sometimes heard him talking to himself like a madman. Such comments upset Dhan Kumari and made her resent both her sniggering neighbours and her deranged husband. Still, compared to her sisters' husbands, who swore at them and beat them in a drunken rage, her sanki buda seemed all right. If only she could rid him of his illness. After consulting her relatives and a few wise elders in Gwangkhel, she concluded that Jemadar had been possessed by harmful spirits while fighting for strange white men in distant lands. Only an experienced bijuwa would be able to cure him with his age-old healing power. To Dhan Kumari's surprise, Jemadar sounded willing, even eager, to take part in the ritual. A bijuwa was invited from Gwangkhel and the ceremony held without delay. A group of relatives came to lend Dhan Kumari a helping hand. They made an altar out of bamboo stalks and banana leaves in the courtyard and gathered everything they needed to propitiate the deities. Dried gourds filled with millet liquor, a chicken, incense, flowers, grain, ginger, mugwort leaves. The bijuwa, a small, grey-haired man, came dressed in an old white robe and a feather headdress. Necklaces made of tiny brass bells and rudraskha beads hung from his neck. He sat Jemadar down before the altar and called upon his master spirits, shaking all over, his voice rising and falling as he slowly went into a trance. Meanwhile, one of Dhan Kumari's relatives slaughtered the chicken and placed it near the altar. Every once in a while, the bijuwa's chanting sounded like the cry of a wounded animal. Dhan Kumari sat in a corner with her relatives and watched with anxious eyes. The bijuwa stood up after some time and danced around the altar beating a brass plate. Still chanting and shaking, he picked up a sprig of mugwort and touched it to Jemadar's head and shoulders. Jemadar bowed his head and closed his eyes. His haggard face exuded a childlike trust that moved and tickled Dhan Kumari in equal measure.

In the following months Dhan Kumari noticed a kind of transformation coming over her husband. The permanently strained look on his face seemed to have softened a little. He smiled at the neighbours he passed on the road and welcomed guests and visitors to his house. The hours he would have spent in dark seclusion he now spent cradling his baby girl and listening to the prattle of his toddler son. He carried the boy everywhere, even to the Indian Embassy where he went to collect his pension every month. His clumsy attempts at affection amused Dhan Kumari. He seemed to have suddenly realized that the mother of his children was a woman whose youth had been stolen from her, a girl deprived of play and laughter. As if to atone for his late realization, he bought her bangles and anklets from a shop on Juddha Road. He urged her to seek recreation with a purpose. On hearing that a women's parade was being organized for the new king's coronation ceremony, Jemadar obtained special permission for her to take part in it. The participants would be trained for three months in the grounds of Singha Durbar. Jemadar insisted on looking after the children and doing the morning chores while she went for the practice. Dhan Kumari detested the monotony of the drill and felt out of place among her fellow paraders. Most of them came from affluent households and wouldn't deign to speak to her. But the glorious precincts of the Singha Durbar palace and the sweet, warm selroti they served afterwards made it worth the pain.

~

On the main day of Dasain, Jemadar donned his brown felt hat, an old gift from a British commander, picked up his walking stick and went with his wife and son to receive tika from a relative. Dhan Kumari had never walked the streets in the company of her husband. She hid her face behind her umbrella all the way. As they were passing through Ason Tol, an old woman leaned out of an upper-floor window and hollered to Jemadar in Newari, 'Gayou bala changu che.' Jemadar stopped, threw back his head and erupted into a hoarse laugh. 'Che makhu,' he said, 'kya kha.'

My son, not grandson. Dhan Kumari covered her mouth and giggled under her umbrella. She had never seen her husband speak to a stranger before, never heard him laugh so freely, never even known he could speak Newari. Could the bijuwa have healed him after all?

But the laughter that seemed to affirm life turned out to be a portent of death. Jemadar fell ill the next day and lay in bed from morning till night, moaning and shivering under the quilts. At night Dhan Kumari heard him clenching his teeth and raving in his sleep again. On the third morning, when she went out and came back with a neighbourhood faith healer, they found him lying cold and still as a rock, his mouth half open, his glassy eyes staring into oblivion.

Dhan Kumari could not make sense of her husband's death, nor why everyone was blaming her for his untold miseries. The neighbours and relatives who had pronounced him a loony now recalled him as a different man. A virtuous soul who never bore ill will towards anyone, and so kind he even talked to stray dogs. As for his silly young wife, she heard them say, she did not even shed a tear over his death. Why would she? He has left behind a house and a lifelong pension for her. Couldn't she at least act like a proper widow? Swanning about town like a newly-wed bride. Dhan Kumari reacted to such remarks with unbridled hostility, sparing not even those who wished her well. One day, when Abdullah, the old bangle-seller in Bagbazar, asked her if Limbu widows were allowed to wear colourful bangles, she flung the bangles at his face and shouted, 'You musulte, what do you think I should wear? A necklace made out of my husband's bones?' Another time, in the middle of a film screening at the first cinema hall in town, she swore at the villain and made heads turn. Blurted out in a hall packed with people, the jet of expletives brought her a queer sense of relief, as though she were hitting back at the unseen tormentor.

The Tamule house was a hive of activity all day. Numa spent the morning dusting the furniture and wiping the objects in the display cabinet. Sumnima scrubbed the bathroom tiles and replaced the misshapen lump of soap with a fat, creamy bar of international brand. By early afternoon, dinner preparations were already in full swing. Premkala sliced, pounded and mixed a variety of ingredients and wiped the dinner set meant for special occasions. The porcelain and silverware sparkled among the old and encrusted pots scattered around the kitchen. A visiting nephew from Lungla had slaughtered a chicken and was singeing it in the yard. Boju sat beside him stoking the fire and giving instructions, 'Hold it closer to the flame, Saila, uff, not that close, you'll burn it.' The smell of charred feathers wafted across the neighbourhood.

Tamule ji bustled around the house making sure everything was in order. He brought the Tibetan carpet out of Boju's room and rolled it out on the living room floor. 'Premkala, is the water tank full?' he said, stopping by the kitchen. 'Girls, hurry up, I have more tasks for you.' He leaned out of the window and shouted, 'Saila, can you remove your mattress from the living room?' He went outside, quickly dusted the shoe-rack near the entrance, then picked up a broom and gave the verandah a brisk sweep. He looked around him and sighed in satisfaction. It was a radiant summer afternoon. The trees in the garden were covered with tight, scarlet plums and downy peaches that filled the air with a fruity, overripe smell. The bramble bushes along the path bore wild berries, some hard and shiny like beads and some so soft they squished between fingers. Thick gourd vines had invaded people's yards. They draped over walls and fences, crept up trees and drainpipes, and looped around verandah railings, their tendrils hanging from the eaves like the ringlets of a woman's hair. A sparrow dove into the wheat field and flew back into the sky in one swift elastic movement. Tamule ji's heart soared along with the bird in flight. If happiness could be measured in days, today he was a happy man.

A year had passed since the people's movement brought down the thirty-year-old Panchayat regime and reinstated multi-party democracy. The change had given rise to new hopes and anxieties. Like many others, Tamule ji felt the need to better his lot, pursue new possibilities. He had decided to quit his job at the electricity corporation and try his luck in the development aid sector. Aid flowed in freely in the loosened atmosphere. Dollar-funded projects were multiplying fast, making 'project job' the most coveted career option among educated Nepalis. Over the past year Tamule ji had applied for jobs with nearly a dozen projects, from infrastructure to irrigation to family planning. After a series of failed attempts, he had finally had a stroke of luck a few months ago. On his way back from Lungla, he had met a middle-aged American couple returning from a trek across the eastern hills. They took an interest in him after learning he had grown up in the region. They sat near him on the flight back to Kathmandu and asked him about his life's journey. Despite his halting English and the roar of the aircraft, Tamule ji managed to describe his trials and tribulations in poignant detail. His story seemed to have impressed the Americans. In Kathmandu, they put him in touch with another foreigner, who advised him to apply for a vacant position at the Global Integrated Development Centre (GIDC), a well-known international NGO. Tamule ji submitted his application, was shortlisted for an interview, and a few days ago received a letter that felt like a boon from heaven. Although the change in his job title—from manager to program assistant—seemed like a demotion, the project job would not only raise his profile, it would also pay him four times his current salary. He had invited the American couple for dinner to show his appreciation.

~

Reverent anticipation filled the air as six o'clock drew near. Tamule ji put on one of his best shirts and went to receive the guests on the ring road, sparking a flurry of last-minute activity in the house. Numa quickly surveyed the living room and tucked in the sofa slipcovers. Sumnima hid the broken buckets and cleaning rags in the backyard. Premkala turned off the noisy stove and changed out of her grease-stained lungi into a kurta surwal. She sat Boju down on a kitchen chair and said, 'Ama, listen. They are our special guests. No foul words, OK? And why are you wearing this old lungi? Wear a sari.' Boju stood up, pointed at her crotch and spat an insult before marching out. Just then the doorbell rang.

~

The faux-crystal chandelier burned bright in the living room. Sumnima and Numa sat squeezed together on a sofa and studied their guests. The man had a pale face with greenish brown eyes and long legs that stretched out under the table. The woman had brown skin, dark eyes and dark hair gathered into a messy bun. Although at first glance she looked almost Nepali, her baggy tie-die trousers, her hemp handbag and something about the way she moved lent her the unmistakable aura of a foreigner. She reached for the bowl of peanuts and held it out to the girls as though she were the host. They bashfully took some and said, 'Thank you, aunty.'

'You can call me Katie,' she said with a smile. 'And he's Brian.'

Numa giggled. Her name sounded funny; 'keti' meant 'girl' in Nepali.

'So, Sumeena, which grade are you in?' Katie asked.

'Seven.'

After a brief warm-up chat, Premkala went to the kitchen and returned with two steaming bowls on a tray. 'This is a Nepali soup,' she said, carefully placing each bowl on a crochet doily. 'Its name is gundruk. It is made of green leaves called as saag.' The guests nodded in appreciation and asked her how it was made. 'First we have to beat the saag,' Premkala beat imaginary saag with her fist. 'Then we put it in a tin and press it very hardly. Then we remain it just like that for a few weeks. In that time it rottens and gets sour taste.'

Sumnima pinched and nudged her sister.

'How interesting,' said Katie. The guests sipped the broth and exchanged quick remarks that escaped their hosts. Even Sumnima and Numa, so proud of their 'good English', had trouble understanding them. Katie looked up and said in an animated voice, 'It's delicious. Day-rai mitto cha!'

'You speak good Nepali,' Tamule ji said with a grateful smile.

Sumnima and Numa murmured in agreement. Everything about their guests charmed them. Their exaggerated friendliness, their mispronounciation of Nepali words, their clumsy attempt to eat rice with their hands, even their forgetting to take their shoes off before entering the living room.

Sumnima felt like a lady as she sipped Coke and dabbed a napkin on her mouth. If only that fleeting moment of elegance defined her whole lifestyle. Tejaswi and Reshma probably drank Coca-Cola with every meal. She had gathered from their conversations that their dining habits were enviably different from hers. Whenever Reshma mentioned her 'breakfast on the lawn', Sumnima imagined her sitting in a beautiful garden buttering her toast while her servant—household staff—poured a cascade of tea out of a real teapot, like in Hindi movies. Unlike the Tamules, who ate a complete dalbhat meal at mid-morning, Reshma's family had toast, eggs and sausages for breakfast and dalbhat only around noon. They used knife and fork, not fingers, and ate out of dishes made of glass and porcelain, not stainless steel. Sumnima would often describe their habits to her mother in a longing and self-pitying tone, and in the same tone her mother would reply, 'Too bad your father is not a ghusya mantri.' Reshma's father, the former Panchayat minister, remained corrupt in the public eye even though he had shifted allegiance and joined the ruling Democratic Party.

'Did I tell you,' Brian said to Tamule ji, 'one of our porters on the trek was also a Tamule. His name was Prem Bahadur Tamule, a really nice chap. Could he be related to you?'

'In my family, no one is porter,' Tamule ji said in a somewhat defensive tone. He thought for a moment and added with a pained expression, 'But porters are the hardest workers. I feel so sorry for them.'

'They're incredibly tough,' said Brian.

'Yes, it is a very tough life,' Tamule ji said. 'In my village they are even twelve years old, thirteen years old. They have no shoes, not even one pair.'

~

Boju heard the sounds of laughter coming from the living room. She had changed into a clean sari, combed her thin hair over her balding scalp, and rolled a dozen cotton wool wicks to pass the time. But no one came for her. Had they forgotten about her? Or were they deliberately excluding her? She who spent her days putting their household in order, she who raised chickens to feed their guests, grew crops and vegetables in their yard, guarded their house against thieves, dogs and ragpickers. If she wanted, she could pack her bags right away and leave for good. After all she had a house of her own in the centre of the city. If only her half-wit son could tame his wife.

A sudden squawk and clatter put a stop to her thoughts. She rushed to the window. The nephew stood outside in the dim light, clutching a hen with one hand and holding the coop shutter with the other. 'O Saila,' she said. 'Did you see the guests?' Saila turned around. The hen wriggled out of his grasp and scampered off. He ran after it and disappeared into darkness. Just then Premkala popped her head in at the door. 'Ama, aren't you coming?' Boju kept quiet. She wanted a proper request, not a throwaway question like that. But her daughter rushed off without waiting for her response. Knowing this was her only chance, Boju gingerly made her way towards the living room.

'Hey Bhagwan,' she said aloud as Tamule ji began introducing her to the guests. 'They came in with their shoes on!' Premkala shot her a warning look and hustled her to a corner sofa. Boju sat there, looking the guests up and down, silently fretting over their shoes soiling the carpet. Tamule ji and Premkala were struggling with their limited vocabulary and made no effort to draw her into the conversation. This seemed to make the guests uncomfortable. Katie turned to Boju and said in her over-friendly voice, 'So what do you do at home all day?' Tamule ji explained the question to Boju and tried translating her answer into English. 'She is saying that she cares the house, grows her grandchildren, feeds the hens. She remembers God. Every morning she listens to holy songs...' The guests looked amused at first, but shifted restlessly in their seats as Boju launched into a lengthy sermon on old age and death. 'Boju, enough,' Sumnima said softly in Nepali, but she carried on. 'What to do, everyone treats old people like scrap. People don't realize they too will grow old one day...' The guests glanced at the wall clock. Their nostrils flared with suppressed yawns.

Then, all of a sudden, Premkala got up and rushed out of the room, causing a welcome interruption to Boju's monologue. She returned a moment later with a tub of ice cream and a stack of bowls and spoons on a tray. 'I forgot to give the sweet dish,' she said, putting the ice cream in the bowls. Two scoops each for the guests, one each for the rest.

As the guests prepared to leave, Tamule ji summoned his

nephew and asked him to escort them to the ring road with a torch. The black starless night rang with a chorus of insects. Tamule ji stood at the gate and watched the three retreating silhouettes till they could be seen no more. Premkala and the girls cleared away dishes and discussed the dinner like actors meeting backstage after a performance. All had gone well. Now they could drop their poses and speak in their own language. They dimmed the lights, turned on the television and collapsed onto the sofa with a collective sigh. The day's broadcast had just ended. The national anthem erupted on the screen, in praise of the Five Times Blessed King whose power had shrunk ever so slightly under the new system. The nephew slipped in through the door carrying a rolled-up mattress and a pillow. Premkala turned off the television, locked the cabinet and hustled everyone to bed.

While Premkala slept, Tamule ji lay awake for a long time, thinking of his new job and the bright days ahead. He thought of the large and clean office building, the spick-and-span bathroom with a hand-soap and a roll of white tissue paper, the staff van that would pick him up in the mornings and drop him home in the evenings. Twelve thousand rupees a month and additional allowances for field trips—he still could not believe his luck. From the hills of Lungla to the offices of an international NGO—Pandit Bajey's prediciton was coming true after all.

~

Tamule ji was only five when Pandit Bajey foresaw that he would rise in the world. On that morning the old priest was officiating at a puja held in the courtyard of the Tamule house. After bundling up the fruit, grain, ghiu and other sacred offerings, he said to Tamule ji's father, 'Your son Gajey has a very lucky forehead. Rest assured, he'll be no less than a Bahun's son.'

'With your blessings, Bajey,' Tamule ji's father said, joining his palms. He turned to the little boy who sat staring at the holy fire.

'Did you hear what Bajey said? Go touch his feet.'

Gajey ran and knelt down before the priest.

It was Pandit Bajey's habit to shower kind pronouncements on destitute clients who made him generous offerings. But to Tamule ji's father, his remark carried the weight of a divine prophecy. All his life he had struggled to attain the Brahmin's godliness. He belonged to the generation of Tamules who had embraced the ways of high-caste Hindus who ruled over their lives in their myriad avatars—as landlords, priests, soothsayers, moneylenders, generals and kings. Tamule ji's father had surrendered himself with the zeal of a convert. The high-caste people in the village neither accepted food from his hand nor allowed him to cross the threshold of their homes, but his faith in their inborn piety was absolute and unshakeable. He chanted Sanskrit mantras during puja, marked his forehead with sandalwood paste and fasted three days a week. His wife, who ate leftovers from his plate on normal days, was barred from coming within his sight when she had her monthly period. He saw his Rai, Limbu and Tamang neighbours through the eyes of his high-caste mentors and maintained a safe distance from them, avoiding meals cooked in their kitchen and excusing himself from their ceremonies. For this reason they had nicknamed him Chimse Bahun. As for the Untouchable people lower than even the lowest of Matwalis, Tamule ji's father left no stone unturned in showing them their place. In their presence he felt almost as pious as a Brahmin. 'Stop behaving like Kami-Damai,' he'd scold his children if they quarrelled or swore at each other. On spring evenings, when they brought home leaf cones heaped with aiselu, Tamule ji's father would cleanse the boys with the sprinkling of sunpani before allowing them inside the house. For he knew the brats went berry-hunting with kids from the Sarki settlement further up the hill. No matter how steep the path, whenever he ran into Pandit Bajey, Tamule ji's father would get down on all fours and press his head to his feet.

8

'Gajey, you have married a Limbuni all right,' Tamule ji's father had told him before he died, 'but don't ever defile your house with pork.'

Those thin slices of spicy pork with succulent layers of skin, fat and meat; smoked and fried pork with dark, crispy rind; tender chunks of boiled pork sprinkled with salt, chilli and lime-juice; pork cooked in pig's blood; and the gentle-flavoured gelatinous stew of pig's feet. Despite his boundless respect for his ancestors, Tamule ji could not resist the pork delicacies that were so popular among his wife's people. Over the years he had convinced himself that his father's injunction against bringing pork into the house did not extend to consuming it. His favourite was the flesh of the black hog of Dharan that Rajan sometimes brought from a special shop in town. On such occasions Premkala would cook the meat in the storage shed and serve it on the terrace.

'Bhai, this is first class,' Tamule ji said, chewing a fatty morsel with relish. They were sitting on the terrace that looked over the paddy fields bathed in orange twilight. Rajan poured out whisky in two glasses and offered him one. Tamule ji dipped a fingertip in his drink and flicked a drop into the air, for the wandering spirits of his ancestors. He took a long sip and sighed with pleasure. He had been on the road all day and was happy to be back.

It had been six months since he started his new job. Every few weeks he had to travel to one of the project areas of GIDC with some colleagues. Although he did not like being away from home, he welcomed these field trips with a sense of adventure. A city dweller exploring the hinterland, bringing literacy, livestock and irrigation to impoverished villagers. He took the inconveniences in his stride and found joy in small things. The greenery that filled his eyes once they left the city behind, the steady motion of the four-wheel drive, the music playing in the car, the fresh wind blowing in from the window. These journeys allowed him to forge friendships with people who might have been mere colleagues in the office setting. The open air and landscape inspired camaraderie, making them seek and enjoy the same flavours throughout the trip. The fried river fish served at small eateries along the highway, chilled beer after a long day of meetings with project beneficiaries and district officials, the delicious local chicken that the field staff cooked them for dinner. Tamule ji could not understand why his colleagues complained about the meagre field allowance. To him, getting paid extra for making these trips already felt like an indulgence. As a matter of fact, he had never felt so calm and secure in his life. Even after paying the utilities bills, monthly loan interest and children's school fees, he managed to save a little in his bank account every month. He no longer squabbled with his wife over grocery expenses. As for his daughters, nothing seemed to excite them more than the boxed meal he sometimes brought home from his office meetings. The little paper box would contain treats from a newly opened restaurant in town. A roast chicken leg or a cutlet nestled among French fries, a ketchup sachet, a napkin, and small plastic cutlery that they would save for future use.

'It must be a big organization, no?' Rajan said, spearing a piece of meat with his fork.

'Yes, they have projects in twelve districts,' Tamule ji said.

'Big organization, big dollars, eh?' Rajan guffawed. 'Where will you put all that money, dai?'

Tamule ji laughed. 'Dollars are only for kuires, bhai,' he said, 'we Nepalis earn Nepali rupees.'

'I hear a car comes to pick you up every day?'

'It's just a staff van,' Tamule ji said with a modest smile. 'It's always packed, so I prefer my motorbike.'

'Is it a fancy office?' Rajan said.

'Not at all,' Tamule ji said with a dismissive frown. He thought for a moment and added, 'Well, it's nice and clean, but not fancy like a five-star hotel. I don't even have my own room. I have to share it with two other people.'

'You work with kuires?'

'No, all my co-workers are Nepali. Only the head is kuire, and a few experts who come and go, the dollar wallahs.' He laughed.

Tamule ji usually took pride in describing his new job and office to his friends and acquaintances. 'Oho, a project job?' they said. Some congratulated him on entering the 'dollar farming' profession. Others complained that even peons and drivers at foreign-funded organizations behaved as though they were a cut above the rest. The tinge of envy in their voice pleased Tamule ji. But with Rajan, he felt the need to downplay his achievement. His brother-in-law still hadn't found a stable job. His efforts to go abroad had fallen through one after another. Only last week he had been disqualified for a prospective job in Korea after his X-ray report showed an old tuberculosis scar. But never one to brood over his problems, he looked relaxed now, sitting on the terrace enjoying his whisky and pork.

The glow of the setting sun washed over the fields and houses, and almost instantly dusk fell, casting shadows on the walls. The hills in the distance grew dim. Birds crisscrossed the air. The sounds of frogs in the paddy fields swelled to a dense chorus. Tamule ji and Rajan sipped their drinks in silence.

The door creaked open and Boju emerged on the terrace, her face set like stone. 'Ama, come join us,' Tamule ji said. Boju cast a severe glance at Rajan and sat down. Tamule ji leaned over the parapet and shouted for an extra glass. Numa promptly brought a glass, placed it on the table and ran back downstairs, crooning a jingle of a family planning ad promoted by the health ministry. At any other time this would have provoked laughter among the adults, but today Boju was not in the mood to laugh. She gulped down the whisky in one go and turned to Rajan. 'Oi mora,' she said, 'you said you'd bring the kids today, didn't you?'

'Eh, did I?' Rajan said absently. 'They're at their mamaghar.'

'Ha, I knew it,' Boju said, chewing a piece of rubbery pork skin. 'Why would she let them visit me?' She poured out another drink and downed it, her face aflame in the gathering dark. 'Just wait, one of these days I'll go throw her out of my house.'

Tamule ji and Rajan shook their heads at the empty threat. They knew Boju had no desire to return to the house that she loved to boast about. As Rajan often said, 'From this distance, she can only bark, not bite.' Although made in a moment of blind rage, her decision to move in with her daughter had set things right.

~

Jemadar Limbu's garden had been lying neglected since his death, becoming a tangled riot of creepers by the time his son got married. Gourd vines crawling up fruit trees, weeds blooming among garlic and onion plants, blue and purple morning glories entwined around reeds and cornstalks. A variety of edible weeds had sprung up in scattered clusters—purple-tinted mint, perilla plants, stinging nettle, curly niguro fern, and taro shrubs with broad, waterproof leaves off which raindrops rolled like transparent beads.

One morning, in the middle of preparing a meal, Shanti went to pick some green chillis from the garden. She moved warily past the thorny bushes, cursing the branches that scratched her arms, watching out for snakes lurking in the thick undergrowth. Time and again she had asked her mother-in-law to prune that unruly jungle, but the foul-mouthed crone would not listen. 'Clear your own bush, not mine,' she'd say with a wicked laugh. Shanti picked a handful of chillis and was hurrying back when she stepped on something that made her shriek. The burning sensation in her leg brought tears to her eyes. Tiny red rashes appeared on her foot, bare except for the thin-strap slipper. She had walked into a stinging nettle shrub! The ugly, prickly plant seemed the very incarnation of her mother-in-law at that moment.

Next day when Boju had gone to visit her sister, Shanti asked two of the lodgers downstairs to clear every shred of unnecessary vegetation in the back field. The boys picked up a hoe and a khukuri and jumped into action, slashing and digging up every plant that looked like weed. Nettles, taro shrubs, mint, ferns, morning glories, brambles, reeds. Shanti helped them stuff the plants in sacks and carry them to the butcher's next door. 'Your water buffaloes got lucky today,' she told the butcher's wife with a self-satisfied laugh. While the boys pulled out the few remaining weeds, Shanti gazed around the clear and empty yard. The air smelled of freshly cut grass. The sky looked bigger and bluer. Instead of the thicket of reeds and brambles, she could see the Tukucha River and the paddy fields beyond.

The shrill cry of a woman shattered her peace. Her mother-in-law stood in the yard shaking like a possessed witch. 'Which son of a whore...' she roared, throwing her hands up in the air. She marched over to one of the boys and tried to snatch the khukuri from his hand. 'You hacked off my plants? Now I'll chop off your fingers.' The boy jumped away crying, 'But Shanti bhauju told us to!' Only then did Boju turn to Shanti, her face purple with rage. 'You think this is your father's property?'

'Ha!' Shanti gave a little laugh. 'My father wouldn't shit on this swamp.'

'Your father who kicked you out?'

'Why wouldn't he? I was stupid enough to marry into a family like this.' Before Boju could reply, she went marching upstairs and banged the door shut. Beneath her anger she felt relieved that the long simmering tension had finally erupted, blowing away any pretence of civility. No feigned courtesies would be needed hereafter, no strained politeness. Lying in her husband's arms that night, Shanti asked in a tearful voice, 'Why was she acting like a madwoman? Is it a crime to rid the garden of weeds?'

'Just ignore her,' Rajan said, staring into her large, doleful eyes. 'She's a sour old lady.' Shanti wasn't consoled. Rajan snuggled up closer and whispered, 'Actually, she's an evergreen stinging nettle bush.' Shanti chuckled, which encouraged him to add, 'You know, whenever I flunked my exams, she used to hit me with a nettle sprig dipped in water. Athha, how it burned! Good thing you destroyed it.' Shanti burst out laughing and started tickling him.

Boju, lying alone in the next room, heard their laughter and spat out a curse in the dark. Those wild edibles had long been a source of delight for her. The zing of silam seeds in her tomato achar, the plain stew of taro leaves and stems, black dal thickened with taro tubers. A meal of sisnu and dhindo brought back memories of her childhood home. The gentle flavours of those free gifts of nature soothed and fortified her. The murderess had gone on a rampage and destroyed them all. It hardly seemed like yesterday that she came slinking into the house, timid as a mouse, with nothing but the clothes on her back. And now she was turning everything upside down. Boju could not stand that bird-like face of hers, the devious smile that had hypnotized her son, her sickly sweet voice and fluttering eyelashes. How proudly she told everyone that her parents had disowned her for marrying a Limbu, as if their rejection proved her superior worth. The string of suitors she had turned down, the fortune and glory she had forsaken...the lying bitch.

Although Boju had weakened her case in advance with her foul mouth and violent temper, Shanti used tact and subtlety to oust her rival. Without stamping her foot, without setting off a confrontation, without even raising her voice she could drive her mother-in-law into hysterics. All she had to do was play deaf when Boju called her, let her orders go in one ear and out the other, wait for Boju's fasting days to cook meat and other choice items, lock the kitchen shelf and hide the key before leaving the house, and then plead innocence with her husband when his mother went berserk. Aware of her waning authority, Boju sometimes yelled at Rajan just to assert her claim over him, reminding him of her motherly sacrifices and the debt of gratitude he owed her, while Shanti, her intended audience, sat in a corner with a smile that seemed to say, 'Cry yourself hoarse, old hag, but he is mine.'

The bad blood intensified after Shanti had her first child. Overjoyed at the birth of a grandson, Shanti's parents forgave her at last. A week after the baby was born, they showed up at Jemadar's house with a set of handmade baby clothes and tiffin carriers filled with nutritious chicken broth and superfoods made of cooked spices and nuts. Shanti's mother embraced her and wept. Her father cradled the baby in his arms and examined its face. 'Thank God,' he said, peering into his grandson's big, startled eyes, 'he looks like us.'

Shanti spent her confinement period in her natal home. She stayed for months on end, enjoying her mother's lavish care, arousing the resentment of her sisters-in-law, who slaved away while she fattened on ghiu and meat and received oil massages in the sun. They began complaining to their husbands and ignoring the orders of their mother-in-law. Tensions arose and tears were shed. Shanti, busy with her newborn, remained blissfully unaware of these subterranean wars.

All this time Boju had been pining for her grandson and pestering Rajan to bring the child home. Rajan ignored her, not wanting to disrupt the newfound harmony in his wife's family. Instead he went and stayed at his in-laws' house every few days. 'Thukka! Have you no pride?' Boju said when he returned. 'Those people kicked their daughter out for marrying you. How can you forget?'

Unbeknown to Boju, Rajan's relationship with his in-laws had been on the mend. At Shanti's suggestion, he had withdrawn his money from the failing restaurant business and loaned it to her brother without interest, rescuing him from a spiral of debt. This had softened his in-laws' attitude towards him. In their eyes, his devotion to his wife sometimes overshadowed his low origins. Besides he was not the lowest of the low. In fact, they had heard children were cleverer in intercaste marriages. 'Our jwai is such a gentleman you won't believe he's a Matwali,' they told visitors with an apologetic smile. But most of their relatives remained sanctimoniously opposed to the union, and Shanti's parents could never fully overcome their shame. In public they might defend their daughter's choice with a few broadminded platitudes. In private they made every effort to dilute their grandson's Matwaliness. On learning that Boju had decided to call the baby 'Yalambar' after the mythical Kirati king, they hastily named him Arjun. Afraid the boy would pick up the coarse and common accent of Matwalis, they taught him to speak the courtly form of Nepali. Aisyo, gaisyo, bhuja khaisyo.

When the baby turned six months old and Boju began planning his first rice ceremony, Shanti informed her that her parents had decided to host the event at their house. Boju felt an urge to bang Shanti's head against the wall, but Shanti's bolstered status as wife, mother and daughter prevented her from taking such a drastic measure. Instead she boycotted the ceremony and threatened to cut off Premkala and Gajendra if they went. The rift deepened. Rajan, increasingly caught between his mother and his wife, maintained a show of balance until he was compelled to take a side.

~

It was Ekadasi, the eleventh day of the lunar month. On this day both mother- and daughter-in-law would observe a fast and feel buoyed all day by a fuzzy, pious emotion. Shanti woke up at dawn, did her puja and left for her parents' home with her son.

In the afternoon Boju went to the kitchen to have her sacred meal of fruit and milk. The mesh-door shelf in which the food was kept was locked. She could not find the key anywhere. She used a hairpin, a crochet hook and random keys, then tried pounding the lock with a stone pestle, nearly crushing her thumb. Baying for instant revenge, she picked up Shanti's new platform shoes, marched downstairs and across the backyard, and hurled them into the Tukucha River. The sight of the eddying waters swallowing the red shoes calmed her for some time. A little while later she heard a knock on the door. She went to the window and peeped through a chink in the curtains. Shanti stood alone at the entrance, hammering the door with her fist. There was no sign of her son. She had left him at her parents' again. Boju sat down, rubbed her fingers with ash and started rolling cotton wicks as if the sound and fury had no power to move her. Shanti screamed and threatened to call the police but Boju did not budge. Almost half an hour passed before she heard Rajan's voice and slowly waddled up to the door and unfastened the bolt.

'Have you gone mad?' Shanti cried.

'It's my house,' Boju said. 'I can shut out whoever I want.'

The two women came at each other's throats, dredging up old slights, hurling readymade lies. Their screams drowned out Rajan's pleas for restraint. Faces appeared at the neighbouring windows. The student lodgers lowered their radio volume to enjoy the shouting match.

'You know what you deserve?' Shanti thundered, using 'talai', the lowest form of 'you'. 'You should be stuffed in a doko and thrown off a cliff, like the old woman in that story.'

At once Boju pounced on Shanti, grabbed her hair by the roots and started yanking it.

'Aiyaaaa!' Shanti let out a guttural scream that made passersby stop in their tracks. This broke the dam of Rajan's patience.

'Ama, stop!' he yelled, pulling his mother away. Boju stopped.

There was a clump of hair in her fist. Rajan picked up a hair-clip from the floor and handed it to his wife. 'Don't cry,' he said, rubbing her shoulder. Then he turned to Boju. 'Ama, I've had enough,' he said with uncharacteristic firmness. 'This can't go on if we are to live under the same roof.' Boju glared at him. There was a ring of finality in his voice that chilled her to the bone. She raised her hand to strike him, but desisted. 'Thukka!' she spat in his face. 'You insult your mother for this slut worth two paisa? Shame on you!'

Early next morning Boju packed her bags and went to her daughter's house, her eyes red and puffy from crying all night.

9

Tamule ji's project job income gradually transformed the look and feel of his house. A double-door refrigerator replaced the small fridge in the kitchen. The noisy, three-legged kerosene stove gave way to a quiet, two-burner propane gas stove. The uncemented space under the counter turned into a base cabinet. The family began eating their meals off melamine plates and put aside the stainless steel utensils for less important visitors. Premkala bought a solid teakwood closet for the bedroom. Her daughters took the Godrej almirah and covered the scratches with stickers and Archies greeting cards. Tamule ji hired carpenters to build them a study desk and a bookshelf. Sumnima, fourteen years old, began to receive a small monthly allowance for canteen snacks, body sprays and sanitary napkins. Yet none of these rewards matched the next surprise lined up for them.

Returning home from school that afternoon, they found the living room bustling with activity. A strange young man knelt on the floor hooking a cord, his brow furrowed in concentration. Their parents, still in their work clothes, stood intently watching him. Boju paced about the room gathering the packaging materials strewn on the floor. It took the girls a moment to realize that the young man was a technician from Nepal Telecom: he was installing a telephone in their house!

'We got a phone! We got a phone!' Numa cried, jumping up and down. Sumnima controlled herself, not wanting to give herself away to the technician.

Getting a phone connection in Kathmandu was no ordinary achievement. The demand surpassed the supply, and one had to wait for up to seven years after filing an application at the Nepal Telecom office. The Tamule family had given up hopes of acquiring a telephone anytime in the near future. But a few weeks ago, Tamule ji had chanced upon a Nepal Telecom official who owned three phone lines and wanted to sell one for a small profit. Included in the deal was a faded green telephone set with a rotary dial. The Tamule family could now call anyone at anytime and talk for as long as they wanted. The days of having to cross the ring road and fumble for change just to make a phone call were over.

Once the technician left and the phone sat like a dignitary awaiting felicitations, everyone took turns making their test calls. Sumnima took out her diary and looked up Reshma's phone number. Her heart thumped as she held the receiver and spun the dial, but she had no wish to betray her excitement to someone who already had multiple telephones in her house.

Reshma answered the phone the moment it rang.

'Eh, you've reached home already,' Sumnima said. 'I just called to ask, um…when is Tejaswi's birthday party?'

'Arey, you forgot already?' Reshma said with an unsuspecting laugh. 'It's on Sunday, silly.'

'Oh, I thought it was on Saturday.'

Numa, who stood waiting her turn, gave a shout of laughter. 'Liar!'

Sumnima glared at her and quickly clamped her hand over the mouthpiece.

For days Sumnima had talked about little else besides the upcoming party. She had spent days crying, begging and cajoling to obtain her parents' permission. Afraid they might go back on their word, she had been obeying their every command. It would be her first visit to Tejaswi's house. She imagined it as a grand old mansion full of whispers and secrets, with shadowy, light-footed servants scurrying through long corridors. Although people sometimes mistook them for sisters, Sumnima and Tejaswi inhabited vastly different worlds. Sumnima could not trace her family tree beyond her two sets of grandparents, all of them hill peasants except her maternal grandfather, a mercenary soldier in the British Indian Army. By contrast, Tejaswi had descended from a long line of blue-blooded ancestors whose names adorned the pages of history textbooks. Her driver addressed her as San'maisaab. The King and Queen were her distant relatives, and her older sister, a Rhododendron alumna, was married to a prince of Rajasthan. There was an aura of mystery about Tejaswi. The details of her life remained hazy even to her best friends. In all these years, they had not understood why she spoke of her mother in the present tense, or why her father, a high-ranking officer in the Royal Nepal Army, seemed more absent from her life than her deceased mother. What little they knew about him came from Tejaswi's cousin Samriddhi, who described her uncle as an abusive, philandering brute who had tormented his wife as long as she was alive. 'He's not even a purebred,' she said. 'His mother was a Bhoteni, our grandfather picked her up from a village outside Kathmandu. Why else do you think Tejaswi looks like a Tib?'

~

On Sunday Sumnima spent the entire morning trying on one outfit after another. Muted shades made her look dull. Bright colours clashed with her dusky complexion. What had she not done to enhance her appearance in recent months? At least twice a day she smeared her face with Fair and Lovely, a whitening cream that was openly popular among girls, and secretly, among boys. Her oily plaits seemed a thing of the distant past. She wore her hair in a low ponytail, with stylish side-swept bangs across her forehead. She had taken off the gold nose-pin that Boju had pierced into her nose long ago, the experience of which she only remembered the shocking sensation of a needle. She showered more frequently than Boju thought appropriate, used scented body sprays, and took meticulous care of her skin and nails. And still the image in the mirror did not satisfy her.

'It's a birthday party, not a Cinderella ball,' Numa said, picking up the clothes scattered on the floor. She folded them, opened the steel almirah and put them in their proper places. 'Why don't you try this?' She took out a long blue dress. 'Didn't Parvati aunty send this?'

Sumnima nodded without enthusiasm. Everyone said Parvati aunty had become too 'forward' since she moved to Hong Kong. Boju said she squandered her husband's hard-earned money on jewellery and fashion and wore skin-tight pants even when she visited her in-laws. Sumnima would fume at such comments. 'It's her life, let her do what she wants.' But she would never trust the taste of a woman raised in the hills of Lungla. The blue midi dress had been hanging in the steel almirah for months, unworn, the tag still intact.

Sumnima slipped into the dress and stood in front of the mirror, reflexively hunching her shoulders to hide her budding breasts. 'Hm, it looks nice on you,' Numa said, pulling up the back-zipper for her. 'But you must stop slouching.' Sumnima straightened herself and gazed at her reflection. Indeed, the flowing dress had transformed her plain and mousy self into an elegant young lady.

~

Rajani aunty was an uncommon Nepali mother: she spoke fluent English and could drive a car. The brand-new Pajero had been imported tax free through her husband's good offices. Reshma sat beside her in the passenger seat, shaking to the beat of an American pop song. Sumnima sat in the back, marvelling at the plush interior of the car—the tinted glass windows that one could open and shut with the click of a button, the dark leather upholstered seats, the stereo system with red and green lights flashing on its sleek surface. Her shoes, soiled by dirt from the fields of Bhaisichaur, were carefully tilted away from the floor mat.

She could see Rajani aunty's face in the rear view mirror. Chin turned up, hair slickly swept back, and eyes covered in sunglasses, she cut a striking figure as she maneuvered the giant car along the potholed roads. People turned to stare at her. President of Rhododendron Alumnae Society, an ace homemaker and an ageless beauty, she had been described as 'a woman of substance' in the lifestyle magazine that Reshma had brought to school last week. Sumnima hoped to exude the same flair and confidence when she grew up, the same air of womanly independence.

It was a sweltering afternoon. The glare from the sunlight reflected off the car's side mirror with blinding intensity. Outside, pedestrians squinted against the sun and shaded their faces with their hands or umbrellas. Dogs poked around in a heap of garbage on the pavement, and directly in front of the Pajero, a battered three-wheeled Vikram tempo spewed a billowing jet of black smoke. The cool, fragrant space inside the car seemed like a moving oasis. And yet Sumnima could not sit back and relax. Perhaps the feeling that she was riding in such luxury was intimidating her, or that she was on her way to attend such a posh birthday party for the time; it could even be the conditioned air, imbued with the smells of freshener and perfume—Sumnima grew nauseous. She sat still and held her breath, alarmed by the churning and gurgling in her stomach.

'Bichawra, look at that man,' Rajani aunty said in a mellifluous accent that made her Nepali sound foreign, an accent she had picked up long ago at her alma mater. Reshma looked out of the window and repeated, 'Bichawra.' Their pity was directed at an old porter who stood near the zebra crossing, bent under a large refrigerator placed on his back. He stretched out his dark, spindly arm to stop the oncoming traffic, but one after another the vehicles rushed past him. Rajani aunty hit the brake to let him pass. All of a sudden Sumnima was jolted forward and a jet of yellow-brown fluid gushed out of her mouth, splattering her dress and the car seat. 'Oh God!' Rajani aunty cried. 'You should have told me to stop!' Sumnima looked aghast. 'I'm so sorry,' she said, and looked around frantically for something to wipe her dress with. The thought of reaching the birthday party in a vomit-stained dress was mortifying. Then she looked up and saw the splatter on the seat and was so embarrassed, she wished she was dead.

'Nanu, give her some tissue,' Rajani aunty told Reshma in a tight voice.

Reshma opened the front cabinet. 'Laa, there's none.'

Rajani aunty drove a little way and pulled up outside a small roadside eatery. She got out of the car and strode inside, drawing puzzled glances from the men who sat there eating. Reshma and Sumnima followed closely behind her. A sweaty faced man stood at the counter, his vest rolled up to his chest to air his belly. He quickly pulled down his vest at the sight of the ladies. 'Where is your tap?' Rajani aunty said without taking off her sunglasses. The man gawked at her, confused. 'Hurry, she just threw up and needs to wash up,' Rajani aunty said, pointing to Sumnima, who stood cowering behind her. 'Ay, I see,' the man nodded, then turned around and hollered, 'Oi, show madam the tap.' A small boy approached them muttering under his breath. He led Sumnima towards the rear of the building, handed her a jug of water and squatted down to wash the dishes piled up on the scummy floor. He dumped some dirty plates into a tub filled with soapsuds, took them out and dumped them in water. His small dark hands moved like a pair of machine parts, quick but lifeless. Sumnima watched him as she washed herself, trying to assess his condition from an educated perspective. How old could he be? Not more than six. Last month she and her friends had participated in a rally organized by Rhododendron Alumnae Society, wearing white t-shirts and baseball caps printed with the slogan 'Stop Child Abuse'. A few street kids had been placed at the front, their white t-shirts clashing against their dark, grimy faces. Rajani aunty, clad in the same t-shirt and cap, held the mic and railed against the exploitation of child workers. Sumnima tried to summon appropriate feelings for the child before her eyes, but his face, hard and unyielding, did not stir any emotion in her. Still, on her way out, she stopped and asked, 'Babu, how old are you?'

'Didi, I am only eighteen years old,' the boy mimicked her concerned tone, suddenly exploding into laughter. The muscles of his face loosened up at once, his eyes sparkled with glee. Sumnima stared at him, a little shaken by his total transformation, and then stormed off, the taunting laughter trailing behind her. Before getting back behind the wheel, Rajani aunty gave her a plastic bag and asked her to hold it until she got off the car. The look of disgust did not leave Rajani aunty's face. Reshma gauged her mother's mood and turned off the music. No one spoke until they reached their destination. Before parting, Rajani aunty planted a light kiss on Reshma's cheek and said, 'Bye, Nanu. Remember, no fatty foods.'

A young man with a military haircut opened the gates of Manjari Niwas, revealing an aged, off-white stucco mansion with a terracotta tile roof, large bay windows and a pillared portico at the entrance. The vast tree-lined property looked pristine and secluded despite being in the middle of a prominent neighbourhood housing embassies and five-star hotels. On one side of the curved driveway was a garden with wild-looking shrubs and a massive bougainvillea bush with variegated pink and purple foliage. At the centre of the garden, a marble cherub peed a thin stream of water into a small, moss-streaked pond.

'Are you San'maisaab's friends?' said the man who had opened the gate. 'She's upstairs on the terrace.' Sumnima glanced at him twice. With his strong jawline, small eyes and evenly tanned skin, he brought to mind a cousin from Lungla who had recently passed the recruitment test for a Gurkha regiment. 'Please enter through that door and take the stairs on your right,' he said, speaking courtly Nepali in a regional rural accent. Like a poorly trained parrot. The grandiose verbs and their unwieldy conjugations sounded laboured coming from his mouth. The girls entered through the main door into a room decorated with old and antique objects. Faded chairs and stools with ornate carvings, porcelain figurines, a bronze lamp, lustreless brass candle-stands, and other such relics that evinced a hankering for a bygone era. In the history textbooks, Tejaswi's forebears came across as a curious breed of despots: Hindu puritans obsessed with European luxury goods, pleasure-seeking dandies who'd cut down their kinsmen on the slightest pretext, mimic maharajahs so insecure about their borrowed grandeur they issued edicts prohibiting commoners from imitating their lifestyle.

'Feels like a museum, no?' Reshma said, looking at the large gilt-framed painting on the wall. 'It does,' said Sumnima, though she had never visited a museum. 'These must be Tejaswi's great-grandparents,' Reshma said in a reverent tone. The painting showed a stern-faced couple dressed like European aristocrats. The mustachioed young man was decked out in British military uniform complete with medals and badges. On his head he sported a jewelled crown with a plume of feathers. The woman beside him wore a velvet blouse covered with pearls and diamonds. It was difficult to tell whether she was sitting or standing because her lower half was buried in a hoop skirt that ballooned out around her like a silk stupa. 'I'd be scared to live here,' Sumnima said. 'It feels haunted.' Reshma pondered this and said in a hushed tone, 'Who knows maybe Tejaswi's mother...'

'Shh!'

They turned into a corridor and climbed two flights of stairs, the wooden steps creaking under their feet. An array of mounted wild animals was displayed on the stairway wall and the landing—blue sheep head, deer antlers, leopard hide, antelope horns, a stuffed pheasant with feathers disintegrating into dust. Tejaswi's stories about her grandfather's hunting expeditions to west Nepal, and her professed fondness for exotic game meats, had never before seemed credible to Sumnima.

When they reached the top of the stairs, Sumnima corrected her drooping posture and smoothed her dress. Thankfully the wet patch had dried. There were about twenty people gathered on the terrace. Middle-aged men and women, children playing hide-and-seek behind the adults' legs, a few elderly people, and a group of young girls and boys. All of them had creamy faces with wide eyes and sharp noses. Some of them spoke courtly Nepali mixed with English. Young men with military haircuts hovered around them with food and drink trays. Tejaswi's grandmother emerged from the crowd to meet the girls, looking stately in her short salt-and-pepper hair and brown silk sari.

'Darshan, Afumuwa,' said Reshma, lightly touching the tip of her nose.

Sumnima, unaccustomed to this form of greeting, copied Reshma somewhat awkwardly. A moment later Tejaswi showed up, wearing a green skirt and a matching shirt with puffed sleeves and large gilt buttons. Her narrow eyes were heavily lined in black. The bow-clip on her hair was made out of the same shiny material as her dress. Sumnima and Reshma showered her with birthday wishes and praised her outfit, for even unlovely clothes looked quirky and interesting on someone as well born as Tejaswi.

'Come, I'll introduce you to my cousins,' she said.

Her cousins sat in a circle sipping Coke from tall, frosted glasses. None of them resembled Tejaswi, whose small, mongoloid features denied her the hauteur befitting a royal family member. After an exchange of hi and hello, Sumnima and Reshma pulled up two chairs and joined the circle. Tejaswi went off to meet other guests. Sumnima felt trapped the minute she sat down.

Samriddhi, the only cousin she knew, was not there. The cousins sat drinking their Coke in guarded silence, casting oblique glances at the two outsiders. Reshma sat tight-lipped with a stony expression. Sumnima shifted her gaze towards a group of women who stood at a little distance. One of them, a young woman in a lemon-yellow sari, was describing something in a pleasantly cadenced voice. Lean and fair, her hair flying in the breeze and her hands flowing in dance-like gestures, she looked the very picture of poise and grace. Presently she turned and hollered at a servant with a tray of water glasses: 'O Bamey, yata aija ta.' The change in her tone and her sudden lapse into rude, peremptory language jarred Sumnima. The servant—a swarthy young man with muscular arms—came up and served her water. The woman then placed a handkerchief on his tray and gave him a brusque instruction, pointing to a child playing nearby. The servant put down his tray and went up to the child. 'San'maisaab,' he said, 'let me wipe your nose.' Her little ladyship glared at him and pushed him away with her little hand. 'Uta jaa!' The guests looked on with doting smiles. The servant followed the kid for a while with a forced grin on his face, and then picked up his tray and resumed his work. Sumnima's heart went out to him. She had heard that soldiers who worked in army officers' homes led tough lives. No task was considered too difficult or too mean for them. There was a widespread rumour that a certain colonel's wife made her ardali wash her family's undergarments.

'Why are you all so quiet?' Tejaswi asked. She seemed disappointed that her friends and cousins hadn't gelled as a group. One of her cousins shrugged her shoulders and gave her a blasé smile. This seemed to peeve Reshma all the more. 'I wish Samriddhi was here,' she said to Tejaswi. 'Didn't you invite her?'

'Afumuwa did but she said she's busy,' Tejaswi said, rolling her eyes.

Reshma and Sumnima exchanged a look. They had never been able to trace the source of resentment between the two cousins. Reshma looked around at the crowd and asked, 'What about your dad? Isn't he here?'

'He's in Lebanon on a peacekeeping mission,' said Tejaswi. She thought for a moment. 'Come I'll show you Mami's picture.'

Reshma and Sumnima gladly took up the unexpected offer. Tejaswi led them down the stairs and stopped in front of a framed photograph hung on the corridor wall. They had passed it by earlier, mistaking it for the ubiquitous portrait of the Queen that hung in all public spaces beside the King's portrait. The woman in the picture sported the same beehive hairstyle, the same pearl necklace and a red rose behind her ear. But this was Manjari aunty, Tejaswi's departed mother, whose name was carved on a bronze plaque on the main gate of the house. Sumnima and Reshma gazed at the picture in solemn silence.

'She's beautiful, no?' Tejaswi said. 'She looks just like Dijju.'

Manjari aunty was indeed the spitting image of Tejaswi's older sister Anushka, who had been married to an Indian prince soon after she finished tenth grade.

'I didn't know she was so beautiful,' said Sumnima, and bit her tongue for using the wrong tense.

10

By his third year at GIDC, Tamule ji had visited all the project areas and begun to grasp the inner workings of the organization. The countless meetings, publications, workshops and monitoring trips no longer excited him. The allure of travel had begun to wear off. The highway, hills and farmlands had grown overfamiliar and the charm of local dining was fading away. He did not enjoy squeezing success stories out of 'target beneficiaries' for the periodic reports. Nor did he like staying at rudimentary hotels in insalubrious towns and training people. Most of them came only for the free meal and transport allowance and yawned throughout. At one training event for local government officials, the participants had emptied two bowls of candies on the table even before the session had begun; Tamule ji had heard plastic wrappers rustling inside the ward chairman's trouser pockets as he rushed towards the biscuits during the tea break. In such moments Tamule ji regretted being a citizen of what he called 'a beggar country'. By now he had worked under many white experts from donor countries. Even the most well-meaning among them, those who avoided treating Nepalis like their minions, couldn't escape their preordained role as masters of the universe. His current supervisor was a friendly American who had first visited Nepal as a tourist and returned the second time as an expert. Tamule ji often forgot the guy was eight years younger than him.

Despite these minor grievances, Tamule ji valued his job. A project job was the safest, quickest and most respectable path to prosperity for a man like him, one who lacked wealth inherited from feudal ancestors, had no connections in high places or the knack for wheeling and dealing. He faithfully performed his duties and kept his criticism to himself.

At the end of his third year, Tamule ji got a promotion,

becoming the only Matwali in the entire organization to have reached the officer level. The three other Matwalis in GIDC included a human resources assistant, a receptionist, and a driver. A higher designation, a fifteen percent raise and a separate office with a computer—Tamule ji could not complain, not even when one of his colleagues cunningly hijacked the sunlit office space reserved for him. At first he was nervous about his new role. His job description was a long list of bullet points that barely registered in his brain even after multiple readings: 'Liaise with international, national and local stakeholders to build synergy in program implementation; provide inputs into the Annual Strategic Planning Framework and the Annual Operational Planning Framework; ensure that project Objectives, Goals and Outcomes are effectively aligned with GIDC's vision and mission,' and so on and so forth. But the new post turned out to be less demanding. Eighty percent of the job involved talking—attending meetings, lecturing partner NGOs, making presentations, holding focus group discussions—and he could delegate the remaining twenty to the program assistant. In the newfound privacy of his small, sunless office, Tamule ji spent his free time playing computer games, and soon got addicted to Solitaire.

The household infrastructure improved further in the following months. Mr and Mrs Tamule installed a second telephone in the landing outside their bedroom; the old rotary phone served as an extension line in the living room downstairs. They revamped the kitchen with tiles and wall cabinets and an extended space for dining. A rice cooker, a toaster and a hot water dispenser appeared on the refurbished counter. The house itself grew in size. They converted the terrace into a TV room and started building a third storey, where Sumnima and Numa would finally have separate rooms.

At long last Premkala saw the possibility of quitting the primary school. One afternoon, a friend of hers fixed a job interview for her at a fairly reputed school in town. The headmistress seemed unimpressed with Premkala's government college degree and her ungrammatical English, but conceded she was good enough for teaching third-grade Nepali and social studies. Premkala chafed at her condescending manner but could not let go of the offer. The pay, although modest, was much higher than her previous salary. She would get a two-day weekend and her daily commute would be shortened by half an hour. She gave her notice at Sunshine Primary the next morning and invited her brother and cousins for a celebratory tongba in the evening.

Thus, amid their moaning and groaning about the daily grind, the Tamule family was doing well for themselves. It was around this time that Tamule ji received a letter from his brother Tikaram.

Dear Gajey,

I hope you are in good health and spirits by the grace of lord Pashupatinath. We are all fine, except your Bhauju's leg continues to trouble her. Ganga's SLC results came out a few days ago. She failed in five out of seven subjects. What to do, she's not bright like her sister Jamuna. I don't know what to do with her. She can take the exam again next year, but I'm afraid she will fail again. It's the same school, same environment, same friends (most of them failed). It would be best if she could get out of the village. I was wondering if she should go to Kathmandu. She's a grown-up now, she just turned eighteen, so I am hoping she won't be a burden on you. She could sit for the SLC as a private candidate in Kathmandu, and if she passes, enrol in a government college. Hopefully she will find a job in a few years. She's a good girl, quiet and dutiful. She can help buhari with housework. What do you think?

Please say namaste to Ama and give my blessings to buhari and my nieces. I will close my pen now. Yours, Tikaram

Tamule ji showed the letter to his wife at a well-chosen moment. It was a Saturday morning. They were in the garden drinking tea and watching the masons laying bricks on the third storey. The previous evening he had gifted her a vacuum cleaner saying he wanted to make her life easier. Her new job would begin in a couple of days. 'What do you think?' he said, after she finished reading the letter. 'This is the least I can do for my brother. We are in a better situation now, don't you think?'

Premkala thought for a moment and asked in a neutral tone, 'When does he want to send her?'

'I guess the sooner the better,' Tamule ji said. 'The rains haven't started yet, so the trails will be dry.'

Premkala nodded her head, her eyes fixed on the bricklayer three floors up. 'All right, but she'll have to sleep in the TV room. Once the girls move up there, maybe she can take their room.'

11

At daybreak, Ganga left the house with Rai kaka, a neighbour uncle who was going to meet his son in Dharan. They walked through the fields in the dim light of dawn, greeting women on their way to the spring, averting their eyes from the empty water pots that might bode ill for the day ahead. After an easy descent through a long, winding forest trail on Gurase Danda, they reached the open fields at the base of the hill. The sun was already high in the sky. Men, women and children were busy reaping wheat in the fields, their sickles crunching through the ripe stalks. Ganga put down her bag and looked back at her village one last time. From this distance it appeared as a dense cluster of mud-and-thatch houses on a terraced hill slope. Hidden somewhere amid that cluster was the house where she was born and raised. Further down below she could see her school, a long, single-storey concrete building with a corrugated tin roof that glittered harshly in the sun. It was her uncle who had donated money for that roof, a source of pride for the entire Tamule community. From that school he had graduated more than twenty years ago, the first Tamule ever to pass the SLC, the School Leaving Certificate exam. The future of many young people hung on the result of this national board exam, also known as the 'iron gate'. But half the students across the country failed the exam each year, and so had Ganga, despite being the oldest student in her class.

Towards mid-morning, before tackling another uphill stretch, Ganga and Rai kaka rested near the suspension bridge. The roar of the river filled their ears as they ate their food. Beaten rice fried in ghiu, hard-boiled eggs, freshly ground philinge achar, and mutton dried and smoked over a wood fire. Ganga's mother had packed them in the most prized container in the house, an airtight plastic box brought from Dharan. 'Don't worry, Chandrey will get us another one,' she had said, her eyes misting over. Before any tears were shed, Ganga's father had interjected in a firm voice, 'O Chandrey's mother, don't you start. Your daughter is not going into exile in a forest, she's going to Kathmandu, to her own uncle's house.'

Days past and present, people near and far, things real and imagined coursed through Ganga's mind as she climbed uphill and downhill through those familiar trails. The steady rhythm of walking stilled her emotions. Only her muscles stayed awake, aching and throbbing as the day wore on. A long journey lay ahead. They would spend the night at Rai kaka's relative's house, leave for Hile next morning, and take the bus to Dharan on the third day. From that point Ganga would be on her own. She wondered if she would make it to Kathmandu alone. Her brother Chandrey might have accompanied her but his wife would go into labour any moment. If he'd come, Ganga would have had a hard time keeping up with him on the trail. His stick-thin limbs concealed the strength of a monster. It was strange to think he would become a father soon. The priest had said it would be a boy. Ganga mourned that she wouldn't be home to welcome her first nephew into the world.

It was late afternoon when Ganga and Rai kaka trudged along the banks of the Arun. The mighty river raged and frothed and shone in a thousand scintillating hues. The sun beat down upon their heads and the smooth, flesh-toned stones on the shore burned their soles. Ganga transferred her rucksack from one shoulder to the other, now carrying it on her back, now hugging it to her chest, now balancing it on her hip like a pail of water. The rucksack belonged to Chandrey, an old gift from Parvati aunty. 'Take it,' he had said, 'you can buy me a nicer bag once you become a rich woman in Kathmandu.' At sundown they reached the village where they would spend the night. High above the wooded hills, the snowy summits of Makalu turned from silver to pink to indigo. They walked past men and women returning from the fields, children herding their cattle home. Birds flew to their nests uttering their last, frantic cries. Ganga felt a stab of homesickness. No matter where she went during the day, at this time she would always be home, making a fire in the kitchen while Jamuna cleaned the lanterns. 'Didi, remember one thing,' Jamuna had said before she left, 'don't let that old witch bully you. It's our uncle's house, our own uncle.'

Arriving at their night stop, they found their hostess chasing hens across the yard. 'Namaste, Nana,' said Rai kaka. The woman stopped and greeted him in a Rai language that Ganga did not understand. An ageing but robust little woman, she wore her hair in a thick braid that reached below her waist. A heavy gold ornament hung from the septum of her nose. A rooster emerged from behind a bush, trailed by several hens and fluffy chicks. Nana caught them one at a time and shoved them all into a bamboo coop, except the one she planned to cook tonight. Meanwhile the guests unloaded their bags and sat on the porch. The children of the house spread a mat for them, brought them water to wash their hands, and served them millet liquor in large aluminium bowls. Ganga held the bowl with both hands and took a large gulp of the drink. It burned her throat and ignited a mild flame in her belly. The heat spread gently, melting pain away. As it was getting dark, Nana lost no time in finishing her task. She knelt down with the hen under her arm and skilfully balanced a khukuri between her chest and the ground. The hen squawked and flapped its wings. Nana grabbed the wings and folded them together on its back, felt for the soft spot under its neck feathers, and with a look of determined concentration, ran its throat vigorously across the shiny, curved blade. A storm of feathers blew around her, blood sprinkled her cheeks. The headless hen flapped and released more down, then relaxed as its life slowly ebbed away. Nana drained the blood into a pot. 'I'll feed you the most delicious chicken jhol tonight,' she said, smiling at Ganga. 'You won't find anything like this in Kathmandu.'

~

On the second day, Ganga and Rai kaka walked all day and spent the night in Hile Bazaar, a road-head town lined with small lodges, shops and eateries. Next morning, after a long wait during which Ganga finished three packets of Wai Wai instant noodles, they finally boarded the bus to Dharan. It was packed with people, vegetables, sacks of grain, chickens, and crying children. The bus drove downhill on the smooth British-aid road, taking a series of sharp hairpin turns. Blooming rhododendrons had reddened the hills in places. Far down below, the Tamor flowed across the valley like a silver serpent. But the passengers could not enjoy the scenic ride. While Rai kaka stood trapped in the crowded aisle, Ganga sat squeezed in a last-row seat, feeling sick to her stomach. The child in the next seat cried nonstop. His mother tried to calm him down, and failing, gave him a slap that made him bawl even louder. Halfway through the ride, Ganga stuck her head out of the window and threw up, spattering the siding under her window with bits of Wai Wai noodles. A feeling of lightness spread over her as she rinsed her mouth and leaned back in her seat.

Rai kaka's son Dammar dai met them at the bus station in Dharan. He greeted Ganga with a warm smile but gave his father a surly look. There was a rumour that Dammar dai had been neglecting his studies and getting involved in ethnic politics. The father and son exchanged a few heated words in Rai language and abruptly switched to normal conversation, as if they had decided to call a momentary truce. It was time to eat. They went to a lively, crowded place that served freshly cooked meals in large compartmentalized steel trays. Steamed rice, potato and cabbage tarkari, mustard greens and radish pickle, each in its own compartment, along with a bowl of dal and a side plate of onion slices, lemon and green chillis. A tired-looking waiter scurried back and forth slapping extra helpings on people's plates. Between mouthfuls Rai kaka gave his son updates from the village, switching to Rai language every now and then. Ganga ate in silence, slowly mixing her food with her fingers. Their imminent parting saddened her. After the meal and a short stroll around Dharan bazaar, Ganga boarded the bus to Kathmandu. Dammar dai handed her a few packets of biscuits and a juice drink for the journey. 'Don't lose your uncle's phone number,' said Rai kaka. 'Call him from a shop if he's not at the bus stop. The shopkeeper can dial the number for you.' Afraid the tears might fall, Ganga forced a wide grin that made the corner of her upper lip quiver like her grandmother's.

The highway beyond Dharan was perfectly straight. On either side of the road were dense forests with dappled sunlight. Ahead lay the vast plains of the Tarai, its flat landscape as alien to Ganga as the dark men and women boarding the bus along the way. At the Biratnagar bus park, a middle-aged woman in tight jeans and a frilly shirt got on and sat beside her. A few hours later, the bus stopped by a wood for a toilet break. Ganga was heading into the bushes with all the women when her seatmate thrust her handbag at her. 'Can you hold this, bahini? I'll be right back.' She ran down a trail and out of sight. Ganga waited, turning away from a man peeing on the roadside. His urine fell on the leaves in a steady patter. Other men paced about, stretched, yawned and smoked. The women emerged from behind the bushes patting down their clothes. Her seatmate didn't return. The driver tossed his cigarette butt, hopped back onto the bus and started the engine. Everyone hurried back on board, and so did Ganga, her bladder full to the point of bursting. The bus was already rolling when her seatmate jumped in. 'I'm feeling so sick,' she said weepily. 'Can I sit by the window for a while, bahini?' Ganga shot her an annoyed glance but heard herself saying, 'Only for a few minutes.' Once in her seat, though, the woman stared out of the window and behaved as though Ganga no longer existed. Ten minutes passed, then fifteen, then thirty. The woman removed her hairclip, shook her hair loose and leaned back. Soon she was asleep, snoring, with her pink mouth gaping open. Her head lolled from side to side. Ganga wanted to wake her up, but after reaching over, hesitated. There was no point fretting over her seat. It now belonged to the woman.

12

Tamule ji found his niece waiting for him at the bus park. She was sitting on her luggage in front of a shop, anxiously peering at another passing motorbike. She looked much the same as she did when he last saw her three years ago—a small, dark girl with thin limbs and tangled hair. He took off his helmet and called her. 'Gajey kaka,' she said, leaping up. 'Namaste.' The skin on her nose was peeling, and despite the warm weather, her lips were dry and cracked. She looked just like Sumnima. Although three years older, she had the same height, the same narrow eyes and a stubby nose pierced with a gold nose-pin. A mountain-bred, weather-beaten, ungroomed version of Sumnima. He got off the motorbike and reached for the large, overstuffed bag on the floor. It was the one he'd left behind during his last visit to Lungla, now worn from overuse. 'Kaka, don't trouble yourself,' Ganga said, 'it's heavy.'

Tamule ji laughed. 'I carried two muris of wheat when I was half your age.' He tied the bag to the back of his motorbike seat and told Ganga to sit on the pillion. She hesitated for a moment and got on the bike. When the bike started and jerked forward, she gave a small cry and gripped his belt. 'Don't worry, you won't fall,' Tamule ji said. He saw her terrified face in the mirror and drove slowly. She sat stiffly, clutching his belt throughout the ride.

When they got home, he gathered the family in the living room to make introductions. Although she seemed exhausted, disoriented, and shaken by the motorbike ride, Ganga greeted her new guardians with enthusiasm. 'Namaste Kaki, yes, it's been so many years. I was only two or three when you visited. Ah, Boju, namaste, so glad to finally meet you. Thuli, Kanchi, how you've grown.' The crack on her lower lip opened, showing a bit of raw flesh.

'Here, use this on your lips,' Numa said, offering her a tube of chapstick.

'You don't have to…' Ganga said shyly.

'Get over it,' Tamule ji said. 'This is your home now, stop acting formal.'

Numa took Ganga's hand, placed the chapstick on her palm and closed her fist. 'Just keep it.'

Boju grimaced. She opened her mouth to say something but a sharp look from Numa silenced her. 'Mother sent this for you,' Ganga said, handing her a bag filled with food. Boju took it quietly, as though she were merely accepting her due, then looked through its contents and put it aside. Tamule ji smiled, relieved that she hadn't flung a jibe at his niece. Ganga seemed eager to please, with a compliment ready for everyone. 'You have such lovely hair,' she said, reaching out and stroking Sumnima's smooth black ponytail. She turned to Numa. 'Kanchi looks even prettier than in the pictures,'—and seeing Premkala enter the room with tea and biscuits on a tray—'just like aunty.' Premkala gave a skeptical smile.

'So how's school going?' Tamule ji asked his niece, unsure whether he should bring up her SLC results. Her face became tight. She took a few sips of tea, as if pondering the question, and said with a smile, 'You know what Birkha Sir always tells his students? He goes—' she raised her voice to mimic the headmaster's high, declamatory tone—'Kids, do you know who put that roof over your heads? Ganga's youngest uncle Gajey. Many years ago he graduated from this school and now he's a big man in Kathmandu.' Tamule ji smiled, then quickly waved the compliment aside and asked in a firm, practical voice, 'Has Mother been taking her medicines?'

It had been three years since he last saw his mother. All bones and wrinkles now, she refused to leave the village even to go to the hospital in the nearest town, fearing she might die on the road, away from the land that held her husband's ashes, the land where she had grown, blossomed and faded. He felt guilty for not visiting her, but his work-related trips left him with little energy for travelling to Lungla, a village remoter than the remotest project area and twice as backward. Every time he returned from a field trip, Kathmandu felt like a grand metropolis, his two-storey house a luxurious sanctuary.

During a lull in the conversation, Ganga said she needed to use the bathroom. 'Come, I'll show you,' said Sumnima, 'it's just off the corridor.' Boju shot her a look of disapproval. Sumnima shrugged and rolled her eyes, then motioned Ganga to follow her. 'Sumnima,' Boju said in a controlled voice. 'She's not a city girl like you. She'll be more comfortable squatting. Why not show her outside?'

Ganga stopped at the door. 'Ganga didi,' Sumnima said, 'don't listen to her, just come.'

Tamule ji silently cheered Sumnima but felt sorry for Boju. She looked hurt. He was thinking of a remark that might console her when his wife said, 'Ama, why don't you go watch TV? It's almost time for *Mahabharat*.'

'Witches, stop ganging up against me,' Boju said, then picked up the bag of food and left the room.

'Thuli,' Ganga begged, 'I can go outside.'

But Sumnima seemed all the more determined to bestow the privilege on her. She dragged her inside the bathroom. 'Here,' she said, lifting the toilet seat cover. 'You push this handle once you're done. The soap is right here, and you can use that towel over there.'

13

Once, when they were nothing but defenseless lumps of flesh, she had taken charge of their lives. She had fed them, clothed them, wiped their shit and vomit, and massaged their limbs with her small but strong hands. She had invented recipes for their health, sewed them cloth diapers and mustard-seed pillows, and made gajal to blacken their little eyes. She had spent countless afternoons watching over them as they slept in the sun, their oiled faces screened by her shawl. While their parents scrambled for crumbs, she had nourished and nurtured them, made them into healthy young women who could go out into the world. And now? They wished her dead, they spat out words that daily lacerated her heart. What was more, her very own daughter gave them the licence to treat her like a rag. As for her son, in all those years he had not even been able to extract an apology from his wife. Was that her reward for a lifetime of suffering?

It was Ganga who rescued Boju from her gnawing sense of defeat. The newcomer represented the land of parasites that leeched off the world that she, Boju, was meant to protect and guard. Unlike other freeloaders who came and went, that little pest would stay on, digging her claws deep into Boju's cherished domain. Boju must watch her every move lest she overstepped her boundaries. The new mission excited Boju, rousing her policing instincts and pushing her into a state of constant vigilance. Every morning as soon as she woke up, Boju would go watch Ganga making tea in the kitchen and give instructions in her drowsy voice: Go easy on milk. Don't stick a wet spoon in the sugar. Can't you stir faster? For the rest of the day Boju skulked around the house surveilling Ganga as she cooked, washed the dishes, burned garbage, hoed the vegetable patches and drew water with the hand pump. The minute Ganga slackened her pace, Boju would shout, 'Oi Gangay Maharani, move your hands. Whose banana are you dreaming of?' Throughout her puja, her attention would be divided between Ganga and her gods, her prayers and bhajans punctuated with—'O Gangata, where are you?' 'Gangotri, did you feed the hens?' 'Gangay Your Highness, can't you hear me?' Sometimes when Ganga was having her meal, Boju would go near her and exclaim, 'My God, this girl's got an appetite.' Then, bending a little, she'd whisper in her ear, 'They say girls who eat too much like to fuck early.' Ganga, who enjoyed such shocking little revelations, nearly choked on her food.

To please Boju, Ganga forsook even the small comforts allowed her in the house. Although allowed to use the indoor bathroom, she used the outdoor toilet at all times. During meals she avoided the table and sat on a pirka on the floor, and ate leftovers out of a cast-off stainless steel plate. She washed her hair with a bar of cheap soap instead of the less cheap shampoo her aunt had bought for her. After realizing Boju loved hoarding, she made it a habit of salvaging all sorts of junk from the garbage pit and safely depositing them in Boju's room. Every day she cooked at least one vegetable to satisfy Boju's craving for wild edibles—stinging nettles, taro leaves, roots of iskus, or fermented delights such as gundruk and kinema. No matter how inane Boju's joke, Ganga would manage a few laughs; she laughed even when the joke was on her.

Within weeks of her arrival, Ganga had made herself indispensable to the Tamule household, assuming the role of cook, cleaner, housekeeper and farmhand all rolled into one. Although a slow, bungling worker, she never stayed idle. If she wasn't cooking, she'd be cleaning something. If she wasn't washing, she'd be drawing water, or pounding maize, or chopping cauliflower leaves to mix in chicken feed. Even when she sat watching TV with eyes riveted on the screen, her hands would be busy shelling peas and garlic, breaking tough stems from mustard greens, or folding dry laundry. Her enthusiasm surprised everyone, most of all Sumnima and Numa. Ganga offered to carry their dirty cups over to the kitchen, ironed their school uniforms, and searched for their missing sock or notebook with a detective's zeal. Initially grateful, they began accepting her unsolicited services as a matter of routine, and soon felt no qualms shouting orders at her: Ganga didi, have you packed our lunch? Ganga didi, there's a spider in my room. Ganga didi, will you please…Ganga's eagerness made every demand seem modest; she left one feeling one should have asked for more.

'She's all right,' Boju whispered to Devi one day. 'If you slap her on one cheek, she'll turn the other.'

Devi nodded incredulously. 'Some people appear so straight and sojho from outside,' she said, 'but they're bent as a sickle on the inside.'

~

Devi was among those who saw a different side of Ganga. In the mornings as soon as Devi showed up at the door with a bottle of milk, Ganga said, 'Didi, slippers outside.' Sometimes she glanced at the wall clock and said, 'Didi, why so late?' After taking the bottle of milk from Devi, she pointed out dirt lodged in its lid, or grumbled about the bottle not being filled to the brim. Then she poured out the milk with a sigh, 'Is this milk or water? Cow milk back home is so thick and creamy.' Some days Devi bore her remarks in petulant silence. Other days she snapped back. 'Then go bring your cow. There are plenty of people who want this milk.' On such occasions Ganga immediately softened like a repentant child. 'Oho, didi,' she said with a weak, placating smile. 'Can't I even joke with you?'

Ganga asserted her authority most forcefully before the young men who were building the rooms on the third floor. 'O bhaiya, wash your own glasses, all right?' she'd shout as she served them tea. 'There's cement all over the stairs, can't you carry it properly?' When the rest of the family was not home, she'd go up several times to make sure the men hadn't sneaked into the bedrooms. She had quickly imbibed the contempt that Kathmandu dwellers felt for those dark-skinned men from the southern plains. Many of them came from the borderland villages and worked as hawkers, tinkers and pedlars. 'Shh, eat this quietly or that black Madise will kidnap you,' she had heard a woman in Bhaisichaur scare her child. One day she had seen a teenage boy punch an old vegetable-seller before snatching his basket and dumping all his tomatoes on the road. 'Saale dhoti, trying to cheat us? I'll give you one kick and send you flying back to India.' Ganga would never trust those dark men. While selling them empty beer bottles, or buying vegetables from them, she called them names and haggled over prices with such vicious energy the poor men sometimes threw up their hands in surrender. 'OK, OK, twenty rupees a kilo!' If she saw ragpickers roaming near the house, she would grab a stick and charge at them yelling, 'Oi Madise! Out, out, out!'

14

The two rooms on the top floor were ready. After much debate, it was decided that Sumnima should get the larger room with a balcony, for she would soon start preparing for the SLC exam and deserved the best space in the house. Tamule ji gladly endorsed the decision. He hoped Sumnima would pass through the 'iron gate' with a distinction, study science at the intermediate level and enter a medical college to become the first doctor in the unwritten history of the Tamule clan. Often in his daydreams he saw her ascending the dais in a white coat and waving a stethoscope to an applauding audience.

He was far less hopeful about his niece's future. It had been four months since she came to Kathmandu. As schools in Kathmandu wouldn't admit her at such a late stage, she would be sitting for the exam as a 'private' candidate. At nineteen she was already older than most SLC candidates. On the day he took her to register for the exam, she had spent a whole ten minutes filling out the form. When he sighed in frustration, she blamed the pen. 'Uff, this thing is useless.' Tamule ji had secretly vowed that if she scraped through the SLC, he would travel to Manakama temple and sacrifice a rooster to Goddess Bhagwati.

~

Sumnima moved to the bright, spacious and secluded room on the top floor. Even before the paint had dried, she plastered the walls with magazine cutouts and posters of world-famous celebrities. Actors, musicians, models, sportsmen, revolutionaries, TV anchors—icons whose particular vocations were somewhat mixed up in her head. She scrawled borrowed and adapted slogans on her new cupboard. 'Who is a rebel? The girl who says NO.' 'Hey parents, leave the kids alone.' A mini stereo stood on her shelf, along with a modest collection of cassettes on which she'd recorded pop and rock-and-roll songs off the FM radio. The room had large windows on two sides. On clear days, the window on the north offered a panoramic view of the hills and mountains. The other window looked out to the open field, which was being dug up for construction and rang all day with the sounds of drilling, hammering and gravel pouring out of a tractor. The room also had a sunny, flower-lined verandah where Sumnima read, napped and hung her undergarments after a shower. Straight down from the verandah stood Devi didi's house, a single-storey cement block with an attached shed. A pensive cow sat in her yard relaxing in the sun all day. Sometimes when Sumnima went out to hang her undergarments, she noticed a boy, probably one of Devi didi's sons, sitting on the roof of the house, plucking the strings of an out-of-tune guitar. The minute she appeared on the verandah, he would strum his guitar and croon a Hindi movie song, dragging out his notes till he ran out of breath. Sumnima would hurriedly peg up her bra and panties and throw a towel over them to protect them from his gaze. Seeing her scuttle inside, he would hit the strings harder and sing louder, oblivious that Sumnima, in her pursuit for a higher taste, had learned to dissociate herself from the world of Hindi cinema. 'No, he's not!' she'd shout every time Numa referred to the boy as 'your admirer'.

Unlike her, Numa had many admirers worthy of her attention. An active member of the scout troop and a skilled athlete, she effortlessly stole the hearts of boys during inter-school competitions and joint student excursions. Lately, she had started receiving 'bluff calls' from boys who enjoyed flirting with her under false names. These anonymous calls always caused a commotion in the house. The new telephone hung on the landing wall right outside their parents' bedroom. No matter how fast the girls ran, they couldn't get to the phone before their mother. On hearing a strange male voice asking for her daughter, she would bang the phone down and then pounce on Numa. Who was he? How did he get your number? Now I know what you do in your after-school meetings! She threatened to cut Numa's monthly allowance and ban her from extra-curricular events. Numa would fly into a rage, screaming her innocence and banging things. Sumnima would shut the door and turn up her music full blast. Sometimes Boju picked up the extension phone and let loose a stream of filthy abuse, throwing Sumnima into a panic. 'Oh God, make her stop!' she would cry to Numa, but Numa would just shrug and repeat her new catchphrase, 'What gives a damn?'

15

The sounds of birds and insects grew fainter as autumn turned to winter, and a quiet descended over the Tamule house. The long festivals finally ended, leaving everyone a bit drained, and a bit fatter, after weeks of feasting and gambling. The marigolds strung across the lintels began to crisp and brown. Ganga and her aunt spent an entire afternoon taking quilts and winter clothes out of storage. Sweaters, socks, wrinkled jackets, plaid trousers, unpaired gloves, monogrammed school blazers, and long-forgotten scarves and shawls came out of the heap as warm, colourful surprises. Startled silverfish scurried out of sleeves and camphor balls dropped from the folds as the garments were aired and hung out to dry in the sun. At night the temperature dropped sharply. The chickens puffed up their feathers and huddled together for warmth.

Sumnima's schooldays were coming to an end. The tenth graders spent their final week steeped in nostalgia. They reminisced about the old days and sang tributes to Rhododendron Girls High School, the institution that had nurtured and shaped them over ten years. They plunged into the task of creating their memory books, hunting for photographs, cutting out magazines and copying farewell quotes. On these bulky tomes made out of hardcover notebooks bound together, senior girls showcased the full range of their personalities. They wrote about their likes and dislikes, shared memorable anecdotes, and posted a well-curated collage of photos of their homes, dogs, hangouts and holidays. On the last day of school, Sumnima and her friends embraced each other and shed copious tears despite knowing they would be meeting next morning at the maths tutor's house.

~

Foggy mornings, sunny afternoons, and long chilly nights—it was a typical winter in Kathmandu. But Ganga felt this was the coldest season of her life. Winter was far mellower in the hills. The sun came out much earlier and the fog never seemed as dense. Their two-storey home, made of earth, wood and thatch, never froze like the concrete houses in the city. Even in the peak of winter Ganga could pace barefoot on the mud floor warmed by the hearth fire. A pinch of sheep fat was enough to protect her skin. Now her face looked dry and flaky even though she slathered on that sweet, sticky, clear fluid she called 'gilsin' every night.

If there was one favourable aspect of winter, it was that the cold had slowed Boju down and made her agreeably passive. She no longer rose at dawn and appeared in the kitchen first thing in the morning. Lying under quilts with her head wrapped in a shawl, she listened to Hindu bhajans and sermons on Radio Nepal until the seven o'clock news began. Her daily puja now consisted of a few perfunctory chants and a truncated bhajan. After finishing her puja, she would ask Ganga to make a fire in a small clay brazier that she kept in her room. She would settle down by the fire with a glass of tea and warm her hands till the sun broke through the fog.

~

Sometimes Devi sat and chatted with Boju after delivering milk to the kitchen. Sipping the watered-down tea that Ganga served her, Devi recounted the latest neighbourhood gossip and stories about innocent-faced refugee relatives who had robbed and murdered their guardians. 'How can people be such black-hearted serpents?' Boju would say. 'I hope we're not raising one under our own roof.' Devi would nod her head, her eyes filled with warning. But Boju did not seem to take her seriously. She betrayed a certain fondness for Ganga despite her professed distrust of the girl. 'I wonder if she'll stay here long though,' she said in a regretful tone. 'If she passes her SLC this time, she'll start going to college. After that, who knows, she may even find a boy and elope with him, don't you think?'

16

For first-time SLC candidates, it was a season of great hope and anxiety. For those taking the exam for the second or third time, a season of joyless repetition. While Ganga felt a kind of dull despair at the approach of the SLC, Sumnima and her friends experienced the panic and excitement shared by tens of thousands of tenth-grade students across the country.

At home Sumnima was pampered like a duck expected to lay a golden egg. Worried that the cold weather and the frequent power cuts might hinder her SLC preparation, Tamule ji bought her a high-voltage emergency lamp and a kerosene heater. 'For our future Doctor Saab,' he said. While Ganga took time out between chores to study for the exam, Sumnima would lie in the sun all day among her books, dozing, daydreaming and ordering countless cups of tea. Every day she came up with a new excuse to squeeze money out of her parents—SLC guide books, 'guess question papers', stationery, alarm clock, tutor's fee, transport fare, and so on. Her small weekly duties, such as emptying the dustbins and cleaning the water filter, fell on Numa's shoulders. In return, Sumnima let her sit in her room all morning and warm her back in front of her heater. The rest of the family only saw Sumnima at mealtimes. She would come downstairs wrapped in a big shawl, a book in hand and a strained look on her face. 'So much to do, so little time,' she'd moan. 'Potato and cauliflower again?' She would eat fast, complaining throughout. 'Which evil person must have invented physics? My eyes are hurting from reading in emergency light.' Her parents accepted all her grumbles and tantrums as symptoms of the SLC stress syndrome. 'I must run,' she'd say after finishing her meal. 'I'm dead if I don't memorize my formulas tonight.' She got away without even washing her dirty plate. No one was to disturb her once she retired to her room on the top floor and closed the door.

Behind the closed door, Sumnima spent most of her time listening to Metro FM, one of the many private radio stations that had emerged in the loosened atmosphere of multi-party democracy. These FM stations were very popular unlike the national radio, which aired bhajans and patriotic songs all morning and broadcast news several times a day in dull, scripted monotones. Metro FM offered an exciting mixed bag of content from western music to Hollywood gossip to phone-in programs where chatty, English-speaking hosts gave tips on health, fashion and relationships. Live debates were held on topics such as 'Is Mr Right a myth or reality?', 'Is public display of affection a bad thing?', or in more intellectually inspired moments, 'How can we foster a reading culture among Nepali youth?', and so on. Sumnima religiously tuned in to these discussions. She never missed the weekly music countdowns and the daily horoscope forecasts, which always seemed to come true for her. 'Give your brain a little rest and let your thoughts wander. You are under Neptune's influence today. It is time to explore and connect with others...'

Even amid these distractions, Sumnima felt she was working hard. She made numerous timetables, met her friends for 'combined study', and tacked up inspirational maxims on her wall. Every evening after dinner, Ganga showed up in her room carrying a flask of coffee and two cups on a tray, and a book under her arm. Both of them liked the idea of drinking coffee and studying deep into the night while the whole city lay asleep. But the seductive aroma of Nescafé distracted them until they drank it to the very last drop. Their zeal faded once they finished the coffee and soon they found themselves packing up for the night, berating themselves for their lack of will.

Sumnima always set her alarm for 5 a.m., but sounds from outside woke her up before the alarm went off. The creaking of the water pump handle, the rattle of pails and buckets, the sloshing of water, the scraping of a bamboo-stick broom—Ganga began working at an ungodly hour. Feeling vaguely sorry for her cousin, Sumnima would pick up a book and turn on the emergency lamp on her bedside table, the light switch being out of her reach. Buried up to her neck under quilts, she would turn the pages with her frigid fingers. Inch by inch she would slip back into her warm cocoon, and soon her head dropped, her book dropped, and off she dropped to sleep again, until she heard Ganga's voice, 'Thuli, get up, tea is here.'

After drinking her tea, Sumnima would get ready for her tutoring class, shivering and moaning as she slipped into a pair of ice-cold jeans. Bundled up in layers of warm clothes, she stepped out into the fog and went striding past the frost-covered fields and unfinished houses. Balram Sir lived on the other side of town. To reach the public bus park, she had to cross the ring road and walk for fifteen minutes past the army barracks. No matter how she timed her walk, she could never avoid the long line of soldiers jogging on that lane. Even when the fog obscured their faces and deadened the drumming of their boots, she could feel their leering eyes on her. She would look straight ahead and furiously quicken her pace until she arrived at the bus park, her cheeks red and nose numb with cold. The fibres of her woollen cap and the stray wisps of her hair would be coated with fine drops of condensed fog. After boarding one of the newer-looking blue buses donated by Japan, she'd sink down in her seat, wipe the frost off the window and look outside as the bus drove across town. At this hour the city would be freshly awake and full of beginnings. In the thinning fog she saw women sweeping outside their front doors, people lighting lamps at roadside shrines, and shopkeepers opening the store shutters. A red-nosed boy cycled past houses hurling rolled-up newpapers over boundary walls. Sumnima would always stop the bus several metres ahead of her destination, lest her friends, who commuted in chauffeured cars, saw her alighting from a public vehicle.

~

Balram Sir taught mathematics at Rhododendron Girls High School, but his primary source of income was the private lessons he gave during the SLC season. A rotund man with broad ears and a thin, piping voice, he had earned many unflattering nicknames during his young teaching career. The way he slurred over the words he could not pronounce, such as 'parallelogram' and 'quadrilateral', the way he advised students to 'just by heart' the equations he could not explain, the pleasure and abandon with which he scratched his crotch or picked his ear—all this made him a source of unending mirth for his students. They spent the tutorial session nudging and kicking each other under the table and convulsing with suppressed laughter. Despite his unseemly habits, Balram Sir was regarded as a 'hot cake' in Kathmandu's education market. A few years ago, one of his tutees from St Francis School had topped the SLC board with full marks in both compulsory and optional maths. The boy's face, beaming with a broad, victorious smile, had been splashed on the front pages of all the newspapers in town. In a widely heard radio interview, he had thanked Balram Sir before reciting a poem about the importance of hard work. 'What a genius poem. Maybe you should become a poet instead of engineer,' the interviewer had joked. The SLC topper turned out to be Balram Sir's mascot. Following the boy's success, well-heeled students from reputed schools began seeking him out before every SLC season. His fees soared. Within two years, his simple two-storey brick house became a three-storey mansion with gilded pillars and many decorative structures jutting out of the façade. His colleagues at Rhododenron called him a fraud. Balram Sir did not care. Let them stew, he said, he was planning to quit that overhyped school and open his own ten-plus-two college.

'It's going to be called Galileo International,' he announced to Sumnima and her friends one morning. 'Do you like the name?'

'It's very nice, sir.'

'We plan to have computers, projectors and all kinds of audio-visual equipment in the classrooms. We'll also bring foreign teachers.'

The girls expressed murmurs of surprise and approval.

'I hope you'll enroll there after SLC?'

The girls looked at each other and mumbled something ambiguous. None of them had any intention of pursuing their higher studies in Nepal. Rajani aunty had already chosen a school for Reshma in Mussoorie. Tejaswi planned to study fashion design in Delhi, and Sumnima's parents had promised to send her to India on condition that she earned a distinction in SLC.

17

'Happy Valentine's! I hope you get many kisses, oops, I mean roses…'

The cheery voice on the radio kept distracting Sumnima from her arithmetic problem. Her SLC exams were only a month and a half away. She stopped smiling and tried to focus on the problem.

'The concert's gonna blow your mind, so be there or be rectangle! Ha-ha-ha…'

Sumnima was hooked. The clever turns of phrase, the one-liners so spontaneous and off-the-cuff, the American slang half of which she did not understand—the new presenter wielded a hypnotic charm over her. She could hear Ganga calling her downstairs for dinner. 'Comiiiiing!' she shouted, then got up from her desk and moved closer to the stereo.

A girl had won a prize for being the first caller on the show.

'Congrats!' the presenter said in a chirpy voice. 'You've won a meal for two at the brand-new, super duper fabulous Café de Kathmandu!'

'Thank you, that is a great news,' the girl said in English. Her nervous gasps echoed through the speaker.

'So is that going to be our dinner date, sweetheart?' the presenter said.

The girl gave an awkward laugh. 'Where can I get the prize, please?' The line hissed and crackled.

'You'll have to come to our office with your ID.'

'I can bring my campus ID?' the girl breathed heavily into the mouthpiece.

'Yup, that'll do,' the presenter said.

'I would like to delicate the next song—' a long squeak drowned out the rest of her words.

'I think your radio set is too close to the phone,' the presenter said above the beeping noise.

'I just want to delicate the song,' the girl said hurriedly through the noise, 'to my family, my sister Devi Bohara, my cousin sister Mina Bohara, Naresh uncle and Sita aunty of Madanpur-6, Palpa, my friend Tina Shrestha of Kusunti and all my family, classmates, friends, family and friends of B.Com first year—'

A prolonged squeak rose from the speaker and the line got cut.

'Oops, looks like we've lost her,' the presenter said with some relief.

Sumnima sighed. Why did people call and ruin the show when they couldn't even speak in English? It rattled her that the presenter's banter about the dinner date had gone unappreciated. She could hear her mother downstairs, shouting about the food getting cold. 'Comiiiing!' Sumnima shouted irritably, then turned to the stereo. Should she call the show to make up for that lousy exchange? What if she made a fool of herself on the air?

'Time to call it a night,' the presenter said, 'but I'll be back again next week.'

Sumnima brought her face close to the speaker.

'Don't forget to tune in to *The Jukebox*, your favourite show, with your favourite host Sagar.'

Sagar. Sumnima said the name aloud and smiled to herself.

~

Sumnima lost interest in all but that one show on the FM radio. The following Saturday, the prospect of listening to *The Jukebox* motivated her to study all day long. As dinnertime coincided with the showtime, she brought her food to her room and tuned in as she ate. Beneath his bright and breezy chatter, she could detect a mind endowed with cosmopolitan wisdom. He knew something about everything, from rock music to Zen Buddhism, from celebrity lifestyles to the Gulf War, from French cuisine to Newari bhattis. Sumnima hung on his every word, seized every scrap that helped her piece him together. Her intense attention brought its rewards. Next week she found out that Sagar was a product of St Francis, the only school in the country that seemed on a par with Rhododendron. Having guessed it from the start, this did not particularly surprise her. What did surprise her was when, a week later, he casually revealed that he had studied in America and returned to Nepal only six months ago. Sagar was the first US returnee she had ever come across.

18

The national telecom services had finally reached Lungla and a phone was installed at the local school. Using the service was a complicated affair though. Tamule ji had to call a day in advance and request Birkha Sir to relay his message to his brother Tikaram. Next day, Tikaram and his family would walk down to the school and wait by the phone at the appointed time. The call went through only after repeated attempts. The line got cut every few minutes. But Tamule ji now felt miles closer to the village and was grateful for the new development. Sometimes he would call Ganga over to the phone to talk to her parents. 'Ama, how's your knee? Did you have your meal? Can you give the phone to Jamuna?' She only asked such mundane questions. Although the SLC exams were in full swing, she seemed determined not to talk about them. To Tamule ji this certainly did not augur well.

Boju cursed the day when those peasants received the telephone. Why did they need a phone for God's sake? To say hello, I fed my cow, have you fed yours? Not only did the frequent trunk calls run up huge bills, her son-in-law now kept track of all his relatives and made hasty commitments to send them money or find them jobs in Kathmandu. Whenever her sixth sense alerted her that he was talking to his relatives, Boju stole into the living room and gently lifted the receiver of the extension phone. She detected an underlying motive in every piece of news they shared. If they said their cow was sick, they meant Tamule ji should buy them another cow. If they said the village school gave too many holidays, they meant Tamule ji should educate their litter in Kathmandu. If they said somebody in the village was ill, they meant Tamule ji should pay for their treatment and prolong their wretched lives. Their remarks made her blood boil and her face twist with rage, but she kept still as a rock, her mouth shut tight.

The rotary phone was falling apart; the slightest movement would make the line crackle and give her away.

~

'Hello, Tika dai, can you hear me now?' Tamule ji shouted into the mouthpiece.

'Yes, yes, I can hear you!' Tikaram shouted from the other end.

'So I was saying,' Tamule ji said, 'you should come to Kathmandu soon. Ganga's SLC exams will finish tomorrow. By the way, is Saila next door taking the SLC?'

'Yes, but he missed his exam on the second day. His sister broke her head so he had to rush her to hospital.'

'Really? How?'

'Poor girl, she slipped off the trail on her way to—'

The line got disconnected. Tamule ji glanced at his watch and quickly redialled the number. His office van would arrive any minute. Every time he called his brother with a clear agenda, their conversation meandered into such unrelated topics. Luckily the call went through. This time he cut straight to the point: 'Should I book your flights for next month? I'll pay the airfare, of course.'

'Flights, well...' said Tikaram. 'We wouldn't like to trouble you, we could come by road, but if you insist...'

Tamule ji turned the page of a wall calendar, which had a picture of GIDC's project beneficiaries in an awareness-raising session. 'How about Wednesday, thirteenth of Baisakh?'

'But Wednesday is an inauspicious day to leave home...'

'OK, fourteenth then,' Tamule ji said.

'That's better.'

Tamule ji hung up with a relieved sigh. As much as he liked catching up with his people, their heavy-footed speech and roundabout way of talking made him impatient at times. He looked at his watch, picked up his bag and made a dash for the door. He stopped outside the puja room, where Ganga sat removing the prayer paraphernalia from the altar.

'Don't you have your maths exam tomorrow?' he asked.

Ganga looked at him and nodded.

'Then what are you doing here?'

'I wanted to quickly wash these for Boju,' she said, gathering the puja items on a brass tray. Small idols smeared with vermillion, a brass hand-bell, an incense holder, a greasy copper diyo, a black fossil stone.

'Didn't your aunt say you don't have to work during the exam?' Tamule ji said.

'She did, but this won't take long,' Ganga said. 'No harm devoting a few minutes to God.'

Tamule ji couldn't help chuckling. His niece's efforts to please Boju amused him. Maybe the girl wasn't as dull as she appeared. She knew how to look out for herself, to use her meekness as a shield. 'I just spoke to your parents,' he said. 'They're coming here next month, on the fourteenth. They'll stay for a month.'

'Really?' Ganga's face lit up like a thousand-watt bulb.

~

The day after she finished her SLC exams, Sumnima dragged Numa to Sewaro Beauty Parlour on the other side of town. The hole-in-the-wall parlour was run by a distant maternal aunt who had migrated from Tehrathum a few years ago. Sumnima got her eyebrows shaped for the first time. Her skin tingled as her aunt pulled and twisted and rolled the thread against her face. After the threading, she got her hair cut into the short, shaggy style of a popular MTV host. She ignored Numa's objections and got her bangs streaked with hydrogen peroxide. 'Thank you, chhema, I love it,' she said, looking in the mirror. Her hair, set and blow-dried, looked worthy of a magazine cover. Just as she had hoped, her aunt refused to accept money from her. 'Stop it, kid,' she said when Sumnima insisted on paying, 'or I'll hit you with this hair-dryer.' Laughing, the girls thanked her and bid her goodbye.

A few days later Sumnima went out with Reshma and Tejaswi to celebrate the end of their SLC exams. They would have three months' break before their results came out. 'Wow, I love your haircut,' Reshma said. 'Eden Spa?'

Sumnima hesitated. Eden Spa was an expensive salon tucked away inside a five-star hotel that Sumnima had never had the chance to enter. 'I didn't have much time,' she said, 'so I went to a parlour near my house. They're very good.'

Reshma and Tejaswi nodded approval; they could be so gullible sometimes.

'Guess what I did yesterday?' Reshma said. She took off her cardigan and showed a small peace sign tattoo on her left arm. Sumnima and Tejaswi gasped in surprise.

'Did it hurt?' Tejaswi asked.

'A little,' Reshma said. 'I didn't know there was a tattoo place in town. They use sterilized equipment, all very safe. My cousin dai took me there. He's visiting from America, he used be to so sojho, now he has long hair and smokes gaanja, it's unbelievable...'

Sumnima tuned out. She was wondering whether Sagar, also a US returnee, had a tattooed arm.

The girls spent all afternoon strolling around Durbarmarg. The clean, wide street led straight to the entrance of the royal palace and was lined with five-star hotels, imported-clothing stores, travel agencies, cafés and restaurants. For lunch they had pizza at an expensive café. It turned out Reshma and Tejaswi were not carrying enough change, so Sumnima had to spend all of the crisp banknotes her relatives had given her after putting tika on her forehead on Dasain. After lunch they went for ice cream at a crowded parlour, and amid the rush and confusion, Sumnima again ended up paying for all three ice creams, silently reproaching her friends for being slow in opening their purses. Ten years at Rhododendron had taught her that the rich could be incredibly stingy. Worried about her depleting cash, she decided to take a tempo home once her friends left. But as they were hugging each other goodbye, Reshma turned around and hailed a taxi for her.

'It's for you,' she said to Sumnima.

'Thanks, but why don't you take it?'

'You take it, my driver's picking me up,' Reshma said with an oblivious smile.

Sumnima had no choice but to get inside the taxi. Throughout the ride she kept her eyes fixed on the taximeter, which ticked up faster than she could keep up. The driver had obviously tampered with the device. Annoyed, she stopped the taxi midway, tossed some money at him and jumped out of the cab. 'O bahini, you can't do this,' the driver said, 'why didn't you tell me before?' His threatening tone faintly unnerved Sumnima but she kept walking with a steadfast gait. He yelled a curse and drove away with a screech.

19

Over the next month Sumnima gleaned other details about Sagar that might have escaped a less devoted listener. She learned about his eclectic taste in food and music, his love for nature, travel and Buddhist philosophy, and the variety of social causes he espoused. He called himself a self-taught photographer and an aspiring filmmaker. Each of these discoveries felt like a small victory and left her hungry for more. Some evenings the two sisters listened to *The Jukebox* together. As Sagar's high and chirpy voice filled the room, Sumnima felt transported far from the humdrum reality of family life. Every now and then she looked to see Numa's reaction. Although Numa professed a total lack of interest in the show, she always listened with an attentive expression on her face. Sumnima felt validated every time she laughed at one of Sagar's quips. If he played a song they both liked, they would hum along in sync with the beat. If the conversation on air turned absurd because of the caller's poor English, they would burst out laughing at once, for nothing sounded funnier to Rhododenron girls than clunky English. Yet Numa's attitude towards her new craze was far from congratulatory. 'God, this guy can blabber,' she'd sigh. 'If you shut his mouth he'll talk out of his ass.' When Sumnima told her he had studied in America, she said, 'Ahhh, hence the lovely fake accent.' Numa's opinions did not make a dent on Sumnima's growing infatuation.

One day Numa tracked down Sagar's home phone number through an extended circle of friends. She charged Sumnima a hundred rupees for the service. After making great song and dance about 'the first phone call', Sumnima realized she did not dare speak to him yet. She decided to write to him instead. Next day she went to Seekers, a bookstore she often passed by but had never entered because she only saw white people coming out through its large glass-panelled doors. She tried to look composed as she went in. The store was bigger than she had imagined. The high-ceilinged space was filled with beautiful objects. Books, wood and metal handicrafts, natural paper products, silk and pashminas, incense, essential oils, etc. A few tourists milled about the shelf filled with self-help books. Soothing instrumental music played in the background and a sweet incense smell hung in the air. Sumnima gradually felt at ease. She spent leafed through paper products—handmade and naturally dyed notebooks, letter pads, bookmarks, greeting cards, envelopes. She compared prices, mulled over different options, and discreetly counted the money in her pocket. Finally, she bought an earth-coloured letter pad pressed with tiny dried flowers. It was the most delicate piece of stationery she had ever bought. She smiled at the thought of Sagar unfolding the paper and reading the message written in her elegant, cursive script. 'Dear Sagar, from the moment I heard your voice...' She mentally composed the letter as she sat in a tempo, smiling to herself, drawing puzzled glances from other passengers. But when she got home and poured her words out on paper, she began to doubt the whole enterprise. Was she being imprudent exposing herself to a radio show host? Would a public figure like him care about her feelings? Besides her mother might skin her alive if she heard him reading out the letter on the air. But then, Sagar would never know of her existence unless she took the risk. Confused, she turned to Numa for advice. 'Show me the letter,' Numa said with authority. Sumnima read her expression as she pored over the letter. Although Numa did her best not to laugh, her mocking half-smile and raised eyebrow did not escape Sumnima. 'Write to him if you must,' Numa said in a restrained voice. 'But maybe you could be less gushy?' Sumnima snatched the letter from her hand and went back to her room. She trashed the letter and wrote a new one, on plain paper, for the letter pad now seemed too flowery.

'*Hi Sagar, I got hooked to your show from the moment I heard it. It's strange, but I think of you all the time. Hands down, you're the coolest RJ in town.*'

That was all. Didn't someone say brevity is the soul of wit? She read the letter over and over, impressed with her own words. She could not bring herself to sign her name though. After racking her brains for pen names, she decided to call herself 'Mona Lisa'. It sounded classy and mysterious. Satisfied, she mailed the letter to Metro FM the next morning.

A week later, Sagar responded to her on the air. 'O Mona Lisa!' he sighed. 'Thank you for your lovely letter.' Sumnima could barely contain herself as he read out her message in his exuberant voice. 'I'm so flattered, Mona Lisa, hands down, you're the coolest girl in town.' Sumnima got up and paced the room, blushing, her heart pounding with excitement. She opened the door to shout for Numa, but stopped—she would only burst the bubble with a pointed barb. There was no one with whom she could share the tumult of her heart. Her best friends would laugh at her if they found out she had a crush on a radio presenter. Reshma certainly would, even though the boys she fancied paled in comparison to Sagar.

20

Although excited about her parents' visit to Kathmandu, Ganga was apprehensive about how Boju might treat them. Two weeks before their arrival, she began a new ritual to appease the old woman. Every day after finishing her kitchen duties, she would spread an old bed sheet on the TV room couch, make Boju lie on her back, and spend an hour massaging her limbs while the television babbled in the background. At first Boju sounded grateful. 'Your poor hands must be tired, have some rest.' But feelings of gratitude quickly hardened into a sense of entitlement. 'Oho, Gangotri, use a little more force, burn the mountains of rice you're stuffed with.' As Ganga's greasy fingers undid the sore knots in her flesh, Boju, lying supine with eyes closed, reminisced about the old days.

'A few weeks after the bijuwa healed him,' said Boju, 'he comes home and tells me, 'Budi, there's going to be a women's parade on coronation day, you should take part in it.' I thought he'd gone mad again, but I couldn't say no to him, could I?'

'Of course not,' Ganga said, rubbing oil on Boju's cracked heels.

'But the problem was I had to wear a kurta surwal for the practice. I wore nothing but sari in those days.'

'Only sari?' Ganga said, tweaking Boju's toes.

'Yes, we were not like today's girls, showing off rumps and bumps in the streets.'

Ganga laughed, and began massaging Boju's calf. A network of purple, swollen veins ran under her pale skin. 'I got a kurta made,' Boju continued, 'but I didn't want the neighbours to see me wearing it. So when I went to Singha Durbar for the practice, I'd avoid the main road and take the path along the Tukucha River. I'd cover my face with a shawl and walk fast fast fast without looking left or right—oho, you're just tickling me, put some more pressure.' Ganga bent forward and pressed her full weight down on Boju's leg. 'Imagine, we got to practice right on the Singha Durbar complex. Ah, such beautiful gardens and fountains. The other women came from big homes. College students, daughters of wealthy sahujis, thula bada folks. Oh, the airs. There were these two women, they stood behind me during the parade and made fun of me in Newari all the time, calling me khencha, like I didn't understand.'

'What does it mean?' Ganga asked.

'An uncouth hill woman. I controlled myself the first day, and the next, and the next, but on the fourth day I couldn't take it anymore, so I turned around and asked directly, 'Ay, who are you calling khencha?' They just giggled. I was so mad I charged at them like a bull and tore big clumps of hair off their educated heads.'

Boju waited, but Ganga did not laugh. Her hands too had gone still. She was staring at the TV screen, where a newlywed couple lay in bed under a canopy of garlands. Ganga's eyes glinted as the groom removed the bride's veil and began unfastening her gold trappings.

'Don't worry, my dear,' Boju said. 'Once you're married, your husband will also do that to you. Then you can massage his equipment instead of my poor limbs.'

'Chhya, Boju!' Ganga cried. 'What are you saying? I don't like men.' She stole another glance at the screen. The bride and groom were locked in a gasping embrace.

'That's what everyone says until,'—Boju burped as Ganga lightly hammered her spine with her fists—'until they find their choice of you know what.'

'God promise, Boju,' Ganga said, using the English words. 'I swear on my mother's blood, I don't want to marry.'

The TV screen buzzed and flickered and went blank, and

simultaneously the refrigerators, radios, water pumps and drilling machines in the neighbourhood stopping running. A new layer of silence fell over the house. For some time, the only sound was the ticking of the wall clock. Ganga took Boju's hand and pressed her palm with her thumbs, slowly working her way up to her fingertips. Neither of them spoke for a while. The silence seemed to have plunged them into their own internal worlds.

'That's why I say,' Boju said, continuing her train of thought aloud, 'one should only eat what one can swallow.' Ganga's face tensed up a little. Earlier that morning she had stolen a pack of biscuits from Boju's room. Or had she seen her eating the scrapings of the milk pot last night? 'Humans are greedy by nature,' Boju went on. She raised herself and straightened her clothes. 'Offer them a finger and they'll bite off your hand.'

'What do you mean, Boju?' Ganga asked guardedly.

'I mean,' Boju said. 'Can't your parents travel by bus?' She leaned forward and wiped her oily palms on Ganga's hair. 'They can barely feed their kids but want to fly on an aeroplane.'

A spark of anger flashed in Ganga's eyes, then disappeared. She forced a smile that made a corner of her upper lip quiver.

'Your kaka can't be their milking cow forever, can he?' Boju said.

Ganga kept quiet for a long moment, then said in an uncertain voice, 'But Boju, they said Kaka insisted on booking flights for them. Buwa prefers travelling by road. Ama is scared of flying.' A shadow crossed over Boju's face. 'You know what Ama said once?' Ganga said with a penitent smile. 'She said—what if the pilot wants to pee really badly?' She released a short forced laugh.

'Oho, look at you siding with your folks,' Boju said. 'At the end of the day, you're all the same. Honey on the tongue, knife in the pocket.'

'But Boju, I didn't mean to...' Ganga stammered.

'Shut up and go feed the hens,' Boju said, motioning her to get out of her sight.

21

Tikaram sat with his brother on the verandah and relayed the news from Lungla.

Life was moving on in the village. His youngest daughter Jamuna had reached eighth grade. The eldest, Chandrey, had become a father; his baby boy had started crawling and kept everyone busy from morning till night. They had been extra vigilant since Setey Kancha's baby burnt to death last month. Poor child, she had crawled right into the smoldering fire in their kitchen. Her parents returned from the field to find a charred lump of flesh instead of their baby. Setey's wife had fainted at the sight and gone almost mad with grief.

Chandrey was growing restless. He thought his child had no future in Lungla. He wanted the whole family to move somewhere, anywhere, but Tikaram's mother would rather die than leave the village.

Their next-door neighbour Rai kaka's wife had passed away at last. She had been suffering for too long. Rai kaka's greatest remaining worry was his son Dammar. The boy had quit his studies and joined a political organization. They opposed the Hindu state, wanted liberation for the Kirati people, and called on all Matwalis to boycott Hindu festivals.

Tamule ji sighed and sipped his tea. News from the village seldom cheered him. 'Dai, your tea is getting cold,' he said. His brother had been talking for nearly an hour. Tikaram lifted his cup with both hands and gulped down his tea. He looked small and worn, his face marked by years of grueling labour. His dark, weathered hands seemed unsuited for the glazed porcelain cup.

'Chandrey is right, Tika dai,' Tamule ji said. 'You can't be stuck in Lungla forever. It's still not too late. If you really want, I can help you start a small business in Dharan.'

'Khai, at this age...' Tikaram looked out to the fields hemmed in by half-built houses.

'Chandrey can help you manage the business.'

'So many houses,' Tikaram said, looking around him. 'In a few years' time, there will be no open patch left. Are they building a school over there?'

Tamule ji resignedly shook his head. It seemed futile trying to change his brother's mind. All those advice-filled letters he'd sent him from Kathmandu, all those ideas he'd given him during his visits to Lungla, all those ardent pleas made through respected elders in the village, all of it had fallen on deaf ears. Tika dai, please buy a small plot in Bhaisichaur before the prices rise, please move to Kathmandu, start a small business, perhaps try your hand at property brokering, send your children to a good school. But no, Tikaram never summoned the drive to move forward in life. Whenever Tamule ji gave him advice, he listened with a smile that seemed to say, 'Spill your guts, my dear Gajey, it's not going to touch a hair on my brain. I have my way of life and you yours, but carry on, empty your mind.' Year after year the prudent ones left the village to escape the unrelenting hardship of life in the hills. Those who could not make it to Kathmandu migrated to small towns in the Tarai plains—Dharan, Itahari, Biratnagar, Lahan. Even Gore Damai had now opened a tailoring shop in Itahari they said. Gore, who used to come to their house every Dasain to collect the tail of the slaughtered sheep. But Tikaram remained in Lungla. By the grace of God he had kept his ancestral land intact while others lost one fertile plot after another to the high-caste moneylenders in the village. On that piece of land he worked from morning till night, harvesting just enough to feed his family two square meals a day.

No matter how he tried to rationalize it, his brother's benighted condition would not stop nagging at Tamule ji's conscience. It seemed unjustifiable that the brother of an international NGO

officer should have to trudge up and down the hills for hours just
to buy a packet of salt. Every evening he sat in the dim light of
a wick lamp while his wife cooked a meal of coarse-grained rice
over a smoking wood-fire. In this day and age he was deprived of
running water, a decent toilet, and even the most basic medicines.
He remained trapped under the yoke of necessity and lived at the
mercy of nature, while his younger brother, sprung from the same
loins, lived a respectable and comfortable life in the capital city.

~

Boju kept a sharp watch on Ganga after her parents' arrival.
Was she giving them special treatment from the kitchen? Adding
extra milk to their tea? Pilfering knickknacks to send to Lungla?
Whenever Ganga was in the kitchen chatting with her mother, or
sitting with her parents in her room, Boju would lurk around the
corner with pricked-up ears, hoping to catch them committing
some act of disloyalty. But even after a week of snooping and
spying, she found nothing incriminating against them. She
withdrew her feelers and softened up a little. Besides they had
brought her such a huge bag of koseli—dried river fish, fiery
dalle chillies, juicy yellow lemons with paper-thin rind, and a
variety of hill bananas she'd never tasted before. In hindsight, it
was good that they came by plane; those lovely, creamy bananas
would have gone bad on the long road journey.

Ganga's mother Sita was a patient and obliging woman. She
would sit with Boju in the yard and listen to her tales for hours
on end. She took no offence when Boju made fun of her tribe, cut
her off in midsentence, or asked her to do small chores around
the house. She had only one flaw: she could not stop complaining
about the pain in her leg. 'Aiya, my leg,' she moaned every time
she stood up, sat down, or took a few steps. 'Oho, this knee is
killing me. Hey Bhagwan, when will this torture end?' She said
her knee had been hurting since she slipped and fell near the

village tap a few years ago, but Boju, who regarded all display of
suffering as a form of self-indulgence, refused to believe her. 'It's
all in your head,' she'd say, 'stop whining, it doesn't suit a hardy
hill woman like you.'

Ganga's father Tikaram was a remarkably disciplined man.
Every morning he woke up in the small hours and washed his face
at the tap outside. His loud hacking and gargling broke the silence
of dawn. After brushing his teeth with a frayed jatropha stem, he
stood on one leg facing east and prayed to the rising sun. Then he
went to the kitchen and drank two glasses of water to flush out
his system. Although Boju did not mind him using the indoor
bathroom, he opted for the squat toilet, being too squeamish to
sit on the communal seat. As a pure vegetarian he refused to eat
off melamine dinnerware (he believed they were partially made
up of bone) and asked to be served on the stainless steel utensils
reserved for less important visitors. No amount of prodding could
get him to eat the packaged titbits served in the house at random
hours, for he had once heard that factory workers, tired of using
their hands, sometimes kneaded dough with their feet and spat
phlegm into the mixture out of impotent rage. His semi-ascetic
habits made a deep impression on his hosts. Even Boju regarded
him with grudging respect. Seeing Ganga's heaped plate during
meals, she said, 'Ganga Maharani, do you have a belly or a sack?
Learn some moderation from your father.'

'Ha, that mule-headed old man,' Ganga replied with a laugh.

~

Ganga had not felt happier since she arrived in Kathmandu a
year ago. Her parents' presence had transformed her uncle's house
into a warm and intimate place. She had never seen them outside
the setting of their home village. Their new surroundings threw
their destitution and unworldiness into stark relief. Uprooted
from their natural habitat, they appeared strange, awkward and

vulnerable. For the first time in her life, Ganga felt a protective urge towards them. But she was careful not to show her happiness or her affection for her parents, afraid her guardians might question her loyalty. At no cost would she let the arrival of those temporary visitors ruin the image she had built of herself. She advised her parents to keep Boju company and assist her in her work in the backyard. She made them watch Indian TV serials with Boju despite their patchy grasp of Hindi. Every so often she would appear in the TV room and scold them for no reason. 'Oho, Buwa, stop asking questions, let Boju watch the serial.' Or she would join Boju in mocking her mother. 'You're right, Boju, whining is no cure for pain.' Her parents smiled at her outbursts, for behind Boju's back she showered them with quiet care and attention.

When they were alone, Ganga would run her eyes over her mother and chide her for neglecting her health. Her mother, only five years older than her aunt, already looked old and frail. The sight of her bent back and wrinkled face filled her with worry and pain. 'Ama, you must eat well,' she would say. 'I'll ask uncle to buy some vitamins for you before you go.' After finishing her morning chores, she would sometimes sit with her mother in the sun and comb her thinning hair. 'Ama, you need a good shampoo. And cold cream for your face.' Every night before going to bed, she massaged her mother's leg with Chinese balm and reminded her to rub glycerine on her cracked heels. Her mother obeyed her like a child. As her father couldn't stand the smell of mosquito repellent mats, Ganga hung a mosquito net above their bed, using scrap ribbons and pajama drawstrings to attach the net corners to walls and window frames. She washed and ironed their clothes, cooked the vegetables they liked, and always set aside small portions of food for her father before adding garlic, onion or strong spices. Every day she added one more of her possessions to the pile of things she planned to send back to Lungla—a few old clothes, a pair of shoes that didn't fit her, half-used bottles of shampoo and lotion, a leather handbag that Sumnima had gifted her, and the rucksack she'd borrowed from Chandrey when she first came to Kathmandu.

Tamule ji took several days off work to show his brother and sister-in-law around town. Premkala joined them once out of politeness. Perhaps to make up for her absence, she asked Ganga to accompany her parents on all their excursions. 'Uff, Kaki wants me to go out again,' Ganga would inform Boju with a frown. She always made sure to wrap up all her chores before heading out. Only after she filled the water tank, stocked up the kitchen, cleared the sink, picked up laundry and scrubbed the floors would she feel relaxed and ready for an outing. She would take a shower and change into a favourite kurta surwal, then go up to Sumnima's room to borrow a few accessories. She would try one earring after another while Sumnima stood at a little distance and appraised her, conveying her opinion through tiny nods or scowls. Ganga would not feel satisfied until Sumnima said with a firm nod, 'Yes, wear those.'

Sumnima and Numa had been treating her with special kindness since her parents arrived. They had stopped giving orders from the landing and hung around in the kitchen trying to help her, unaware that they obstructed rather than aided her work. They held hot pans with cleaning rags, wiped the countertop with potholders, used three different bowls when one sufficed, and threw dirty dishes in the sink without wiping off greasy remnants. They used water as if it flowed from an inexhaustible mountain spring. Late risers, they had not seen how laboriously Ganga collected water every morning, how she sweated and panted and ached as she pulled the water-pump handle up and down. 'Thuli, Kanchi, please go, you've done enough,' she would implore her cousins, allowing them to retreat into their rooms with a lightened conscience.

What Ganga enjoyed most was being out in the city with her parents. Spring had arrived and the trees all over the city had bloomed purple, red and yellow. Riding around the ring road on a public bus, Ganga realized that Kathmandu was smaller than she had imagined. If the traffic was light, one could circle it in less than two hours. Inside the ring road, the heart of the city thumped with life. Markets, eateries, office buildings, hospitals, temples and squares. Every day Ganga and her parents saw a different face of the city—the maze of narrow alleys with old, cramped houses, the busy thoroughfare filled with pedestrians and hawkers selling their wares, the clean street near the royal palace lined with exclusive stores and restaurants, and the quiet neighbourhood where wealthy folk lived behind high walls, their homes and gardens hidden from view. Tamule ji took them to all the major temples inside the city and on the outskirts. They returned with sanctified leaves, grains, flowers and smashed coconuts in tiny plastic bags, and plastic bottles filled with murky waters from the sacred rivers of the valley. Tikaram made a special packet of offerings for the village priest, who had advised them on the protocol of worship.

Early one morning they boarded a trolley bus bound towards Suryabinayak temple in Bhaktapur. The landscape became greener and the air fresher as they moved away from the city centre. They drove past farmland overrun by concrete settlements, farmland crisscrossed by streams and dirt trails, and farmland dotted with brick kiln towers emitting thick swirls of smoke. While Tamule ji and Tikaram stood in the aisle, Ganga and her mother sat together near the window and chatted all the way. 'Look, it's like our bensi field,' her mother said to Ganga. Ganga leaned over and looked outside. Beyond the road, luminous green paddy fields ran to meet the foothills at the edge of the valley. Above the hills, a row of snowy peaks shimmered faintly like gauze in the morning sky.

22

In a moment of effusive amiability, Sumnima had promised to show her uncle and aunt around town. But every week she gave them some excuse to escape the commitment. She couldn't spend her post-SLC break herding her village relatives around town.

She had been writing to Sagar every week for the past month. Brief, light-hearted letters peppered with snappy phrases lifted from songs and magazines. Sagar read them aloud on air. His sprightly voice and foreign accent made her words sound all the more alluring. Sometimes his true response seemed hidden in the songs he played on the show.

'Hello, I love you, won't you tell me your name?'

'Mysterious girl, I wanna be close to you…'

During scheduled power cuts, she sat on the verandah and listened to his show on her father's old transistor, which no longer received a signal inside the house. The minute she stepped out into the verandah, the dark shape of a boy wearing a cap emerged on Devi didi's rooftop. He stood near the balustrade, lit a cigarette behind a cupped palm, and took long, slow puffs, his head lifted in her direction. In the darkness Sumnima could see nothing but the burning tip of his cigarette, yet she felt his eyes fastened on her. Cursing him under her breath, she lowered the radio volume and ducked behind the flowerpots. 'Sumnima, did you take my radio?' she could hear her father shouting from somewhere. 'Bring it back, I want to listen to the news.' But Sumnima clung to the gadget as if her life depended on it. There was something magical about listening to Sagar's voice on a quiet summer's night, candle flames flickering in the windows all around her.

'Mona Lisa, amore mio, the next song is for you.'

~

One morning Sumnima's uncle met her in the landing and caught her off guard.

'Thuli, are you going out today?' he asked.

'No, why?'

'We haven't been to New Road, so we were wondering if you could go with us.'

Sumnima felt ensnared. 'Um…what about Baba? Or Ganga didi?'

'Your Baba has an important meeting,' her uncle said. 'Ganga's stomach is upset.'

Right at that moment Numa ran downstairs and stopped in the landing. She was in her school uniform, on her way to the bus stop. 'Tika kaka, you still haven't been to New Road?' Numa exclaimed. 'Sumnima, you should take them today. They only have two days left.' Then she waved them goodbye and dashed downstairs, leaving behind the lemony fragrance of her body spray. Sumnima glared at her; her sister could be insufferable at times.

Sumnima spent an arduous day in New Road with her uncle and aunt. They spoke in a crude village accent, addressed her as 'Thuli' in public, and wanted single and group photos taken in front of every temple and monument. At Bishal Bazaar, the multistorey supermarket so popular among Rhododendron girls, they made her take pictures of them riding the escalator, making her wish she could sink into the ground. For hours they walked through the crowded lanes of Indrachowk, Ason and Bhotahity, gaping at everything in sight: the dazzling array of clothes, footwear, spices, metalwares, beads, tassels and plastic goods, the buff-meat momos cooking in giant steamers over roaring stoves, the hawkers crying their wares and shoppers haggling over prices. Tikaram bada stopped to worship every shrine along the way. He hummed bhajans and mumbled the names of gods as he jostled against passersby. Sita badi peeped through shop windows and made him ask the price of every item that attracted her eye, eliciting rude answers from sahujis, who could tell customers from window-shoppers like wheat from chaff. Sumnima strode fast to spur her charges, but Sita badi dawdled along. 'Aiya, this cursed leg,' she said again and again. At one point, overcome with exasperation, Sumnima said with an affected laugh, 'Badi , at this rate we'll need three days to look around New Road.' Sita badi smiled apologetically and tried to quicken her pace, hurting her knee. Tikaram bada saw his wife's face contort in pain. 'What to do, Thuli,' he said in an offended tone, 'your badi is not a city woman. Do you know she broke her knee last year?'

Sumnima blushed and gave him a guilty nod. During their month-long stay in Kathmandu, she had not once seen her uncle lose his temper. There was something disconcerting about the anger of a man as simple and guileless as him. A moment later when Sita badi suggested looking inside a jewellery shop, Sumnima swallowed her reservations and led them into the store. Behind the counter stood a comely young man in a white shirt and glasses. He had an air of confidence that left no doubt that his father owned the shop. He greeted them with a smile, offered them chairs and asked them which items they would like to see. Just as Sumnima had feared, her aunt wanted to hold and examine every piece of jewellery that caught her fancy. 'Aha, what a lovely necklace. Babu, can I see that ring? And those earrings over there?' After looking through a dozen items, she decided to buy a puny silver bangle for her baby grandson in Lungla.

'Five hundred fifty, last price,' said the shopkeeper, who'd been solicitous throughout, less for the sake of his customers than for their young chaperone, who looked rather charming in her peace sign t-shirt and canvas shoes, her orange bangs held back with a floral hair band.

'Kaki, that's a very good price,' Sumnima said. 'You should take it.'

Sita badi turned to her husband. Tikaram bada took the bangle and measured its girth with his fingers. 'Take it,' he said, 'I think it will fit him by next year.'

'Okay,' Sita badi said with some relief. She dug her hand into the layers of cloth tied around her waist and pulled out a small drawstring purse. Sumnima watched with mounting impatience as she clumsily pulled the strings and opened the purse. The cash was wrapped in a dirty handkerchief tied in a knot. Sita badi could not undo the knot and passed it to her husband. He tried to open it and passed it back to her. Sumnima shook her head at the shopkeeper to let him know she shared his exasperation, and then glanced at her uncle to make sure he hadn't noticed. In the end, they cut the knot with scissors. The bills, freed at last, were old and crumpled, some of them faded almost beyond recognition. 'Kaki, let me count them for you,' Sumnima said, grabbing them from her hand. She counted them hurriedly, darting an apologetic glance at the shopkeeper. Sita badi was short of fifty-two rupees. Sumnima supplied this amount from her own pocket and hustled her charges out of the shop, vowing never to return there.

~

A night before the guests left, Ganga and Tamule ji helped them do their final packing. Sumnima and Numa hovered around them trying to help, but felt overwhelmed by the clutter. 'Looks like a flood relief campaign,' Numa whispered to Sumnima. New and second-hand clothes, medicines, first-aid kit, inexpensive footwear, tea, sugar, spices, toothpaste, soap, instant noodles, stationery, batteries, candies and trinkets. Some were random spare items lying about the house, such as a pair of scissors, a calculator, a few steel mugs, a torch, an umbrella, and plastic bags with store labels. Everything would be put to good use in Lungla. As their travel bags didn't have enough space, Tamule ji stuffed some of the items into nylon shopping bags and tied them with strings.

The guests left early next morning. Everyone came out to wish them a good journey. Ganga held herself together and avoided meeting her parents' eyes, but at the very last minute, she noticed her mother's small, forlorn face and broke down. 'Don't cry,' her mother said, hugging her tight. Sumnima and Numa looked on regretfully. It hadn't occurred to them that the seemingly casual farewell could be so painful for their cousin. 'Now stop it,' Tikaram said. 'We should part with smiles not tears.'

'True. All this crying-shrying only brings bad luck,' said Boju.

~

Tamule ji felt sad and empty as he walked back from the domestic terminal. Fom a certain vantage point, his brother's life appeared more whole and meaningful than his. He had stayed in the village and carried on the legacy of their forebears—they who planted their roots and nurtured the land, kept alive kinship and community ties, they who lived large, expansive lives even amid want and hardship, extending themselves to connect with other lives. It was Tikaram who'd offered their father the last drops of water during his final moment. Dependable and dutiful, he now looked after their aging mother, tended to their sick relatives, helped carry the dead in the village. In contrast, he, Gajendra Tamule, had joined the herd of city folk who spent their days scurrying in and out of their holes, hustling and hoarding for themselves. A small, shrunken existence. As for his daughters, they belonged to the generation that would never know the true meaning of generosity. But who could blame them? The times had changed. One must embrace the changes and move on, Tamule ji thought as he got out of the taxi and strode towards his office.

23

It was getting dark when Sumnima reached home. The shoes near the entrance indicated that her parents had returned from work. She went around the house and slipped in through the back door. Ganga was in the kitchen, grinding spices in the granite mortar. 'Are they in their room?' Sumnima asked in a whisper. 'Khai, maybe,' Ganga said, feebly rocking the pestle back and forth. Her parents had left only a week ago and she seemed homesick.

Sumnima took off her shoes and tiptoed upstairs. Her father stood on the landing, talking—no, scolding someone on the phone. 'Don't you have better things to do? If you call again, I'll report you to the police.' Thankfully even his threats sounded civil compared to Boju's free-flowing obscenity. He hung up and turned to Sumnima. 'Some loafer was looking for your sister. Why does she give them her number?'

'She doesn't give,' Sumnima said. 'They find out.'

Her father looked unconvinced. 'And you?' he said. 'Why so late? You said it was lunch.'

'I had to go buy a book.'

'Book? But your SLC got over two months ago.'

'Uff, it's not a textbook.'

'What is it then? Story book?'

Sumnima shrugged and climbed the next flight of stairs.

'When I was young,' Tamule ji raised his voice, 'I too read many story books. But madam, reality is different from fantasy.'

Sumnima walked up to her room and slammed the door shut. The two hours she spent at the bookstore had filled her with an unusual sense of peace and well-being, but in one stroke her father had destroyed it. She threw her bag on the floor and began undressing, fuming and banging things. Her eyes fell on book that had fallen out of her bag. She brightened up. *Moments of Awakening: Experiencing What Is.* The cover showed a beam of soft light emanating from a lotus flower. On her way back from Reshma's birthday lunch, she had dropped by Seekers for a quick peek, but once inside, lost all track of time. The hypnotic Buddhist chant and the scent of essential oils had carried her away. She was strolling about the aisles trying on silver jewellery and fingering silk and pashmina scarves when she spotted the book that Sagar had recommended on his last show. Pure serendipity. She had blown her last remaining cash on the book.

Sumnima hopped onto her bed, leaned back against a pillow and started reading it. With laboured concentration she read the blurbs, acknowledgments and the long epigraph poem.

How does a part of the world leave the world?
How can wetness leave water?

The words on the page grew dimmer as darkness descended.

No matter how fast you run
Your shadow more than keeps up
Sometimes, it's in front!
Only full, overhead sun
diminishes your shadow.

The door opened and someone turned on the lights. Sumnima looked up. Her mother stood near the door with a stack of neatly folded clothes. 'Eh, you're back,' she said. She walked towards Sumnima and placed the clothes on the bed. 'Here, all folded and pressed.'

'Thanks,' Sumnima said, returning to the book.

'Breathe. Sit still. Watch how the mind jumps from thought to thought.'

'So what did you girls do today?' her mother asked.

'Hung out in Durbarmarg,' Sumnima said, drawing the book closer to her and furrowing her brow. That didn't deter her mother. She pulled up a chair and settled down.

'I'm preparing my lesson plan,' she said. 'Will you go through it once I'm done? I have to show it to the principal.'

Sumnima nodded without looking up.

'Just want to make sure the English is okay,' said Premkala. 'I should make use of my angrezi expert daughter, no?' She chuckled.

Sumnima forced a smile, then narrowed her eyes and ran a finger along a passage. '*It is everything and nothing. It is being, not doing. It is the present moment.*' The barrier between her and the book made its content seem all the more profound.

'Guess what?' Premkala said. 'Your friend's mother, what's her name, the minister's wife. She's going to be chief guest at our annual day event next week.'

'I see,' said Sumnima, not surprised in the least. These days Rajani aunty got invited as a special guest, keynote speaker and inaugurator to many events in town. Her photos and interviews appeared so frequently in local media that Reshma didn't even mention them to her friends anymore.

Premkala gazed at Sumnima, as though pondering the next topic of conversation, then lunged forward and brushed a stray thread off her shoulder. Sumnima shrank at the touch. She turned a page, grimacing, her impatience rising. 'Sometimes I wonder,' her mother said, 'what all I could've done if only I could speak fancy English. Everyone knows your friend's mother is not even IA-passed. But look at her rising and shining. Just because she can rattle off in English pa-ta-ta-ta-ta...'

'Mummy, please!' Sumnima broke out. 'Can't we talk about all this later? I'm trying to read.'

Premkala's face grew stiff. She tilted her head and glanced at the title of the book. 'Those stories won't get you anywhere,' she said, rising. 'And what have you done to your hair? You look scary, like a lakhey.' Premkala waited for her response, but Sumnima kept quiet, not wanting to prolong the dialogue. Premkala turned around and huffily left the room. Sumnima continued reading, hoping to make the most of her hard-won solitude, but couldn't get past a few pages despite her earnest effort. She put the book away and wrote to Sagar, thanking him for recommending such an extraordinary book.

~

Each of us is alone after all, thought Premkala, as she stood on the verandah after dinner, letting the wind blow her fury away. The moon shone down on Bhaisichaur, casting an ethereal silver sheen on unexpected objects—the steel water tanks on rooftops, the white rag of a scarecrow in the field, the hillock of sand at the construction site, and the steel pressure cooker Ganga was scouring near the drum.

Premkala was only twenty when she gave birth to Sumnima in a missionary hospital in town. She had never really been fond of children. Having had to teach and tame swarms of unruly children at work every day, she saw them as a chore and responsibility. The sight of children, even those bursting with health and laughter, left her indifferent. She felt no urge to coo over them like most women did. Instead, her first instinct was always to quieten them and teach them discipline. And yet when she first laid her eyes on her child, that bluish, bruised mass of flesh screaming in her arms, she had experienced a strange and exquisite joy. Here's a being that's completely mine, she thought naïvely. A year later Numa was born, and Premkala welcomed her with the same happy illusion, amazed to see her own reflection in that wrinkled little face.

The two children took over her life for the next decade and a half. Children at work, children at home. Their cries and laughter formed the background to her waking moments. Their tantrums, their constant demand for care and attention, their noise permeated the innermost recesses of her mind, leaving no space for quiet reflection. She enjoyed brief spells of peace only in rare moments. The silence that filled the house after her daughters fell asleep, the calm that washed over her once she hustled them off to school and closed the door behind her. And yet life without them seemed unimaginable. Every fall and bruise they suffered hurt her more, and she punished them by inflicting more pain. Slipper, knuckles, broomstick, ruler, and the rage unleashed by her bare hand—the girls had endured it all.

Over the years the beatings had stopped. Her daughters feared her less and talked back at her. She could no longer make them behave with a sharp glance or a raised hand. They cared little for her company or attention. In fact it seemed time had reversed their roles. Now it was she who yearned for their friendship and confidence, while they pushed her away and shut her out of their world. The older they grew, the farther they moved away from her.

Indeed one could never own another being. Love, marriage, motherhood, they were simply illusions. Each is separate, alone, thought Premkala, as Ganga rinsed the last pot, got up and carried a tubful of dishes inside the house.

24

A day before the SLC results were to come out, Sumnima and Ganga visited the Ganeshthan temple. It was Tuesday, the day for Lord Ganesh, and the temple was more crowded than usual. They stood in line for a full hour, elbowing rival devotees and guarding their place against pious housewives adept at jumping the queue. When their turn for worship finally came, they knelt down before the elephant god, burned oil lamps and stuffed sweetmeats into the crevices of his trunk. Head bowed and eyes shut tight, Sumnima asked the lord of success for a distinction. Ganga pleaded for at least pass marks. Scarcely had they begun their prayer when a woman tapped on Ganga's shoulder and said, 'Oi bahini, move aside. Can't you see the queue?' The girls ignored her. They bowed their heads at the deity's feet, dabbed vermillion tika on their foreheads and stuck sanctified petals in their hair before rising and offering one last quick prayer. They left the sanctum buoyant with hope, unfazed by the hostile glances directed at them as they pushed their way past the crowd.

Next day the SLC results were published in a national daily. Soon after she woke up, Ganga went to a nearby stationery shop and bought a copy of the paper. Sumnima had suggested they get their own copy instead of borrowing Tamule ji's. The two of them convened in Sumnima's room and carefully went through the lists of roll numbers. To their great chagrin, Ganesh Bhagwan had not answered their prayers. Sumnima's roll number was in the second division list, a far cry from a distinction. Ganga went through the lists three times but could not find her roll number. They looked at each other, confused and crestfallen. Outside a cuckoo burst into a full-throated song. It echoed through the green expanse but brought no cheer to their hearts. 'I should go make tea now,' Ganga said, hurrying downstairs, pretending it was just another day.

Sumnima tossed the newspaper aside with a world-weary sigh. What would she tell her parents? A part of her felt she had got what she deserved and should humbly ask their forgiveness. The other part said she should feign incomprehension and outrage, and claim that the dimwits who marked her papers had clearly made a mistake. The door opened and Numa came in, looking tense. 'Mummy and Baba have seen the results,' she said in a tone of mild reproach. 'They were making jabs at me as if I'm to blame. Go talk to them.'

Sumnima dragged herself down the stairs, feeling like a sacrificial lamb on its way to the altar. A pall of disappointment hung over the house. Her mother was on the phone in the landing. She glowered at Sumnima as she passed. Inside the bedroom, her father sat holding a newspaper with a funereal expression on his face. He got up and flung the paper at her. 'Shame on you!' Sumnima caught a whiff of fresh print as the paper hit her face and fell to the floor. The next half an hour went as expected. She suffered the verbal onslaught in silence, head hung down, eyes focused on the colourful dragon patterns on the carpet. A moment later her mother came in. 'My colleague Reema just called,' she said, glaring at Sumnima. 'Her son got first division.' The intense loathing in her eyes made Sumnima suddenly conscious of her appearance—her Fair & Lovely bleached face, the fiery glow of her dyed bangs, her thinned eyebrows and ears pierced in three places. 'Fashion queen,' her mother said, 'where will you go with your second division?'

Sumnima thought for a moment and said in a placating tone, 'That school in India, the one where Reshma is going, I think they accept second division.'

'You think we'll send you to India?' said Tamule ji. 'There are plenty of government colleges in town, go choose one.'

Sumnima shrugged off that wildly improbable threat, then picked up the newspaper and marched downstairs. Ganga stood at the kitchen counter, staring blankly at a pot of boiling tea. 'Thuli,' she said. 'I'm dead, I don't know what to do.' She lifted the pot and poured out tea, tapping the strainer on the rim of each cup. Sumnima sat in a chair and spread the newspaper on the table. 'Come, let's check again,' she said, trying to sound hopeful. 'We'll start at the bottom this time.' Ganga set down the spoon and sprang to her side. Long, symmetrical columns of five-digit numbers filled the broadsheet pages from top to bottom. Sumnima traced her finger down the long list of third-division candidates, then down the second division list, where Tamule ji had circled her number so angrily the nib had ripped the paper, and finally down the first division list. Ganga's roll number was nowhere to be found.

~

Ganga could not believe it. What had she not done to pass the exam? She had churned out the longest possible answer to every question because people said SLC markers measured the answers with a ruler instead of reading them. She had used her best handwriting and drawn margins on each answer-sheet because she had heard messy papers were automatically penalized. She had prayed and fasted and spent whole nights cramming passages and formulas into her head. And yet the 'iron gate' had slammed shut in her face for the second time.

Sunlight flooded the kitchen and glinted off the utensils and the curve of the sink tap. The bell at the Mahadev temple sent forth its clanging peals. A pressure cooker whistle blew loud and long next door, and the smell of steaming rice wafted through the window. Everything else in the world was going on just as it always did. The ordinariness of these sounds made Ganga feel more alone in her sorrow. 'Thuli,' she said, turning to Sumnima.

'I can't face Kaka Kaki. Will you please take them their tea?'

Sumnima did not respond. She was looking over the lists again, her eyes darting back and forth between the newspaper and the numbers scribbled on her palm. 'Arey,' she said, smiling a little. 'Reshma and Tejaswi both under third division. No wonder they haven't called yet.'

'Thuli, will you take this?' Ganga said, holding out the tea tray.

'Okay, but first I have to call my friends,' Sumnima said, and ran upstairs.

Ganga avoided her uncle's eyes as she served him tea. 'Second time, eh?' he said. 'Do you have brains or cow-dung?' Ganga walked over to her aunt. She sat slumped in a chair, too consumed by her daughter's results to worry about her niece. Ganga offered her tea and hastily turned to leave. 'Wait,' her uncle said, 'tell me, what are your plans now? What should I tell Tika dai?' Ganga stared at the dragons on the carpet. 'Maybe you should return to Lungla,' he said. 'Your mother is weak. Chandrey's wife is overburdened with work. I'm sure they need an extra hand in the house.'

The prospect seemed frightening enough to make Ganga whimper, 'No, Kaka, I can't...'

Tamule ji stared at her small and dejected face. 'No SLC, no job skills, no ambition, what will you do in life?'

Ganga kept quiet; a tear fell on the carpet. Her uncle collapsed into the chair with a sigh. Her aunt sipped her tea in grim silence. The phone rang but nobody picked it up. Outside, the cuckoo trilled and trilled, mocking their tragedy with its joyous song.

25

Private education was in high demand and schools were sprouting like weeds all over Kathmandu. At least two schools had been opened in Bhaisichaur alone. One was a preschool called International Montessori, a two-storey residential building with ill-proportioned cartoon characters painted on its walls—a Mickey Mouse with a head too small, a scrawny Donald Duck, a dog with a rectangular snout, and so on. All morning the children screamed out rhymes about Baa Baa black sheep and Mary's little lamb. The other was Oxford Academy, a three-storey building from where little boys shot paper aeroplanes and instant noodle wrappings on the remaining patch of the open field. Sumnima sometimes leaned out of her window and shouted, 'Don't you have a dustbin in your school?' The kids glanced at her and continued their sport as if she did not exist. This was enough to hurt Sumnima in her current state. She had become a kind of non-entity since her SLC results came out a month ago. Her parents only spoke to her in curt monosyllables. They had transferred all their hopes to Numa, who would be taking the SLC in a few months and been advised to stay away from the 'rotten apple'.

Looking for solace in friendship, Sumnima met Reshma and Tejaswi at a café one afternoon, only to be left even more distressed. Their third-division scores had made no dent in their original plans. Tejaswi, though vacillating between fashion design and hotel management, had decided to look for a college in Delhi. Reshma's parents had made a large donation and secured a place for her at a posh residential school in Mussoorie. She would be leaving in two weeks. Sumnima listened dispiritedly as Reshma prattled about her new school and the big farewell party her mother had planned for her.

Next morning Sumnima went up to her father and said, 'Baba, my friends have already booked their tickets to India. If we don't rush, we'll miss the admission deadlines.' Tamule ji looked up from his newspaper and shook his head. 'Still dreaming?' he said. He reached for his wallet and took out some hundred-rupee bills. 'Here, you should go enroll in Lalitpur Multiple Campus before you miss *their* deadline.'

Sumnima stamped her foot and stormed off. Lalitpur Multiple Campus. Wasn't that the crummy old building near the bus park? The one with a rusty signboard over the gate and 'No pissing here' painted on the boundary wall? She recalled only the air of neglect and decay that hung over the place. She spent the rest of the day sulking in her room, filled with a sense of impending doom. Did her father seriously intend to send her to a government college? She imagined herself sitting in the mildewed classroom while some fusty old professor lectured mechanically in highfalutin Nepali. She imagined herself hanging out in cheap teashops with students from small towns and villages. And what would they talk about? Nepali film stars? It all seemed like a cruel joke. Above all, how would she face Sagar as a student of a shabby government college? Half a year had passed since she first heard his voice, but she remained as smitten with him as ever. His cheerful banter lifted her out of her gloom. Her sorrow melted at the sound of his laughter. The love songs he played for her every week, his messages so frivolous yet charged with meaning, and the caressing tone in which he uttered her pen name—they felt like brief spells of sunshine on a dark rainy day.

26

The hotel staff hadn't even laid out the buffet when Sumnima arrived for the farewell lunch. Reshma was still getting her hair done at Eden Spa. The few guests in the banquet hall stood talking to Rajani aunty, now director of a well-funded NGO. She looked glamorous in a bronze raw-silk sari and a low-cut blouse, her skin gleaming in gold and honey tones. Sumnima took a seat in a corner and waited, eyes fixed on the door. It was to meet Tejaswi that she had come rushing to the party. After thinking it over for a week, she had decided to share her secret with her friend. She wanted advice on whether she should call Sagar or wait till he gave a clear signal.

Half an hour passed but Tejaswi did not show up. The waiters started serving snacks. They kept circling around the little group gathered around Rajani aunty. Were they deliberately ignoring her? Sumnima felt small and insignificant sitting by herself unattended in that exclusive setting. She fiddled with her nails, crossed and uncrossed her legs and swept her bangs this way and that. People were streaming into the hall, smiling and exchanging pleasantries. They radiated an air of easy affluence that blended well with their surroundings. Some of them spoke fluent English. The crowd was so homogeneous, so uniformly elegant it made Sumnima wonder—didn't Reshma have any poor relatives? As far as she knew, Reshma's father too had grown up in a remote village in the far west. He had won the last election from his home district and still owned vast bighas of land in the region. Yet Reshma moved in a social world that bore no trace of such links, except for the retinue of dark-skinned servants brought from the village.

'Sumnima!' Someone called her name. She turned around and saw Reshma's plump figure teetering towards her on high heels. Her dark lipstick and artificial curls made her look much older than sixteen. Sumnima rose and kissed her on both cheeks, a gesture that had come into vogue among Rhododendron girls.

'Do you like my hair?' Reshma asked.

'Absolutely gorgeous,' Sumnima said, then looked around to make sure nobody had heard.

The girls chitchatted for a few minutes before Rajani aunty brought some guests over to meet Reshma. Sumnima stepped aside and watched the mother and daughter entertain the guests. It had never struck her before that each of Reshma's gestures and manners bore the unmistakable stamp of her mother. The tone of her voice, her accented Nepali, her laughter, her hand movements. Even the way she screwed up her eyes to express disapproval seemed an exact impersonation of Rajani aunty. Only without Rajani aunty's good looks and refined grace, she appeared like a sad parody of her.

Tejaswi arrived at last, looking a bit overdressed in a brocade kurta surwal. Rajani aunty went rushing towards her, the long, voluminous anchal of her sari trailing behind her like a silken waterfall. 'Tejaswi, you're late,' she said, grimacing in mock anger. Tejaswi smiled and apologized for the delay. Rajani aunty led her by the hand and introduced her to the guests, subtly prompting her to shed some light on her bloodline. At any other time Tejaswi would have gladly obliged, but she seemed out of sorts today. Her smile disappeared too quickly. Her eyes wandered round the hall while Rajani aunty spoke for her. 'Right, she's Anushka's sister. No, General Pratap is her uncle, not dad. I'm not sure. Tejaswi, does Anushka have children yet?'

Tejaswi politely excused herself when she saw Sumnima waving at her. 'Let's go out, I have to tell you something,' she said as soon as they met, and led Sumnima towards the verandah that overlooked the back garden. Emerging into the bright sunlight, Sumnima finally noticed her pale and troubled face. She asked her what was wrong. Tejaswi leaned over the railing and took a deep breath. 'I had a fight with my dad before I came,' she said.

'Why?'

'He wants me to get engaged before I go to Delhi.'

Sumnima felt deflated. Tejaswi had broached a matter more consequential than her girlish infatuation for Sagar. 'Really?' Sumnima said, although early marriages were the norm in Tejaswi's family. Her sister Anushka had been married off at the age of seventeen, after she was caught strolling with her Newar boyfriend on the outskirts of Kathmandu. Tejaswi's cousin Samriddhi, two years older than her, was already engaged to a major in the Royal Nepal Army.

'He says it's an excellent proposal so we shouldn't let it pass,' Tejaswi said.

'Who's the guy?'

'A distant cousin, I've only met him at a few parties. He just completed his training at Sandhurst.' She paused for a moment and said in an irrepressibly reverent tone, 'He's the son of Prayag Shumsher, former army chief, and his mother is closely related to the Queen.'

'I see.' Sumnima wanted to make her confession, but Tejaswi kept talking about her potential fiancé. 'My parents showed me a photo of him. It was taken at Ratna Sumshere's eldest son's wedding party, the son who's a doctor. He married General Thapa's middle daughter, do you know them?' The incestuous world of the highbred always aroused a mix of awe and suffocation in Sumnima. 'He looked really short in the photo.' Tejashwi sighed. 'But all the women of my family have had arranged marriages—how can I not? I don't know what to do.' Then her posture softened, and her words lost their edge. 'Maybe marriage isn't a complete disaster,' she said. She became more optimistic: 'It'll close some doors, but it'll open others, won't it? And every woman has to marry, after all.' She finally turned her attention to Sumnima, 'Now tell me how you've been.' By then Sumnima no longer felt like confessing.

27

The booming education market rescued Sumnima from the dreaded prospect of attending a government college. One afternoon she called Balram Sir to ask for advice. He spent almost half an hour encouraging her to enrol in his newly opened ten-plus-two college. At Galileo International, students could sign up for any subject as long as they paid the six months' fees in advance. There were no cut-off marks for enrolment in the science stream. Despite her third-division scores, Sumnima could study science and prepare herself for a medical college.

'Baba, that means I can still study science,' Sumnima said to her father, smiling at him for the first time in several weeks.

Tamule ji tried not to look too pleased. 'OK, I'll give you one last chance,' he said in a firm voice.

It was a moment of reconciliation. Tamule ji sat her down beside him and recounted his journey through the vicissitudes of life. Sumnima listened and nodded as if she was hearing it all for the first time. Galileo International may not have earned a reputation yet, but it was at least a private English-medium institution, housed in a decent-looking building with no moss patches on the wall. It attracted students who shared her background and could possibly become her friends. Also it was a co-ed institution. After spending ten years in an all-girls school, even the thought of sitting next to a boy thrilled Sumnima, her feelings for Sagar notwithstanding.

'Baba, I promise I'll work hard this time,' she said.

'You had better,' said Tamule ji, and added in careful English. 'Opportunity does not knock on the door twice.'

Next day Balram Sir gave Sumnima a complete tour of the school. The amenities and facilities exceeded Sumnima's expectations. The classrooms smelled of fresh paint and had brand-new desks and chairs. There was a small computer lab where students could practice typing on large keyboards. The canteen was under construction. 'It will be very hygienic,' Balram Sir said. 'All kitchen staff will be required to wear plastic gloves.' Balram Sir's office was on the top floor. It had windows on three sides and a terrace with a view of the mountains, just like Sumnima's room at home. What impressed Sumnima most was the vast, fully equipped lab. A life-size human skeleton greeted her at the door. Instead of the usual blackboard, there was a smooth whiteboard that Sumnima had only seen in American high-school movies. Five wide counters ran along the length of the room, with sinks, gas outlets, and rows of sparkling beakers and test tubes. The shelves on the wall cabinets contained a variety of equipment and specimens preserved in jars. Sumnima pictured herself standing at the counter and carrying out advanced experiments, like a professional scientist

~

At the start of autumn, Sumnima entered eleventh grade. Her new possessions heralded a new chapter in her life. Thick textbooks with colourful diagrams of human anatomy and atomic structures, hard-backed science notebooks with smooth blank pages on the left and ruled pages on the right, a white lab coat in which she already looked like a doctor, a dissection set that resembled the manicure kit that Parvati aunty had gifted her, and a uniform consisting of a tight-fitting white shirt and a black skirt of unprescribed length.

Beneath its imposing façade, Galileo International had an air of ambiguity that seemed to suit Sumnima's temperament. Its institutional motto changed every few weeks, the latest being 'Eastern hearts, Western minds'. The teachers moonlighted in several colleges and kept little track of the students' family background. The students bunked classes and smoked cigarettes in the toilet. They listened to their Walkman during class and pulled pranks in the lab. Balram Sir had stopped teaching and taken to wearing a suit every day. He seldom emerged from his top-floor office and bothered no one as long as they paid their fees on time. He had yet to recruit foreign teachers as promised, but no one seemed to mind.

The coveted style and attitude in Galileo International contrasted with the primness of Sumnima's old school. Girls at Galileo left their shirts untucked over their fitted skirts and wore their socks scrunched down to their ankles. They slung their bags carelessly over their shoulders and assumed slack postures that conveyed a blithe indifference to the world. Sumnima's peers came from average families with average means and aspirations. Their daily joys and sorrows had similar shades and textures. None of them inhabited the world of chauffeured cars and five-star parties, or style their hair at Eden Spa. Like Sumnima, most of them commuted to school in public buses and tempos. The new environment loosened something up in Sumnima, freed her somewhat from the constant need to gloss over her reality, a freedom she had not known at Rhododendron, where one's surname, mode of transport, the quality of lunch one brought, and even the cut of one's uniform betrayed the subtle gradations of social rank.

~

As the school year progressed, Sumnima continued writing to Sagar, still undecided whether or not to call him. One day during a chemistry practical, Manisha, her lab partner, discovered a letter she'd drafted to Sagar. Sumnima had not realized it had fallen from her notebook. She was pouring a solution into a test tube when she saw Manisha leaning over the counter and reading it with an amused expression on her face. Sumnima jumped up and grabbed the letter from her hand, spilling some of the blue solution.

'Hmm, a love letter to a radio jockey,' Manisha said with a teasing smile.

Sumnima blushed, unsure what to make of her tone. Manisha was among the most diligent students in class. She always took charge of their collaborative lab projects, lent Sumnima her notes and spared her the horror of dissecting frogs and cockroaches. Occasionally she took the liberty of patronizing Sumnima. If Sumnima tried to set up an experiment, or adjust the bunsen burner flame, Manisha would gently push her aside and say, 'Move, I'll do it.' The other day she had shown Sumnima a newspaper comic strip and said laughing, 'Look, I found a picture of you.' The comic strip showed a stick-figure scientist staring dumbfounded at an exploding beaker, his lab coat pitted with burn holes. Sumnima, hesitant to contradict her, had faked a laugh.

'It's not a love letter,' Sumnima said. 'Promise me you won't tell anyone?'

'Why would I, I've never even heard his show,' Manisha said. 'It seems every other girl has a crush on some radio host these days.'

The remark stung Sumnima, but she could not deny it. Indeed she was no different from the legions of fan girls who sent letters to popular radio jockeys in town. If she wanted to distinguish herself from them, she would have to overcome her fears and meet Sagar in the flesh.

28

The fog lifted around late morning, and the houses, fields and trees of Bhaisichaur gradually came into view. The slow-moving cars on the ring road began racing and honking. School children rushed outside and climbed the wet monkey bars, smearing their palms with rust. Sumnima was sitting on the verandah with her back to the sun, her books spread on the floor. '*Molar heat capacity is the amount of heat required to*'—she read. The sun slowed down her senses. Yawning, she lay flat on her stomach. '*Molar heat capacity is the amount of heat required to raise the temperature of one mole of substance by...*' —her eyes glazed over, the words began to swim on the page. She forced her eyes open and propped herself up on her elbows, but dozed off before she realized it. A green fly circled over the dregs in her teacup. In her dream, Sagar stood beside her right on that verandah, looking out to misty, pine-covered hills somewhere in India. His face was blurred and his words came out in a babbling stream, but she could feel herself soaring in ecstasy. She slept through the familiar sounds of the neighbourhood—the children singing rhymes at the school, the hammering and drilling at the building sites, the plaintive cry of a scrap hawker walking down the lane, 'Khali shishi, purana kagaj, phalam ke tukde.'

All of a sudden something fell from the sky and hit her leg. Sumnima awoke with a start, her cheek flushed and imprinted with the braided pattern of the floor-mat. The fly sat on the floor-mat. Fixing her gaze on its metallic green abdomen and its throbbing little eyes, she picked up a book, raised it over her head, and in a single hard blow smashed it to pulp. She left the book there, not wanting to see the mess, and started gathering her things. Books, sweater, shawl, pens, chapstick, Walkman, water-bottle. Just then she noticed a strange object lying on the floor—a stone wrapped in a sheet of paper and tied with a rubber band.

It was a short note written in English. The letters were uneven and tilted in different directions as though fanned by the wind.

Dearest Sumnima,

When I see your adorable face in the baranda and the road, it makes my heart beat. I think about you whole day. At night I see you from the window after you put on the light. You are an amazing and marvellous girl. I only want to say that I like you very, very much. If you don't have same feeling to me, you can abnegate me from your heart. If you have same feeling, please reply me soon.

Your ardent admirer,

Rishi

Rishi. The name sounded vaguely familiar. Sumnima got up and scanned the rooftops around her. On the first terrace, an old woman was napping in the sun, her head covered with a bunched-up shawl. On the second, a middle-aged man was engrossed in a newspaper. On the third, a family of four sat eating peanuts and oranges, setting up little mounds of peanut shells and orange peels on the floor. None of them seemed a likely suspect. She leaned over the railing and looked at the newly expanded road—only some workers spreading tar that shone blue-black in the glare of the sun. She turned to Devi didi's house. The terrace was empty. A cow sat in the yard, chewing cud and waving flies away with its tail.

All at once Sumnima had a flash of recognition.

Didn't Devi didi have a son called Rishiram? Of course! Rishi was Rishiram, *that* Rishiram! The knowledge came as an assault on her whole being. She inspected Devi didi's terrace again, noticing for the first time that they were adding a new storey to their house. Their rough, unplastered roof had half-built concrete pillars from which naked rods jutted out towards the sky. The spot where Rishiram usually sat banging his guitar was piled with bricks and wooden planks. But he was nowhere in sight. Sumnima scrunched up the letter and marched into her room. Her earliest impressions of Rishiram came flooding back. The sickly, snotty boy who sat on the floor and stared at the television, his eyes popping out, his butt-crack showing above his sagging trousers. Was it him or his brother who used to ride her discarded bicycle? There was one incident that stood out vividly in her memory. That morning he had come to the Tamule house with Devi didi to watch an episode of *Ramayan* on the Doordarshan channel. Perhaps emboldened by his mother's presence, he had mustered the courage to sit on their brand-new sofa. Sumnima and Numa had watched bemused as he leaned back in his seat and lightly bounced on the springs, grinning with delight. But at the sound of Boju's voice in the corridor, he had jumped off the sofa and sat down on the floor with such lightning speed they were left gaping in confusion.

Sumnima laughed at the memory. At some point later, Devi didi had bought a television, and the boys had stopped visiting the Tamule house. Sumnima had gradually stopped noticing them over the years. They had receded into the distant background of her mind though their mother still delivered milk to their house. It had not even occurred to her that the boy who had stolen the fleeting pleasure of sitting on their sofa and the guitar-toting lad who stared at her from Devi didi's terrace was one and the same person. She had not imagined, even in her wildest dreams, that he would have the gall to fancy—no, hurl a love letter at her!

After considering all possible ways to put him in his place, Sumnima decided that silence would be the best response. She had heard somewhere that indifference was more powerful than hate. She tore the letter into pieces and threw it in the dustbin, only to regret it—she could have shown it to Numa and had a few good laughs.

29

The winter moved slowly. The vines in the backyard gradually shed their leaves, exposing dried knots and tangles. The farmlands of Bhaischaur turned into stubble fields. At the building sites, the hammering and drilling carried on at full force, and the frostbitten hands of children sieved sand and hauled bricks all morning. At sundown the bare jacaranda trees looked like intricate charcoal sketches; every bird perched on a branch, every abandoned nest, and every leaf awaiting its fall was starkly visible against the sky.

Sumnima sat at her desk with a plate of dalbhat she'd just brought from the kitchen, a thick woollen cap pulled over her ears. The room was freezing. Numa had taken the heater as she was studying for the SLC exam, along with Ganga, who had decided to give it one more try.

'Hellooo everyone,' Sagar chirped. 'It's Saturday night and I'm back with *The Jukebox*, your favourite show on Metro FM.' Sumnima smiled as she always did on hearing his voice. She took off her cap to hear better. With a swift, deft movement of her fingers, she mixed rice, dal, mustard greens and a piece of chicken on her plate. She ate absently, taking small bites. 'I've got some great songs lined up for you but—' Sagar paused and heaved a long sigh—'I also have some sad news for you.'

Sumnima sat up, alert.

'My dear, beloved listeners,' Sagar said, 'I hate to say this, but this is my final show on Metro FM.'

The news struck Sumnima like a bolt of lightning. She sat motionless for a while, her hand frozen in midair between her plate and her mouth. 'I had a fantastic year running the show,' Sagar said in a subdued voice, 'now it's time to go.' Sumnima got up, dropping a few grains of rice on the carpet, and turned up the volume with her left hand. 'Bye bye love, bye bye happiness,' Sagar hummed, 'hello loneliness, I think I'm gonna cry.' Sumnima laughed, pretending it was one of his jokes, but he began to sound more and more serious. 'I'd like to thank all my listeners for making *The Jukebox* the greatest show in town. A huge thanks to Naresh dai the station manager and to Rajendra dai, Hari dai and Renuka didi, our wonderful technical support team, for all the...' Sumnima stared at the speaker. Her food was cold and her fingers were crusted with dal. As the show neared its end, she anxiously waited for Sagar to mention Mona Lisa, invite her to continue their romance through another medium, or at least reveal his future whereabouts, but all he said before signing off was, 'Ciao, friends, I'll miss you all. I leave you with this last song.'

'Yesterday, love was such an easy game to play
Now I need a place to hide away
Oh I believe in yesterday'

Sumnima listened to the song in a state of total disbelief until it was cut off by the loud theme music of Metro FM. The show was over. She would never hear Sagar's voice again. Never. She washed her hand and took her food back to the kitchen. The news had destroyed her appetite. Why had he quit so abruptly? All those sweet things he'd said on air, all those songs he'd played for her week after week—did they mean nothing to him? It was her fault. She had given him no clue to find her, not even her real name. It was still not too late. She had his phone number.

Sumnima went to Numa's room. Numa and Ganga sat huddled near the heater bent over their books, their eyes bloodshot from the effort to stay awake. 'You know what?' Sumnima said 'Today was Sagar's last show.'

'Really?' said Numa, her eyes wide. The news seemed to have

woken her up completely. Ganga looked up from her book but asked no questions.

'Yes, he announced it just now,' Sumnima said. 'I must do something or else I'll never see him. Should I call him?'

Numa thought for a moment and said, 'Did he drop any hint that he wants to meet you?

Sumnima shook her head.

'Then don't call,' Numa said.

'But he doesn't even know my—'

'Oh, Mona Lisa,' Numa sighed. 'Why don't you understand? If he really wants to meet you, he'll find a way. Kathmandu is small, it's not hard to track people down.'

Sumnima left the room distraught and dissatisfied.

Next day she couldn't help sharing her dilemma with Manisha, the only person in her school who had some inkling of her feelings for Sagar. She brought it up while they were preparing a frog skin slide during zoology practicals.

'By the way,' Sumnima said, as if the thought had occurred to her just then, 'Sagar, the radio host I've been writing to, he quit the show, you know.'

The look of surprise on Manisha's face encouraged Sumnima. 'I have his phone number. You think I should call him?'

Manisha picked up the almost imperceptible section of frog skin with forceps and carefully placed it on the glass slide. 'You can't let go of that radio guy, can you?' she said, smiling. That radio guy. The phrase snubbed Sumnima, but there was no point arguing. Manisha was already bent over a microscope, examining the frog tissue.

~

Next day Sumnima feigned a headache and stayed in bed until her parents left for work. She spent hours shoring up her courage before making the dreaded call. She rehearsed her opening lines and carried out a mock conversation with Numa, with Numa pretending to be Sagar. She stood in front of the mirror and corrected her posture as if Sagar would see her through the telephone. Around noon, after Boju retired to the TV room, she went downstairs and placed Ganga on guard. 'Didi, I'm about to make an important call. Can you make sure Boju doesn't pick up the extension?' Ganga gave her a complicit smile but asked no questions. Sumnima went to the landing and picked up the phone. Numa sat on the stairs, her skeptical gaze fixed on Sumnima. The call went through, but Sumnima hung up. 'What if he doesn't remember me?'

'Uff,' Numa said, 'who gives a damn?'

Sumnima cleared her throat and dialled again. Her heart beat wildly when she heard the ringtone. Once, twice, thrice.

'Hello.'

It was Sagar.

'Hello, is this Sagar?' she asked in a trembling voice.

'Yes?'

'Oh, hi, this is Sumnima, I've been writing to you, not sure you remember.' Like Sagar, she spoke English peppered with Nepali.

'Sumnima...' Sagar said in an uncertain tone. 'Sumnima what?'

'Tamule,' she said. She didn't like the sound of her last name. Sundered from her first name, the word sounded a bit jarring. It brought to mind a rugged and unrefined people of the hills. 'But I wrote under a different name,' she added shyly. 'Mona Lisa.'

'Ah, Mona Lisa, of course I remember,' Sagar said in a lukewarm tone. Sumnima felt a pang of regret. No, she should not have called him. She felt exposed and diminished. They spent a few minutes exchanging polite generalities, as if the secret intimacy they had developed through the airwaves meant nothing in real life. She glanced at Numa and pulled a face. Her sister had been right all along.

But as Sumnima was about to hang up, determined to flush Sagar out of her system, the conversation took an unexpected turn. 'Nice talking to you,' Sagar said. 'Now that we know each other, may I have the pleasure of meeting you in person?' Sumnima looked at Numa and opened her mouth wide. Numa jumped up, came to her side and tried to listen in, pressing her cheek against Sumnima's.

'Free for lunch on Saturday?' Sagar said.

Sumnima pushed Numa away. 'Yes,' she said, smiling and blushing, as though the whole world had suddenly burst into blossom.

30

It was a bright winter afternoon. The houses in Bhaisichaur looked deserted. Not a soul stood on the terraces hung with colourful rows of washing. Behind the curtained windows, families sat enjoying the Hindi feature film that Nepal Television broadcast every Saturday. The high-pitched songs and dialogues resounded through the neighbourhood, confusing stray dogs and chasing sparrows away from verandah railings. There were no children on the open playground, no workers at the building sites. No bulldozer or tractor plied on the dirt lane that was being widened into a motor road. All was empty and still, except Sumnima's heart, which flapped beneath her chest like a decapitated hen. In a black mesh top with flared sleeves, fitting jeans and cross-strap block heels, she was dressed in the height of fashion. Tiny gemstones sparkled on her ears, neck and hands. Her long, straight, henna-dyed hair shone like burnished copper. Her nails, painted black until yesterday, were now a subtle shade of pink. Several years of using Fair & Lovely had made her face a shade lighter than her neck. Sumnima felt nervous but confident of her power. 'Open your heart and embrace what lies ahead,' she remembered her horoscope prediction for the day. 'The universe is speaking to you.'

She walked past the closed shutters of Bhairey's shop, now smartened up and renamed Fancy Mart. Without its usual traffic, the ring road was an avenue of bare trees that stretched as far as the eye could see. Sumnima wandered around for some time looking for a taxi. 'Oi sexy, need a ride?' a conductor yelled out of a bus window. Next a truck came tooting and expelled a ball of smoke into her powdered face. Was it her mesh top or were her jeans too tight? Sumnima pulled down her top to cover her butt. She crossed her arms over her breasts.

Finally a taxi came by. She flagged it down and got inside. The driver, an excitable young man, honked and swore and adjusted the rear-view mirror to look at his passenger. Sumnima shook and jolted in her seat, lost in thought. Was she going on a 'date' or was it a casual meeting? Sagar had sounded distant and nonchalant for the most part, though in the end it was he who proposed they meet. A strong, familiar stench wafted in through the window and knocked her out of her reverie. They had arrived near the Bagmati, the putrid river drifting through the valley like a symbol of collective decay. Sumnima clamped her nose and looked out as they crossed the bridge. Above the river the sky looked serene, and in the far distance a row of mountains stood out over the hills like uncut jewels. The taxi turned and sped past a white, high-domed temple that Sumnima couldn't name although she had walked past it countless times. A golden griffin perched on each corner of its roof, ferocious and open-mouthed, ready to fling itself into the sky. Sagar's voice kept echoing in her head. *Now that we know each other, may I have the pleasure of meeting you?*

The shops and offices along the road were all closed, but further up in Sundhara, men and women were doing brisk business under the open sky. Crowds gathered around the small heaps of clothes, kitchenware, footwear, and plastic toys set up on the pavements. Sumnima looked the other way. Her mother might be here buying clothes to send back to Lungla. In the morning she had asked her to help her with the shopping. Suminma, who wouldn't be caught dead haggling with footpath shopkeepers, had trotted out an excuse and passed the duty onto Numa. Her heart pounded as she neared her destination. She took out a perfume sample vial and rubbed it on her wrists, releasing a burst of musky fragrance that made the driver steal another glance at her. The sacred thread from Janai Purnima festival, now dirty and discoloured, was still tied around her wrist. She broke it with her teeth, nearly nicking her gum, and put it in her pocket, to discard it later in an unpolluted site. They drove past Shahid Gate. The taxi stopped in Durbarmarg near the statue of the late king Mahendra, whose name decorated many a road, bridge, school, college, and even the series of Nepali textbooks she had read at school.

As Sumnima got out of the taxi, the Ghantaghar clocktower sounded two melancholy peals, chasing the crows out of the nearby trees. They flew away cawing and flapping their heavy black wings. She had arrived on the dot. Not wanting to look too eager, she strolled around for a while. She smoothed her hair, checked her reflection in the shop windows and bought a pack of chewing gum from a stall. The mint cooled her throat, but she could feel her cheeks burning as she entered the restaurant. She stood near the entrance and waited for Sagar to rise from one of the tables and introduce himself. 'Don't worry,' he had said on the phone, 'the minute I spot a lovely, lost-looking lady walk in through the door, I'll know it's you.' She waited, but no one came. It was seventeen minutes past two. She paced the floor wearing a lost expression. A group of girls, also in mesh tops with flared sleeves, sat talking in an accent that she traced to Rhododendron Girls High School. She realized with relief that she didn't know any of them. At the next table a woman was helping two little boys slice a pizza. 'Knife on the right, babu,' she said. 'Peet-za, not pija.' It was nearing half past two but Sagar was nowhere in sight. Sumnima could not decide what a self-respecting girl ought to do in such a situation: sit and wait, call him from the phone at the counter, or just go back home. Had he forgotten or was he playing a practical joke on her? Tears tingled in her eyes and blurred the faces around her. She turned her head up to the ceiling before they ran over and ruined her makeup. With painful effort she gathered herself together and turned to leave. Just then a man walked in through the door and stopped in front of her. A nondescript man of medium height, not fat but a bit on the plump side. He was wearing a creased shirt and dark pants and holding a jacket in his hand.

'Um…Sumnima?' he said, looking at her with his big round eyes.

'Yes,' she said with a smile that concealed the fleeting pang of disappointment.

'Sorry, I'm late, was busy putting on my makeup, you see,' he guffawed.

Sumnima laughed, recognizing the voice with a rush of tenderness that swept away all doubt and confusion. Yes, it was him. The man who had held her captive with the first sound of his voice; the man who had cast a spell on her through the airwaves. He may not be good-looking in a conventional sense, but she believed in the old adage that handsome is as handsome does. 'I got caught up in a meeting, sorry,' he said. He chose a table in a sunny spot and asked her to sit down, ready to take charge. Her heart raced, her stomach churned. Unable to look him in the face, she turned her gaze towards the next table. One of the boys was accusing the other of grabbing the larger slice of pizza. The mother was discreetly trying to teach him good manners, but each time she whispered in his ear, he screamed louder. Sagar and Sumnima looked at each other with amused smiles. For a brief moment Sumnima felt as though they were an old couple, communicating without words, drawing the same conclusions about the outside world. Sagar picked up the menu and asked her what she would like to eat.

'Just coffee,' she said shyly.

'C'mon, you're slim enough,' he said, his eyes twinkling with laughter.

'I had a big breakfast,' Sumnima said, even though 'breakfast' seemed like a somewhat deceptive term for her mid-morning dalbhat meal.

'I'm starving,' said Sagar.

Sumnima looked at him as he pored over the menu. He had a roundish, slightly chubby face with big eyes and thick eyebrows, a sharp nose and full lips. He appeared about ten years older than her, probably in his late twenties. His open collar revealed a sprinkling of chest hair. His breast pocket contained a pen and a floppy disk that made him look busy and professional, as if he had more important things to do than sit around chatting with a strange girl who adored him. Sumnima felt grateful for his presence.

'I'll just get a burger,' he said, looking up, 'but you must try their potato chilli. They're awesome.'

'I'd love to,' Sumnima said with matching gusto, even though she did not like the dish.

The boy at the next table yelled at his brother and threw his fork on the floor. 'What a brat,' Sagar said, lowering his voice. 'That's why I never want to have kids.'

'Really?' Sumnima said, curious.

'Yes, never marry, never have kids.' Sagar leaned back in his chair with a deep sigh. 'I'm a rolling stone, you see, I gather no moss.'

A rolling stone. Sumnima knew the phrase but not its precise meaning. Was she supposed to laugh? 'So why did you leave the radio show?' she asked, changing the subject.

'Oh, I just have too much on my plate. It was a fun job, I'd have loved to continue if I had more time.'

'What are you busy with?'

'Lots of things. I'm making a documentary film on women trafficking. Working on my own photography project. Doing a consultancy for the UN. And might start writing a newspaper column.'

'Oh God,' Sumnima gasped. 'You've only been back for a year, no?'

'Yup.'

'Were you sad to leave America?'

'Not at all,' Sagar said energetically. Sumnima could tell she had raised a topic dear to him. 'I had a pretty decent job at a think tank in D.C., most people thought I was crazy to leave, but I have no regrets.' Sumnima did not know what a think tank was. 'There's so much people like us can do in this country,' he went on. 'So much room for experiment and innovation.'

Sumnima nodded sagely, a little sorry that she did not belong with 'people like us'. The waiter came and placed their food on the table. While Sumnima picked on her potato chilli, Sagar opened his mouth wide and took a big bite of his chicken burger.

'Man, I miss real hamburgers,' he said. 'And good steak. In other words, cow meat is the one thing I miss about America.'

Sumnima laughed but couldn't help being mildly scandalized. She had never met a Nepali, let alone a high-caste Hindu Nepali, who ate cow meat. Strangely this made him all the more desirable in her eyes. A rebel spirit, a breaker of taboos.

The next hour flew by before Sumnima realized it. The radio host's ebullient charm was no less overpowering in real life. He spoke without rest, mixing English and Nepali, making witty asides. He jumped from one topic to another with such ease Sumnima couldn't keep pace with him. She laughed and nodded even though some of his jokes and American colloquialisms went over her head. He only stopped at intervals to chew his food and sip water, and these brief silences made her so shy she could barely lift up her eyes.

A waiter cleared the plates and asked if they would like to order anything else. 'No thanks, we'll take the bill,' said Sagar, putting on his jacket. Sumnima felt dismayed that he wanted to leave so soon. They had not even started talking about themselves. Were they going to part as mere acquaintances? As if he had read her mind, Sagar suddenly lunged across the table and looked into her eyes.

'So, does Mona Lisa have a boyfriend?' he asked.

Sumnima dropped her eyes and shook her head.

'Ah,' said Sagar. 'So you only go around breaking hearts.'

Sumnima laughed a nervous little laugh, her senses all in a whirl.

'Will this heart-breaker give me her number?' said Sagar.

Sumnima was extremely delighted to hear this, but also a little worried. There was every chance that her parents or Boju might answer the phone when he called. The thought of Boju heaping obscenities on him made her shudder. 'I mostly answer the phone myself,' she said, writing her number down on a paper napkin. 'But just so you know,' she added with some hesitation, 'my parents are not used to boys calling me.'

'Don't worry,' Sagar said with a knowing smile. 'I'll know when to hang up.'

The waiter came and placed the bill in front of Sagar.

'Should I…' Sumnima said, reaching for her purse.

Sagar considered this for a moment. 'Thanks,' he said, passing the bill to her. 'I don't have change today, but next time it's on me.'

31

Sumnima stood near the intersection and watched Sagar ride off on his motorbike. She crossed the street in a daze and almost bumped into another motorbike. 'Do you want to go up?' the driver yelled, pointing his chin at the sky. Sumnima saw his mouth move but couldn't make out his words. She was seized by a feeling she had not experienced before, a kind of rapture mingled with the terror of the unknown. Sagar had taken her phone number and opened up a world of possibilities, yet how unattainable he seemed already. She had never read the books he had read, never travelled outside Nepal, never even been on an aeroplane. She hailed a taxi but remembered she did not have enough money left. She let it pass and headed towards the bus stand, walking past the slogan-covered walls of a government college. An event had just ended on the campus and students were spilling out of the gates into the pavement. Sumnima quickened her pace, conscious that she stood out from the crowd with her well-groomed appearance. A group of boys lingered near the bus park waving political party flags. One of them leaned forward as she passed and hummed a teasing little song.

'Musu musu hasi deuna lai lai…'

'Stop it, yaar,' another said, 'Didn't you just hear a speech on women rights?'

They gave a shout of laughter and chanted, 'Naribaad jindabad! Saribaad Jindabad!'

Sumnima controlled herself. No point descending to the level of riffraff, she thought, and boarded a bus that was about to leave. The bus was packed. She stood near the door hoping to get some air, but at the next stop the conductor took in more passengers and shoved her towards the back of the crowded aisle. 'Uff, so irritating,' she said, in English, at which two girls standing near her sarcastically rolled their eyes. A rush of passengers pushed her further back at the next stop. Backs, breasts, hips and crotches pressed against her from all sides. She could see nothing except the armpit tuft of a man holding onto the overhead bar. As the bus rolled along through the city, she found herself settling into that oddly comfortable position. Her head cushioned against the back of a fellow passenger, she tried to relive the dreamlike moments spent with Sagar. The jokes and laughter, the intensity with which he had peered into her eyes, the relief on his face when she told him she didn't have a boyfriend. Maybe he was not out of her reach after all.

Dusk had fallen and a chill set in when she got off the bus and walked towards the ring road. Under the sky smeared with sunset, the earth seemed steeped in magic. The fields and houses and passersby, the children playing on the open field, and even the bramble bushes growing by the wayside seemed imbued with newness. She went galloping along the fields, smiling at the children whose jubilant cries rose and merged with the symphony rising within her. She inhaled the cold air, received the wind in her face, and let her hair fly hither and thither. The ecstasy ebbed a little when the three-storey house came into view. The mammoth dish antenna on the roof bore the last remaining sliver of sunlight. Sumnima looked at her watch. Five thirty. Her mother was already cross that she had refused to go shopping with her. Sumnima planned a course of action. She would enter through the back door, steal up to her room and quickly change into her pajamas, then go downstairs with a drowsy expression, pretending she'd just woken up from a long nap. Ganga would corroborate the lie by asking, 'Thuli, you're finally up?'

Sumnima opened the gate as noiselessly as possible and went around the house, frowning at the faint odour of chicken manure. The hens squawked as she passed the coop; she jerked her head forward and shushed them. She took off her shoes and gently pushed the back door that opened into the dining room. And who else should meet her gaze but the one she most wanted to avoid? Her mother sat at the dining table wrapped in a shawl, drinking a cup of tea with a frosty expression on her face. 'Eh, Mummy, there you are,' Sumnima said. Her mother pursed her lips. Sumnima couldn't tell if she was mad at her, or just irritable for no particular reason. 'I'm so exhausted,' she went on, trying to hide her nervousness. 'I scoured every bookstore in town, but couldn't find the chemistry book I need.' At moments of crisis, lies spooled out of her brain so effortlessly she almost believed them herself. Her mother remained quiet. Had she found out about Sagar? 'You look drained, Mummy,' said Sumnima. 'Are you unwell?'

Her mother's face finally relaxed. 'I'm okay,' she said, 'but we're going to have another permanent guest in the house.'

That was all? Sumnima could barely hide her relief. 'Who?'

'Your Maila bada's daughter Manlahari. She's coming from Dharan.'

Sumnima tried to look concerned, though all she really wanted was to run upstairs to Numa and recall every last detail of her time with Sagar.

Her mother sipped her tea and said, 'She was four or five when she left her home in Assam. Your bada couldn't take care of her, so he sent her to Dharan, to his wife's parents. Now they're both dead, and the rest of the family doesn't want her.'

'Oh.' Sumnima was only half listening.

'Your bada doesn't want Manlahari to return to Assam. There's some unrest. So he asked your father if she could come here, and your Baba just can't say no.'

'He really can't,' Sumnima said absently. She got up to go.

'She's around your age. Wait, no, she was born a year later, so she must be Numa's age.'

Her mother began to calculate the years on her fingers. Sumnima slunk out of the room, leaving her mother to brood over the impending burden.

~

Maila had been writing regularly to Tamule ji over the past year. A series of misfortunes had befallen that already hapless man. First he had lost his job at the tea estate after his fellow workers beat up the manager over wages. Next, an acquaintance had coaxed him into investing in a small business venture and swindled him out of his life's savings. And a month later, his wife's people in Dharan had said they could no longer support his daughter, who had just finished her SLC exam. To crown it all, the armed conflict in Assam had spread to his district and some families of Nepali origin had come under attack.

Premkala had read his letters. Those sad, artless accounts of his misery awakened both her sympathy and her instinct of self-preservation. She wanted his troubles to end soon, before they began creeping into her world. She had already prepared her husband for the inevitable. 'Maila dai, I understand your problem,' he was meant to say when Maila made his request, 'but what to do, I have my own worries. Kathmandu has become so expensive, you see. I have to send two daughters to college. Sumnima plans to study medicine. Numa wants to go to India. And we also have Ganga to look after.'

For once Tamule ji had completely agreed with his wife. At the back of his mind he felt he owed nothing to a brother who had turned his back on his community for the sake of a disreputable widow. He had never met Maila's wife, but heard enough from his relatives to form a poor opinion of her. They described her as a lowly Tamangni, a Bhoteni from a cow-eating tribe, an ill-omened creature who'd 'eaten' her first husband within two months of their marriage. On the day Maila brought her home, their aunt

Thulkaki had spat on her face and accused her of ensnaring her gullible nephew. The new bride had kept quiet then, but soon brainwashed Maila into leaving the village and moving to India. One of her relatives worked in the tea gardens of Assam. Maila had heedlessly followed her, ignoring the pleas of his family. He had always been impulsive and irresponsible. Looking back, Tamule ji could see how his brother had been doomed to failure right from the start. Maila had spent his school years playing marbles, picking berries and branches, and running around the village like a tramp. It was Maila who had taught him to climb trees and swim in the fast-flowing river. Tamule ji remembered those summer afternoons at the river. They would fling their clothes off and dive into the cold, rushing water, laughing with shock and delight as the current carried them downstream, and later emerge on the shore panting from exertion, their hearts content, their legs quivering like jelly. Afterwards, they washed their clothes and spread them on a large boulder. Loose, mud-coloured tunics and trousers made of homespun yarn. They sat on the shore and waited for their clothes to dry, chatting about all things under the sun, their shrunken penises hidden behind their folded knees.

A few days after Tamule ji made up his mind, Maila had called from Assam and made his desperate appeal on behalf of his daughter. 'Don't worry, dai,' Tamule ji had heard himself saying. 'She can come stay with us. What is family for?'

32

Sumnima sat at her desk calculating her love compatibility with Sagar when a girl burst in through the door. 'Are you Sumnima didi?' Her eager tone irked Sumnima. She was not in the mood to entertain anyone, least of all poor cousins from strange towns. It had been two weeks since Sagar took her number, but he had not called her. She had calculated the love match three times, using Sagar's first name, then his last name, and then his date of birth, but all three times the result had disappointed her. Still she looked up at her cousin and forced a smile. The girl had a confident air about her despite her alleged helplessness. It was the middle of January but she was wearing a flimsy top and a knee-length denim skirt fastened at the waist with a large safety pin. Her wrists were crowded with plastic bangles and colourful woven bracelets. Her red nail paint was chipping off.

'You are Maila bada's daughter, no?' she asked. 'When did you arrive?'

'An hour ago,' said the girl.

'You came alone?'

'No, with Amrit mama, my mother's youngest brother. He's downstairs chatting with uncle and aunty.'

'I see,' said Sumnima. The greatest advantage of living on the top floor was that she could stay removed from the petty affairs of the household—the squabbles and commotions downstairs, the small, mindless tasks that came up without warning, the visitors who showed up unannounced, and the trespassing children, beggars and stray dogs that made Boju howl curses that rang through the sky.

The girl looked around the room with curious eyes—the door covered with magazine cutouts, the clothes hanging inside the half-open cupboard, the stereo and the stack of audiotapes, the makeup items scattered in front of the mirror. 'Hm,' she said, looking at the poster of an American rock band on the wall. 'I also like English heroes.'

Sumnima pressed her lips to stifle a laugh.

'Can I see this?' her cousin asked, pulling a large photo album from the shelf. Sumnima nodded. Her cousin sat on the bed and flipped through the album, swinging her crossed leg. Sumnima ran her eyes over her smooth, muscular calf, wondering if she shaved them or if they were naturally hairless like hers.

She felt a jolt of recognition when her eyes fell on her feet.

Broad and flat, with short, stubby toes splayed like a ginger pod—her cousin's feet looked exactly like hers, as if made from the same mould. They appeared like a rude evidence of their shared origin, of their unbreakable kinship.

'Ah, this must be Numa,' her cousin said, peering at the album. 'So fair and pretty. She's just a few months older than me, so I won't call her didi.' She glanced at Sumnima and smiled, as if to make up for the almost cheeky remark. 'She's not home?'

'No,' Sumnima said. 'She went out with friends.'

'She also finished her SLC exam last week, no?'

'Yes. Seems you know so much about us, whereas I don't even know your name.'

'Manlahari.'

The name sounded strange and pastoral to Sumnima's ears. 'That's quite a long name,' she said. 'Don't you have a nickname? Something shorter?'

'I do, but I prefer Manlahari,' her cousin replied.

Sumnima picked up a fallen towel and folded it, searching for words that would cut the girl down to size, but Manlahari seemed to have realized her mistake. Before Sumnima could react, she said in a remorseful tone, 'All my friends in Dharan call me Manlahari, but you can call me Sanu if you want. That's what my mother calls me.' Sumnima's ruffled pride was instantly smoothed.

She tossed the towel aside and said with a smile, 'Don't worry, I'll call you Manlahari. Do you know what it means?'

'Yes, it means a song of the heart,' Manalahari said with a note of pride. 'You know what Sumnima means?'

Sumnima shook her head.

33

One February morning Manlahari slipped into Sumnima's room and handed her a large pink sealed envelope. 'The guy next door sent this for you,' she said with a significant smile. Manlahari waited for her to open it, but Sumnima tossed it aside and said, 'I'll look at it later.' Manlahari frowned and left the room. Sumnima shut the door and hurriedly opened the envelope. It was a greeting card with a candle burning between two red hearts. '*Dearest Sumnima, Happy Valentine's Day. Lot of love, Rishi.*'

Sumina tore the card to pieces and threw it in the dustbin. Just then she heard a polite rap on the door. Ganga was the only person in the house who heeded her instruction to knock before entering. The door opened and there she stood, her eyes bright and cheeks red from the cold. Multiple layers of ill-assorted clothes padded her small frame. 'Thuli, come fast,' she said in an excited voice. 'There's a call for you.'

'Who is it?' Sumnima asked.

'It's a boy,' Ganga said with a mischievous smile.

Sumnima flared up at once. 'How dare he!' She rushed downstairs, almost knocking over some dirty teacups on the floor. Ganga followed her to the landing.

'Will you stop bothering me?' Sumnima yelled into the mouthpiece.

After a brief silence, a voice said, in English, 'Hey, are you mad?'

Sumnima's knees went slack. Up rose the flame she had been trying to smother all these months.

'Oh, sorry, I thought...' she stuttered. 'I didn't know it was you.' Ganga picked up a broom and started sweeping imaginary cobwebs off the wall.

'You disappeared,' Sagar said.

'You're the one who never called.'

Ganga cast a furtive glance at her cousin. Her blushing face, her pouting lips. She held the broom upright, stood on her toes and swept the ceiling in wide strokes. Her cap fell to the floor but she did not notice.

'If only you knew,' Sagar said. 'I wanted to call you the day after we met. But guess what?'

'What?'

'I lost the napkin on which you wrote your number! Can you believe it?'

'Really?'

'Yes, it was so frustrating. I've been looking for the precious napkin ever since. And now, out of nowhere, I found it inside a cushion cover. I have no clue how it got there!'

Sumnima laughed.

'I guess we were destined to meet again,' Sagar said.

'I think so.'

'What are you doing this evening?'

'Why, nothing,' said Sumnima.

'Then let's meet for dinner. It's Valentine's Day!'

It was an exciting but unsettling proposal. Sumnima had never had dinner in a restaurant, only a few lunches with her friends. Would it be too late in the evening? How would she get back home?

'Sure, where should we meet?' she said. Her heart pounded partly with elation and partly out of fear that someone might have picked up the extension phone. The line crackled and the phone volume went down. Could it be Boju? She motioned Ganga to go check while Sagar suggested restaurant options. Ganga flew down the stairs, honoured to be part this clandestine mission.

'Bye, I'll see you tomorrow evening,' Sumnima hung up.

Ganga returned a moment later. 'That was Manlahari,' she said.

'She fled the minute she saw me. Look, she still hasn't picked up the cups. Why don't you tell her?'

Sumnima shrugged and went upstairs, her mind occupied with far more pressing questions. Sagar had chosen a restaurant on the opposite side of town, which meant the taxi fare would be expensive. Riding on a grimy bus or tempo on such an occasion was out of the question. She might also have to cover the meal if he allowed her to pay as he had last time. Her pocket money was dwindling. Asking her parents for more would provoke a barrage of prying questions. The tightfisted old woman would not spare a paisa. Sumnima spent the afternoon cobbling together funds. While Boju sat in the sun chatting with Devi, she sneaked into her room and rummaged under her mattress and pillows, in her crammed shelves, among the things piled on top of her locked cupboard. Finally, in a dusty corner between the windowsill and the cupboard, she found a faded envelope that contained a few hundred rupees smeared with tika, probably dakshina money from Dasain that Boju had put aside and forgotten. In the same corner she also chanced upon her khutruke, in which she and Numa used to save their money as children. She brought the pot to her room, and with the aid of a hairpin and a tweezer, pinched some notes out of the slit in its top one at a time. The painstaking effort bore little fruit. Those bills and coins amounted to no more than one hundred and forty-seven rupees and fifty-five paisas. In the end she pestered Ganga into lending her money from the grocery budget. 'Thank you, Ganga didi, you're so kind. I promise I'll pay back soon!'

~

The red sun glowed through haze that hung over the city. While monkeys leapt freely from temple roof to tree branch to telegraph wire, horns blared and tempers ran high on the street below. Sumnima looked out of the window and frowned at the stalled traffic. A bus with passengers hanging off the door; motorcycles trying to squeeze through gaps between vehicles; an overloaded Vikram tempo tipping off balance; a large SUV with the United Nations logo; and private cars from whose windows the car-owning folk sized each other up.

'Dai, why's there such a jam?' Sumnima asked, but the driver, a graying middle-aged man, was listening to the radio news at full volume. A man with a loud booming voice read out the headlines. Her Majesty the Queen had inaugurated a new bank in the city. The prime minister had reiterated the importance of strengthening Nepal-India ties. The opposition party's no-confidence motion against the prime minister had not received enough votes in parliament. A group of Maoists had attacked police stations and government offices in several districts outside Kathmandu, announcing the launch of a People's War.

Sumnima could not wrap her head around the last headline. People's War? It sounded grandiose and far-fetched. The idea of some people in far-flung districts waging a war against the government seemed somewhat ludicrous. 'Dai, can you lower the volume?' she said, but the driver didn't hear her. She could see his face creased in concentration in the rearview mirror. The traffic hadn't moved an inch and the honking was getting louder. Sumnima took a compact mirror out of her bag and replenished her lipstick. She still couldn't believe that Sagar had asked her out to dinner on Valentine's Day.

A man swore out loud from the adjacent Vikram tempo. 'Saale, chor mantri!' Only then did Sumnima realize why the traffic was being held up. A minister's convoy was passing through the next street and all surrounding roads had been blocked for the time being. After an agonizingly long wait during which all the people on the street, from public bus conductors to foreign expats to private car owners seemed united in their rage against the minister, the jam cleared all of a sudden and the sea of vehicles rushed onwards. There were shouts of relief in the air. The taxi driver changed gear and set the wheels in motion. The newsreader signed off with a namaste and an old Nepali song came on the radio.

'There can be thousands of lovers
But love there can only be one
Be careful when receiving love
There is only one you can return...'

Sumnima leaned back in her seat. The music enclosed her and formed a beautiful soundtrack to the images floating past her—rows upon rows of dusty shops and signboards, a strip of crimson sky above a new high-rise, a black glass window that looked aflame, leaves sprouting on a roadside tree, a traffic policeman flailing his arms. The song ended just as they reached the entry point of Thamel. The fare was lower than Sumnima expected; the driver had not tampered with his meter. She gathered the faded and tattered notes that had long been sitting in her purse, placed a crisp twenty-rupee note on top, and handed them over with a friendly smile. The driver, preoccupied with his own thoughts, did not even count them before stuffing them in his pocket.

Sumnima had passed through the neighbourhood a few times but never ventured into Thamel proper. It was seen as a somewhat shady area, a favourite haunt of hippie tourists, marijuana dealers and rakish local guys. But ever since Sagar referred to it as 'the coolest part of town,' she had been longing to see it through his eyes. She walked through the maze of narrow alleys lined with a hodgepodge of old buildings. There were cafés, bars and restaurants hung with glittering heart-shaped balloons, second-hand bookstores, jewellery and handicraft stalls, stores that sold colourful clothing and trekking gear. Strains of reggae music and Buddhist chants floated from the CD shops. Tourists of all shapes, sizes and colours thronged the lanes. Shopkeepers standing at the storefronts called out to Sumnima.

'Hello, musi-musi, please come in.'

'Japan? Thailand?'

'Ni hao, look, madam, very good price.'

Sumnima was flattered; she had never been mistaken for a foreigner before. After walking back and forth on the same street a few times, she spotted the sign for the restaurant on the second floor of a renovated building. La Portobello. Sumnima climbed the stairs and straightened up as she walked into the restaurant. The dimly lit space was filled with foreigners and a scattering of young Nepali men and women. A candle burned on each table, its flame glinting off the glasses and silverware. A faint jazz tune rose above the hum of the diners' conversation, the clink of cutlery and muted laughter. One portion of the wall displayed framed black-and-white pictures of Hollywood legends. The other carried symbols of a Nepali hill village—a sickle, a pair of braided straw mats, and a little festoon of dried garlic and red chillis. Sumnima quickly scanned the faces of the Nepalis. To her relief, she recognized no one. As Sagar had not arrived, she went to the bathroom to touch up her makeup. The stylish ambience of the restaurant did not extend to the bathroom; it was cramped and smelly. She took out her lipstick and went in, tiptoeing over a scummy patch on the floor. Before she reached the mirror over the sink, her eyes fell on the fizzy, beer-like urine in the toilet bowl. The sight almost made her gag. She rushed out of the door, nearly bumping into a tall white man who stood outside. He gave her a brief nod before going in. Sumnima hurried back to the dining room, hoping she wouldn't have to face him again, and sat by a window that overlooked the street.

Nearly ten minutes passed before a waiter approached her with a menu. She smiled and straightened her posture, ready to accept his apologies. Instead of giving her the menu, he pointed to a corner table and said, 'Bahini, can you please move there?' Sumnima's face became tight, but there was a note of authority and impatience in his voice that impelled her to obey him. The waiter left and came back shortly with a white couple. He ushered them towards the window table, helped them with their backpacks, and announced the Valentine's Day specials. 'Wee,' he said with a grin, 'jay parlay fransay, but only little little.'

Sumnima fumed and squirmed in silence. She shot the waiter a menacing glare as he passed her table, then tried to convince herself that she had struck back well. But her anger did not dissipate. Not until she saw Sagar walk in through the door.

'Happy Valentine's,' he said with feeling.

'Thank you, same to you,' Sumnima said.

He looked younger than she remembered, and not unhandsome in a rust-coloured sweater and faded jeans. He apologized for the delay, complained about the traffic jam, and sat down across from her, full of effervescent energy. 'O bhai,' he called a waiter. 'Why isn't our candle lit?' It was the same waiter. To her surprise, he hastily came over, pulled a match out of his pocket and lit the candle. 'Sorry, sir.' He gave them the menus, announced the specials, went to the next table, then came back the instant Sagar raised his hand.

'I'll go for the pepperoni and mushroom pizza,' said Sagar. 'What about you?'

'Me?' Sumnima said, all flustered. She had assumed they would be sharing a meal. She quickly looked through the menu. So many expensive dishes with such fancy names, it was difficult to choose. The waiter had already arrived with his order pad. 'I'll just have this,' Sumnima said in confused haste, pointing to a dish she had never heard of.

After the waiter left, Sagar took a moment to gaze at Sumnima. Her eyes, lips, hair, skin, nails, all of her gleamed tonight. Two specks of diamond sparkled on her earlobes. A small ruby stud hung from a thin gold chain around her neck. She wore a matching ring on her finger.

'That's not an engagement ring, I hope?' he said.

'Of course not,' Sumnima said with a small laugh.

'Thank God,' Sagar said. 'Else I'd be done for.'

Sumnima blushed and lowered her eyes.

Sagar was in a splendid mood. His documentary film on women trafficking had been selected for the upcoming film festival. He had managed to get funding for his independent film project, which was about the Kamaiyas, the bonded labourers of west Nepal. 'It's modern slavery,' he said in an outraged tone. 'I wrote an article about it last week. Did you get a chance to read it?' 'Oh no, I missed it,' Sumnima said, silently vowing to make a habit of reading newspapers. After Sagar finished expounding on modern slavery, their conversation drifted into sweet nothings which Sumnima found infinitely more pleasant. Sagar complimented her on her smile, confessed he was being 'corny,' and asked her what perfume she used. He stared deep into her eyes as he spoke, as though searching for some answer. Sumnima's heart felt flooded.

'Ah, here comes our feast,' he said, rubbing his palms. The waiter came with a pizza in one hand and a steaming pasta dish in another. 'Pepperoni mushroom pizza for you, sir,' he said, placing it before Sagar. 'Bahini, here's your spaghetti napolitana.' Sumnima felt disappointed. She had expected something more special than noodles splattered with tomato sauce. There was a tiny dish with whitish powder on the side; she had no idea what it was for. 'Ah, this looks awesome,' Sagar said, beaming at his pizza. The thin, crisp crust was layered with melted cheese baked to a golden brown and topped with mushrooms and round slivers of pepperoni. He quipped about the gastronomic wisdom of Italians, added various condiments on his pizza and separated the slices with a knife. He pulled the biggest slice, breaking a long cheese string with his fingers, and ate with great relish. After wolfing down three slices, he looked at Sumnima and asked somewhat tentatively, 'Wanna try?' Sumnima passed the offer and stuck to her spaghetti, making a sincere effort to enjoy the strong tomato tang and the flavour of strange herbs. There was no ladylike way to eat those noodles. At every bite they slipped off her fork and trailed from her mouth. She had to lift up her chin and push them down with her hand. She left the white powder untouched. Thankfully Sagar seemed too absorbed in his meal to notice her ordeal.

'Should we get coffee and dessert?' he said after finishing his pizza.

'Sure,' said Sumnima, pleased that he wished to prolong the hour.

They shared a large piece of Valentine's Day chocolate cake. Sumnima merely nibbled it while Sagar polished it off between sips of coffee. When it came time to pay, the waiter handed the bill to Sagar. He briefly went through it, did some calculation in his head and took out his wallet. Sumnima wondered if she should let him pay, but asked anyway, 'How much is it?' Pat came the reply, 'About four twenty-five each.' Sumnima tried to look unfazed. It was by far the most expensive meal she'd ever had. 'The VAT's already included,' Sagar explained, 'so the total is roughly eight fifty if we add a fifteen percent tip.' Sumnima didn't understand what the fifteen percent tip was all about. She took out her purse and placed three clean hundred-rupee notes on the table, relieved that she'd already used the torn bills.

'Thanks for coming,' Sagar said, looking into her eyes. 'It was a wonderful dinner.'

Sumnima's heart pounded as they climbed down the dark, narrow staircase, their arms brushing against each other. The moment had arrived. Her throat became dry in nervous anticipation. She wiped her clammy hand on her jeans, almost certain he would reach for it, but even after climbing halfway down the stairs, he made no such move. Sumnima slowed down her pace, trying to lengthen each remaining second, but in no time they emerged out of the building into the bright, bustling street. Sumnima's heart sank. The moment had passed.

'Too bad we live on opposite sides of town,' Sagar said, 'but maybe you can walk me to my bike?'

Sumnima smiled. Yes, she would walk to the ends of the earth, crawl if necessary, as long as he was with her. They walked together for some time, both curiously silent. The crowd of tourists had swelled. Loud music floated from the bars and restaurants.

'Didi, five rupees.' A little boy dressed in rags approached Sumnima and stretched out his hand. In the other hand he held an empty plastic milk-packet with the logo of the dairy corporation. Sumnima reached inside her handbag. The boy grinned and sniffed the packet.

'Don't, I don't like to encourage them,' Sagar said in a tone of principled conviction.

Sumnima put her purse away, a little embarrassed. The boy chased them for a moment, then stopped and yelled out loud, 'Didi so nice! Dai so kanjoos!'

Sumnima and Sagar laughed and kept walking. They turned into a dark lane behind a ramshackle tourist lodge where Sagar's motorbike was parked. And that was where it finally happened. As they stood face to face saying goodbye, Sagar suddenly pulled her towards him and kissed her, gently at first, then passionately, probing the inside of her mouth with his tongue. His stubble pricked her chin, his teeth grazed her lips and his warm, coffee breath mingled with hers. The novelty of the sensation stunned Sumnima and sent electric shivers down her spine. She closed her eyes, reeling in ecstasy. They did not stop until they heard some boys giggling on the lodge terrace.

34

Ganga felt a growing resentment towards Manlahari. The girl couldn't stop giving her advice although she was half a decade younger than her. Ganga didi, you should boil milk longer to kill bacteria. You must soak daal before you cook them. Better to fry garlic before onions. 'Don't act smart, I know what I'm doing,' Ganga would say, though deep down she felt she could not match up to her junior counterpart. Her dogged efforts dazzled no one. While she skillfully aped the neighbourhood women in quibbling over the price of onions and yelling at dark-skinned vendors, she lacked their housewifely thrift and shrewdness, and often got short-changed by wily shopkeepers like Bhairey. She panicked at the slightest disruption in her routine, and despised visitors who turned up just before mealtime, forcing her to make tea and snacks in the midst of preparing a meal. By contrast, Manlahari seemed capable of juggling any number of tasks with calm dexterity. She had been assigned the morning duties in the kitchen, and it took her less than two hours to go from room to room serving tea, cook an irreproachable meal, hold a gossip session with Devi and read the tabloid supplement of the daily newspaper. On the stroke of nine-thirty she announced the meal, hustling everyone out of their rooms, and after offering them extra helpings, joined them at the table and ate at a leisurely pace, listening to Sumnima and Numa chat about music, movies, fashion and other such topics that aroused her envy and fascination. She finished cleaning up just in time to go upstairs and tune in to *Bollywood Dhamaka* on Sumnima's radio. Even while doing her preordained duties, she exuded command and authority that brooked no interference. But let anyone set her a task outside of her routine and she would put her foot down and give a hundred excuses to avoid it, so that it was Ganga who ended up doing all the unforeseen chores, from making tea for visitors and shutting windows in stormy weather to shooing stray dogs from the yard.

~

While the rest of the family regarded Manlahari with cautious approbation, Boju saw her as vice incarnate. She had rallied against Manlahari from the day she heard about her. A few days before she arrived in Kathmandu, a dispute had erupted over where the newcomer would sleep. Premkala had suggested putting a bed in the TV room. Boju thought even the kitchen floor would be a luxury for a destitute stray like her. In the end they decided to accommodate Manlahari in Ganga's room. The old bed in the storage shed and the steel almirah in Numa's room would be handed down to her. Boju, still unsatisfied, had calmed down after she saw the almirah; it looked sufficiently battered, with a loose handle, scratched surfaces and dried-up glue stains all over the mirror. When Manlahari finally showed up, wearing a see-through top and a skirt that exposed her legs, Boju congratulated herself on her prescient powers. 'See,' she told Ganga. 'I knew she was the slutty type.' Everything about Manlahari, from her face and voice and laughter to the way she moved and ate seemed like an act of defiance to Boju. While Ganga still had her meals sitting on the kitchen floor, the little fledgling presided at the table like Her Majesty and chomped away without a trace of humility, as if it was her grandfather's harvest. How she glared back if you glanced at her overloaded plate! One felt like gouging her eyes out. And why everyone sang praises about her cooking Boju did not understand. Even stones taste good when drowned in oil and spices, don't they? 'Of course they do,' Ganga would say. 'Kaka Kaki shouldn't pamper her. She'll start dancing on their heads.' Boju would nod her approval. By now Ganga had allayed her fears that the two dependents might gang up and shake the order of things.

Some days, after finishing her chores, Manlahari would join Boju and Ganga in the TV room. The minute she sat down, Boju would pick up the remote control and switch from the Indian channel to BBC World Service. Jabbering white reporters, starving black children, grey war zones, men in suits giving speeches. 'Boju, why are we watching this?' Manlahari would say, 'please put the serial back on.' But Boju did not mind forsaking her favourite Indian serial to deny Manlahari her amusement. She would stare at the images on the screen despite grasping not a word in the commentary, until Manlahari got up and stamped out of the room.

35

As the date for the SLC results came closer, Mr and Mrs Tamule did their best to rein in their expectations of Numa. The blow they received from Sumnima last year had sobered them. They refrained from making guesses about Numa's scores or exploring colleges for her in advance. Every morning Tamule ji lit a lamp in the puja room for Numa's success, but he did it quietly, without even letting his wife know. So when the results came out and they found Numa had passed with a distinction, it felt like a reward for the good deeds of their past lives. 'My brilliant chhori,' Tamule ji said, patting her on the shoulder. 'Go bow your head before the gods.' Premkala embraced her daughter in an unusual show of affection. They called their relatives to share the news, distributed sweets around the neighbourhood and hosted a celebratory dinner for close family and friends. 'How did your daughter do in SLC?' This question, which had made them want to shrink and hide until not so long ago, now became music to their ears. 'We would have been happy with first division, but she got a distinction. Eighty-one percent,' Tamule ji would inform people with a humble smile. When they voiced their astonishment, he would quickly try to generalize his experience. 'Sometimes parents tend to underestimate their children.' During casual conversations he felt restless if people didn't bring up the SLC results. His tongue itched to mention his daughter's success, and he mentally reproached those who denied him the opportunity.

Ganga felt relieved that Numa's results had deflected all attention away from her. She had flunked for the third time, and the news rooted out any last vestige of hope that she might someday pass through the 'iron gate'. What enraged her most was that Manlahari had scored a high second division. On the morning the results came out, her uncle gave her a long lecture and threatened to send her back to Lungla. But the dominant mood in the house was euphoric, and by evening he seemed to have forgotten his threat. Ganga lay low, trying to melt into the background as she went about her daily chores.

Sumnima celebrated Numa's achievement although it exacerbated her feelings of inadequacy. Throughout school they had been students of equal calibre. Now in a single leap her little sister had outdone her. Soon she would go to school in India, the first member of the family to study outside Nepal. As a matter of fact, everyone in their circle who had taken the SLC that year had beat Sumnima, except Ganga. Even Manlahari, a student from a small government school in Dharan, had scored a high second division, putting Sumnima to shame.

~

Numa chose a college in Shimla, the famed summer capital of British India. Some of her senior friends were already studying there. Misty weather, pine-covered hills, wooden houses with gabled roofs—she had seen many Hindi movies set in the picturesque landscape of Shimla.

After going through the list of subjects in her college brochure, she decided to study English and psychology. She announced her decision during dinner one evening.

Her parents looked up from their plates, mortified.

'You want to study such lightweight subjects?' her mother said. 'What's the point of getting a distinction?'

'Science is not for me,' Numa shrugged. She mixed rice and dal with her fingers and ate a mouthful. 'I'll end up killing many innocents if I become a doctor. If I become an engineer, my roads and bridges will collapse and cause death and destruction.'

Sumnima chuckled.

'This is how privilege spoils kids,' Tamule ji said. 'Education becomes a hobby and fashion. In my time, if I'd had the opportunity to study medicine or engineering—'

'But this is not your time,' Numa said. 'And I'm not like Sumnima, no can force me to study science.'

The argument lasted for several days. In the end they reached a compromise. Numa would study commerce. Her parents agreed it was less lucrative than science but far more useful than those airy-fairy subjects that brought neither money nor prestige.

~

'How about we go drop Numa off at her school?' Tamule ji asked his wife one morning. 'We can help her settle in, and it'll be a good excuse to see the place.'

The suggestion thrilled Premkala. As a child she had once stepped across the Nepal-India border on her way to Dharan. She was travelling with her mother, brother and some relatives from Tehrathum. The east-west highway didn't exist at the time, and to reach Dharan they had to pass through India. She did not even realize when they had crossed the border. They drove through hot, dusty towns with small shops, paan-stained roads, and crowds of dark-skinned people whose very appearance evoked a deep-seated dread and suspicion in her. Those places seemed far removed from the India she had seen in Hindi films. In Raxaul, they had boarded a dirty, dilapidated train and shared a second-class compartment with a family from one of the border districts. Dark men in dhotis and kurtas, women in garish-coloured saris. They spoke a mix of Hindi and Maithili, and Premkala and her relatives could only pick up snatches of their conversation. 'Better watch out,' one of her uncles had warned her mother, 'these Madiseys are third-rate people, all thieves and crooks.' All the way to Jogbani, Premkala and her relatives had kept their eyes fastened on their luggage. Now, three decades later, she was finally going to see the India that matched her girlhood dreams, a place where beautiful, light-skinned men and women took romantic strolls among pine trees and snowcapped hills.

Premkala requested leave from work two weeks in advance. 'Dropping your daughter off or going on a late honeymoon?' said the headmistress. She whined about the bad timing and the difficulty of finding a substitute. Premkala listened with a tolerant smile but did not back down. That evening as soon as she reached home, she went up to Numa's room. She was lying in bed reading a thick, glittery novel by Sidney Sheldon, the bestselling author whom Premkala imagined as a voluptuous blonde.

'Your Baba and I are going to Shimla with you,' Premkala said. 'My leave got approved.'

A shadow of disappointment crossed Numa's face. 'Eh, I didn't know that.' She put the book aside. 'That's great but...are you sure you want to waste your time and money?'

'You don't want us to come?' Premkala said sharply.

'No, no, I didn't mean that.' Numa got out of bed and sat on a chair, restless. 'But my friends are going with me, they can help me get around. We've already made plans.'

'What plans?'

'Sorry, I should've told you earlier,' Numa said eagerly. 'We'll fly to Delhi together and stay at a friend's place, it's near Delhi University, a very safe area. We'll hang around the city for two days, then take the night bus to Shimla on the third day. You don't have to come—unless you really want to.'

Premkala kept quiet.

'Don't worry, Mummy, I'll be fine,' Numa said with a smile. 'I'm not a kid anymore.'

Premkala left the room. Next day she went up to the headmistress and said, 'Ma'am, you looked so upset about my honeymoon I decided to cancel my trip.'

36

It was Ganga who had to cook the morning meal while Manlahari prepped and primped for her registration day at the college. After an hour-long shower during which she ignored Boju's repeated knocks on the door, Manlahari put on her best clothes and makeup, and went to Sumnima's room to request a few squirts of her body spray. She threw some books in her handbag, checked herself one last time in the mirror, and went bouncing down the stairs. 'Bye bye, I'm off!' she shouted to Ganga, who stood outside aiming a stone at a dog that had wandered into the yard. Ganga watched her sprint out of the gate and down the lane until she was out of sight. Then she turned to the dog that was still nosing at the garbage pit. With a savage scowl she raised her arm high above her head, bent slightly backwards and threw the stone at the dog with all her strength. The dog fled cowering and yelping. 'Show up again and you'll be dead!' she roared.

Ganga had never felt so wronged in life. Her routine had been changed and her duties increased just to accommodate Manlahari's morning classes. While she stayed home and did all the donkey-work, Manlahari would go to college, make new friends and spend her days romping around town. This thought made her irritable all day long. She shouted at the gas delivery boy for no reason and nearly strangled a hen while taking it out of the coop. Towards afternoon, as the clouds darkened and brought showers, Ganga ran up to the terrace and pulled all the clothes off the lines except Manlahari's, rejoicing in the thought that Manlahari had forgotten to carry her umbrella. She stood on the verandah and watched the drizzle, wishing it would turn into a hailstorm. Princess, she thought, we have guests tonight, you better show up in time to cook the meal, or else—she could not finish her thought.

The evening brought some consolation. Ganga was in their shared room dusting her shelf when the door flung open and in came Manlahari, her hair damp and clothes muddy, her face overcast. Without so much as a smile at Ganga, she closed the curtain and began undressing facing the wall. She wrapped a towel around her waist and changed her trousers first, drawing sharp breaths, then threw the towel over her breasts and swiftly removed her damp top and bra, holding the towel in place with her chin. Ganga watched her bare back, filled with puzzled delight. What could have riled her up? Manlahari took off her earrings and bangles, put them inside the almirah, and spat at the broken handle before banging it shut. She threw the door open and went stamping downstairs, leaving her wet clothes on the floor. Soon after, Ganga heard her banging pots in the kitchen, pounding spices as though she wanted to pulverize the granite mortar. She heard her aunt come out to the landing and shout, 'Stop that noise, will you?' Ganga chuckled. Someone had really knocked the wind out of her.

When the noise abated, Ganga went downstairs. Manlahari was peeling a potato with a fixed expression on her face. 'I see you have a lot to cook today,' Ganga said, looking around the kitchen. 'If you want, I can cook the meat while you do the vegetables.' Manlahari looked surprised. 'OK, that will be nice,' she said. 'I'm so tired.' Ganga rolled her eyes. In her view, only the rich and fortunate were entitled to feel tired without doing strenuous physical work. She put a pot on the stove and heated some oil in it. 'So how was your first day of college?' she asked.

'That place is a shithole,' Manlahari said. 'The classrooms are like dungeons, the furniture is broken, the toilets stink.' She wiped her tears with her sleeve.

'Eh, really?' said Ganga, stirring the pot.

'And the filthy scrawls on the toilet walls. Bahini, want to suck my dick? Hello sister, how big is your—'

'Shh,' Ganga said, shaking with giggles. She picked up a piece of meat between her thumb and forefinger and tossed it into her mouth, nearly scalding her tongue.

'It's a cheap, *khatey* college,' Manlahari said, scrunching up her face. .

Ganga rolled her eyes again. It always irked her when Manlahari dismissed something as *khatey*, as if she deserved better.

'So are there better colleges in Dharan?' Ganga asked.

Manlahari shot her a look. 'I was hoping to go to a *standard* college,' she said, using the English word. 'A *standard* ten-plus two college, like Sumnima didi.'

'Like Sumnima?' Ganga said. 'How can you compare yourself with her? You should thank God they're at least sending you to college.'

After a moment's silence, Manlahari said with a simpering smile, 'I should thank God I didn't fail the SLC three times.'

Ganga shuddered from head to foot. Almost involuntarily her hand reached out and landed a resounding slap across her cousin's cheek. Manlahari froze for an instant. Then, gritting her teeth, she lunged forward and caught hold of Ganga's hair. Ganga struggled and tried to bite her arm while Manlahari pinned her against the counter and pummelled her with her fist. They only came back to their senses when one of their elbows knocked a large glass bowl off the counter. The crashing noise brought their uncle and aunt darting into the kitchen.

'Have you both gone mad?' their aunt cried, staring at the glass shards scattered on the floor.

'Launching a war, eh?' their uncle said, half amused. 'They say Maoists have started a war in Rolpa-Rukum, you want to start one here?'

37

At the start of the new school year at Galileo, Sumnima received a letter from Numa. It was Numa's first letter since she left for India two months ago.

Hi Sumnima,

I am settling well in this beautiful place. Old buildings with ivy creeping up the walls, dark pine trees, steep and winding paths where mist hovers from morning till night, it makes you feel like you're walking in the clouds. Our dorms are clean and spacious. I share a room with two Indian girls. My roommate Radhika Chadda is a character you'd enjoy. The first day as I was unpacking my suitcase, she came up to me and said, 'Is that a foreign shampoo? Can I take a look?' I said sure. Then she went through my toiletries one by one. Cream, lotion, body spray, facewash. She smelled them, examined the packaging, checked the labels. Then she said, 'Last year my parents went to Kathmandu for Shivratri. They brought me so many foreign goods.' I didn't know what to make of that remark. Later I learned that you can't find foreign-made goods in India. Girls here are crazy about things we bring from Kathmandu, things made in Thailand, Singapore, Malaysia, Hong Kong. We Nepalis have something to be proud of besides Mt Everest and Gautam Buddha!

I've made two close friends. Kesang from Kalimpong and Pauline from Shillong. We met at the welcome party and hit it off right away. Both of them speak Nepali. During our first week we had to put up with mild 'ragging' from senior girls. They stopped us along the way and made us dance to stupid Hindi songs in front of a large crowd. Kesang was so mad she almost had a fight with one of the seniors. Pauline just stood there and pretended to dance, but I was a great sport, I gave them such a performance they were all rolling on the floor by the end of it.

Majority of girls in our college are from Punjab and Delhi. Some of them are here with the goal of becoming convent-educated brides. They call us 'chinks'. I don't mind it so much, but other Nepali girls, those of the 'non-chinky' variety, can't stand being lumped together with 'us'. The other day I heard Aparna yell at her roommate, 'My eyes are bigger than yours. From which angle do I look like a chink? Not all Nepalis are chinky, OK?' But it seems these behenjis see no difference between her highness and me. Most of them think Nepal is just another Chinkland within India.

Take care and give my warm regards to everyone at home. Please remind Mummy-Baba to send me money. Love, Numa

P.S. I'm enclosing a photo we took last month. The one with short hair is Pauline—isn't she cute?

Sumnima carefully looked at the photo. It showed Numa and her friends sitting on a couch in their pajamas, their arms over each other's shoulders, their cheeks pressed close together. They looked like sisters. All three had fair skin, narrow eyes and straight dark hair. Yet the first to catch one's eye was Pauline, with her short bob haircut and dimpled smile, and the mischievous gleam in her eyes.

~

Although she loathed her college, Manlahari knew she did not have the luxury of choice. Every morning she would sit in the mouldy classroom and assiduously take notes while the lecturer droned on about the concept of development and the paradigm shifts in the field. Her teachers were dull, harmless breadwinners who hustled from one college to another trying to supplement their meagre incomes. The English lecturer notoriously taught at five places, including at an English-language institute that guaranteed mastery of the language in four weeks. The sociology lecturer took extended leave every few months to work as a consultant for an aid agency. Some mornings Manlahari would come rushing to class only to learn that the lecture had been cancelled. Other days she would hear that the lecturer had shown up only to find the class almost empty. Despite all efforts, she felt her motivation waning over the weeks.

Every other week the campus would be abuzz with protests organized by the student wings of political parties. They railed against the fuel price hike, against corruption and Indian interference. Half the time Manlahari did not understand what they were shouting about. Sometimes clashes broke out between students from different political parties and police had to be called in. A few times the student leaders of the opposition party had tried to coax Manlahari into joining their party. Manlahari stayed away from these political types. She had made friends with two of her classmates who shared her indifference to politics. Like her, they were outsiders to the city and yearned for 'standard' things in life. Rashmi, from Ramechhap district, was a short, plump and energetic girl who came with her eyes painted like a Kathak dancer's at six in the morning. Sunita was from the nearby district of Kavre. She worked at a beauty parlour three days a week and knew all about haircare and skincare. Both of them lived with their families in rented quarters in the narrow alleys of the city. Every morning they would meet outside the college to decide whether or not they should attend classes. Often they spent the hours roaming around town. They lingered outside shop windows admiring clothes, shoes and jewellery they could not afford to buy. They frequented teashops and dingy eateries that served freshly cooked bara, chhoela and buff momocha. They strolled around Patan Durbar Square watching tourists and passersby, and when they finally got tired, sat down under the eaves of one of the temples. Manlahari enjoyed this routine from Sunday through Friday, and on Saturday morning made it a point to announce in front of Ganga: 'Uff, today is my *hatest* day.'

The wound of resentment festered inside Ganga. While she suppressed her humblest desires for the sake of the household, that cunning girl broke every rule on the pretext of attending college. Manlahari spent hours preening and posing in front of the mirror, acquired pretty clothes and accessories from Sumnima, and went gallivanting around town all day. She now considered her occasional duties, such as cleaning the latrine or digging the field, beneath her and expected Ganga to do them. How quickly the stranded waif had turned into a fussy little queen. A bit of stale rice? No, thank you. A leftover chicken neck? No, thank you. It was as if nothing except dainty treats could go down her delicate throat, as if her college had wiped out her not too distant memory of hunger.

38

One morning Manlahari and her friends were about to enter a teashop near their college when they saw a throng of people gathered on the pavement staring at something. Curious, they walked over towards them. The onlookers were reading the slogans painted in red across the boundary wall of their college. 'Death to the murderer government. Death to the feudal, reactionary state. Long live the People's War and New Democratic Revolution.' At the bottom of the slogans was the name of a party that sounded vaguely familiar to Manlahari—Communist Party of Nepal (Maoist). A few months ago some people who called themselves Maoists had thrown a petrol bomb at the Pepsi factory on the outskirts of Kathmandu. Were they the same people?

'Of course,' Sunita said as they slowly made their way back to the teashop. 'Last week they looted weapons from a police station in Ramechhap. It happened close to my uncle's house, he's a ward chair from the Democratic Party.' She stopped and looked at Manlahari, widening her blue-shadowed eyes. 'They might have killed him had they found him, imagine! Luckily he was in Kathmandu.' Manlahari put her hand to her mouth and gasped.

They went into the teashop, greeted the woman at the counter and sat at a corner table, away from the boys who hung about the door smoking and laughing loudly. Flies sat on the tea stains on the table; Manlahari waved them away. 'They came to Kavre too,' Rashmi said, running her fingers through her hair, which was tightly permed and looked like Wai Wai noodles. 'I think it was in February. I heard they took away several lakhs of rupees from a landowner's house, and they burned all the loan documents.' The woman brought them strong milky tea in transparent glasses.

The girls smiled and thanked her. 'Why did they burn the loan documents?' Manlahari asked, sipping her tea.

'So the poor wouldn't have to pay back,' Rashmi said somewhat approvingly. 'They say they're fighting for the poor and oppressed. Khai, there were a few women too, and they were all shouting long live people's war, death to this, death to that, like those slogans on the wall.'

The guys paid up and left, and the place suddenly became quiet. Manlahari imagined huge troops of Maoists storming the city, throwing bombs and firing their machine guns at VIP homes and buildings. 'Do you think they'll attack Kathmandu?' she said in an excited tone.

'No way,' Sunita said with a dismissive frown. 'My uncle said they'll be finished soon.'

'Finished? Is your uncle God or something?' Rashmi said with a small laugh.

'Who's saying he's God?' Sunita shot back. 'But he's into politics, he knows what's going on. He said the police have already killed two dozens of Maoists in Rolpa, Rukum and other districts in west Nepal. And they've arrested thousands of people who could be Maoists. There's no chance they'll come to Kathmandu.'

They had finished their tea. Manlahari took out her purse—a fold-in hemp wallet that Sumnima had handed down to her. 'Leave it, I'll pay,' Sunita said, patting her shoulder.

Next morning when Manlahari arrived at the campus, the slogans on the wall had been painted over, some of the letters still faintly visible beneath the whitewash.

~

Within just four months Manlahari and her friends had grown almost inseparable. Yet she was aware of the gulf between her life and theirs. Her friends did not come from well-to-do households, but as full members of their family, they enjoyed a sense of entitlement that was denied her in her uncle's home. Unlike her, they could wheedle money out of their parents to perm their hair, buy the latest music tapes, or go to the cinema. They took English classes at a private language institute and harboured dreams of going abroad. They could bend or break the rules of their house without fearing they might be carted off to some remote village. She by contrast knew no such freedom. While the rest of the family wallowed in bed all morning like lazy water buffaloes, she had to get up at the crack of dawn and serve them tea before leaving for college. She might lie, dodge, sulk, bang pots and pans, or spoil a job on purpose, but she could never escape the duties assigned her. She could tire herself out cursing that old crone behind her back but never dare snatch the remote control from her hand and change the channel. Nor could she spew the blistering replies that made her tongue itch while her aunt hailed cooking instructions from the landing. Forget perming her hair, the pocket money she received barely even covered her monthly bus fare.

Perhaps realizing this, Rashmi and Sunita always offered to pay for her tea and snacks. They had seen three Hindi movies at the theatre so far and each time refused to let Manlahari pay. Manlahari appreciated their generosity but occasionally detected a shade of condescension in their manner, in the way Sunita patted her shoulder and said, 'Don't worry, yaar, we'll take care of it.' Or that self-approving smile on Rashmi's face as she offered her half-used makeup items gathered from the beauty parlour. Anxious to redeem her pride Manlahari found herself boasting about the very family against which she fulminated at all other times. She dropped subtle hints to remind her friends of their status. They lived in mean, rented lodgings while she dwelled in a private house equipped with modern amenities. Their fathers did lowly fixing and plumbing jobs while her uncle worked in an office alongside white people. She had cousins who knew all about English movies and music and spoke English better than their English lecturer. All things considered, her lifestyle was far more 'standard' than theirs.

~

'You know how much Sumnima didi spent on a bra yesterday?'
    'How much?'
    'Six hundred.'
    'Baa! Six hundred?'
    'Yes,' Manlahari said, taking a lip-gloss tube out of her bag. She removed its cap and let its rolling ball-tip glide over her lips. 'Sumnima didi only wears foreign brands.' She rubbed her lips together to spread the shine. 'See this chibistick, I got this from her. It's also foreign.' Sunita and Rashmi took turns examining the product, murmuring appreciatively. 'You can try it if you want,' Manlahari said. Rashmi removed the cap and rolled its ball-tip over her lips, then passed it to Sunita.
    The three pairs of lips shimmered identically in the sun.
    It was a warm, breezy afternoon. They sat on a high temple porch watching the muted bustle on Patan Durbar Square. Around them children rode the stone lions that guarded the old palace. Elderly men sat in a row gazing at passersby. Tourists in hats and sunglasses clicked photos while curio hawkers pestered them to buy their wares. At the bottom of the temple steps, a woman stood scattering handfuls of rice on the floor. Pigeons pecked around her, their heads bobbing, colours shifting on their iridescent necks. Clouds floated above the golden spires on the temple roofs, and the red trimmings that hung from the eaves danced in continuous little waves.
    Manlahari was drifting into sweet lassitude when she noticed a figure that jolted her awake. 'Oh no, I'm dead!' she said, quickly ducking behind Rashmi's back.

'What happened? What happened?' her friends asked in unison.

'Shhh,' Manlahari said. Rashmi's stiff curls tickled her nose but she stayed put. She slowly raised her head. Yes, it was Sumnima, in a short sleeveless top that exposed a sliver of her tan belly, her long hennaed hair shining in the sun. She held a black motorcycle helmet to her chest, her arms wrapped around it as though it were a precious object. Whose could it be? Manlahari stood up and looked more carefully. Sumnima was not alone. She was walking with a man whose face was obscured by sunglasses. From his dark hair and brown skin, Manlahari guessed he was a Nepali, though his khaki shorts, the mineral water bottle in his hand, and the big camera slung around his neck made him look like a tourist. He walked with a jaunty step and talked continuously, while Sumnima laughed, shook her head, and ran her fingers through her hair. Even from a distance, Manlahari could tell Sumnima was completely under his spell. She let down her guard, climbed down the steps and followed them with her eyes. The couple exited the square and stopped at a roadside parking area. The man got on a motorcycle and took the helmet from Sumnima's hand. Sumnima hopped on behind him. She reached in her handbag for a scarf and wrapped it around the lower part of her face before they rode off.

39

'So is Sagar officially your boyfriend now? Is he a good kisser? Now that I've landed in a girls' school again, my chances of experiencing a first kiss are next to nil. The guys we see in town are the opposite of kissworthy. Yesterday when the three of us were walking down the Mall Road, one guy called out to us, 'Chingchong kingkong pingpong!' Kesang wanted to go punch him but Pauline and I stopped her. Kesang is feisty as a bull. As for Pauline, she's so calm and soft-spoken no one would guess she's actually the daredevil among us. She suggested hitchhiking to town on our first day of school, can you imagine? What if we had been—'

Numa could not concentrate on the rest of the letter. Was Sagar officially her boyfriend now? It seemed that the higher he rose in her estimation, the lower her chances of winning his love. Within just two years of returning from America, he had established such excellent connections in Kathmandu he now received invitations to cocktail parties. At twenty-eight he rubbed shoulders with donors, diplomats and politicians. He landed one lucrative consultancy after another and was invited to workshops and seminars abroad. Only last month he had gone to Bangkok for a workshop on 'conflict resolution and peacebuilding', a topic that he said would become 'hot' in Nepal, as the Maoists were spreading beyond their remote stronghold and the government was using force to wipe them out. Sumnima loved hearing about his cocktail dinners and foreign travels, about the praises he had won and the people he had met. It flattered her that a man as worldly as Sagar, a man ten years older than her, deigned to share his experiences with her. His company enlarged her small, mundane existence.

Until she met Sagar, she had never thought about the price of love in monetary terms. Now money constituted a chief hurdle in her amorous pursuit. The exorbitant taxi fares, the frequent restaurant bills and the little presents—books, music cassettes, pens and diaries—she gave him every now and then. Add to this the cost of personal grooming—clothes, makeup, accessories, lotions, body sprays and the lacy satin lingerie she had been saving for 'the right moment.' The monthly pocket money she received from her parents was a mere fraction of the cost of romance. She had to constantly invent plausible lies to squeeze extra cash out of them. Lab fees, school picnic, mandatory donation for flood victims, exhibition tour, farewell gift for a departing teacher, and so on. Occasionally she stole from her parents' wallets, or ferreted out the faded bills that Boju hid in the nooks and crannies of her room. If that did not suffice, she persuaded Ganga to skim her grocery fund.

And yet she could not extract an unequivocal declaration of love from Sagar. He remained, in his own words, a rolling stone, a nomad spirit, driftwood floating through the sea of life. On most days he treated her simply as a close confidant, sharing not only his career plans and political scoops gathered from his high-level contacts, but also the long-drawn sagas of his past love affairs. There was one ex-girlfriend whom he remembered with particular fondness, an American seeker he'd met during his college years. 'She was different,' he'd say, making Sumnima feel like a nondescript lump. 'I brought her to Kathmandu one summer. Oh, we had some crazy fun.' Sumnima refrained from asking what they did, but he told her anyway. 'We spent one full moon night near Aryaghat. Watched the burning pyres, discussed afterlife over a bottle of wine.' The cremation ground on the foetid banks of the Bagmati didn't seem like an ideal spot for spiritual romance, but the story tormented Sumnima for days.

Yet there were also days that held all the promise and wonder of mutual love. On such afternoons, Sagar took her to the edges of the valley, away from the noise and dust of the city. She would sit behind him on his motorcycle with her arms wrapped around him, and feel the wind in her face as he drove past the open fields at a low, steady speed. They would stop by a leafy, secluded spot, eat a quick lunch at a resort, and stroll through the woods kissing and holding hands. Sometimes he brought his camera and took pictures of her, capturing her smile, eyes and gestures in intimate close-up shots that he would print and show her later, resurrecting her dying hopes.

Away from him, she existed in a state of perpetual anxiety and anticipation, waiting for his phone call, planning her outfit for their next meeting, or pondering the deeper meaning of his words and gestures. By now many a dark stairway, lonely alley and taxi driver in Kathmandu had witnessed them blinded by desire. Sagar's ravenous mouth, his crushing embrace and the rhythmic movement of his hands. The memory of his touch stirred her even on bleak Sunday afternoons when the wail of a drilling machine and the distant drone of an aeroplane measured the tenor of life. But even as passion blazed inside her, Sumnima feared crossing the limit, and appreciated that in all those months Sagar had not strayed below her beltline. 'When will this mermaid become a woman?' he had once teased her as he fondled her breasts in a restaurant corridor. 'When the time comes,' she had whispered with a smile.

40

Monsoon turned to autumn, bringing clear skies and a slight chill in the air. Sunlight came down at a different angle and illuminated new sections of the fields and houses. Marigolds bloomed everywhere and kites appeared in the sky, heralding the long festivals. Tamule ji planned to travel to Lungla with his niece and booked their flights to Tumlingtar weeks in advance. Schools and offices began to close. People returned to their villages in droves, leaving the city streets empty and quiet. Ganga spent her days in joyful anticipation.

~

Ganga heart skipped a beat as the plane took off with a roar and a shudder. She gripped the seat in front and shut her eyes. 'Don't be scared, nothing will happen,' her uncle said above the noise. She took a deep breath and wiped her sweaty palms on her lap. The loud hum filled her ears and made her dizzy. The airhostess—a trim and tidy young woman in a sari—began serving airline candies on a tray, walking hunched over down the cramped aisle. Ganga shuffled in anticipation. The airhostess held the tray out to her with a professional smile, which disappeared when Ganga grabbed two fistfuls of candies. Ganga wanted to put the candies back right away but it was too late. She ate one and put the rest in her pocket for the kids back home. 'You can look out of the window,' her uncle said, glancing up from his newspaper. Ganga did as she was told. Far down below she could see rows upon rows of green hills, toy-size houses, miniature terraced fields hewn out of steep hillsides, and a thin winding river like a shiny thread. The hills grew smaller and smaller as the plane gained altitude, and soon disappeared under a bed of clouds. At one point the clouds parted and revealed a range of icy peaks glinting in sharp sunlight. Half an hour later, the plane landed and juddered to a halt on the dirt runway. 'Here we are,' her uncle said with a smile. Ganga got up. Wind brushed her face as she walked out of the aircraft. She looked around at the quiet green valley and the surrounding hills. Her limbs grew light, every cell in her body seemed to relax.

Chandrey and Jamuna were waiting outside the airport, along with Saila, a distant cousin who would serve as their main porter. Jamuna, a thin, flat-chested girl until two years ago, had grown into a slender young woman. Chandrey looked as lanky as ever, and a little ridiculous with a bright green plastic bucket hanging from his arm.

'Dai, what's this for?' Ganga said with a laugh.

'We just bought it in the market,' said Chandrey. 'Gajey kaka will need it while bathing.'

'Harey, you needn't have troubled yourselves,' said Tamule ji. 'It's a full day's walk. Why saddle yourself with unnecessary things.'

Chandrey and Jamuna refused to let their uncle carry any luggage. They tied up the heavier bags and placed them on Saila's back, then slung the remaining bags over their shoulders. Jamuna offered to carry Ganga's backpack too. 'Give it to me didi, you must have forgotten how to carry loads,' she said with a mocking smile. Ganga slapped her on the shoulder. 'Shut up,' she said. 'I can carry you to Lungla if I must.'

～

There was a festive air around the village. The paddies had ripened to a fluorescent green. The orange trees bore raw, greenish-orange fruit. The houses were whitewashed and painted with red clay along the borders. The roofs had fresh layers of thatch. The sheep tethered in people's backyards bleated throughout the day as if they knew their end was near. A high bamboo swing had been put up near the school. All afternoon young boys and girls played on it shouting and laughing while small children clamoured for their turn. Dragonflies buzzed around the fields and fireflies lit up the nights.

Ganga's family had worked hard to make the house comfortable for the visitors from Kathmandu. They had spruced up the rooms, brought new blankets and sheets, and kept clean towels, slippers and torches handy. Tikaram had replaced the thatch screen in the latrine with a proper door made of tin and wood. And yet for the first few days, Ganga had a difficult time adjusting to her old space. The room she shared with Jamuna had no table or cupboard, and her clothes and things lay scattered around the floor. Ants nested in the cracks of the mud wall and bit her at night. The house had no running water, and she had to walk up a hill for ten minutes to reach the public tap. Smoke from the wood fire in the kitchen burned her eyes. At night the village would be plunged into total darkness, and she had to grope her way around the house in weak lantern light. In the absence of a television, there was nothing to do but sleep once the evening chores were over. Although she did not look forward to returning to Kathmandu, she could not imagine staying on forever.

Still, the days passed by more quickly than she wished. Her relatives treated her like a special guest, as though she shared the same status as Gajey kaka. They greeted her effusively, sat her down beside him and served her millet raksi and snacks. 'How plump and fair you've grown, Ganga,' they said. 'Kathmandu air suits you, eh?' At home her mother and sister-in-law Malati forbade her to do any housework. Ganga had nearly forgotten the amount of work that women had to do in the village. Feed the buffaloes, cook and clean and wash, make countless trips to the water tap, collect grass and wood from the forest, carry heavy loads up steep trails, brew and distill raksi, look after the children, and work the fields in the planting and harvesting seasons—life, for them, meant endless, crushing toil. Ganga felt sorry for them, but was glad to distance herself from their oppressive routines. 'You're a guest,' they said, and she behaved like one. She slept in late, visited friends and relatives, told them stories about Kathmandu, and basked in their hospitality. At home she spent a lot of time playing with her little nephew. She loved to watch him totter around on his unsteady legs, to hear him lisp out her name, 'Nonga puppu'. The child quickly grew fond of her and wouldn't leave her side. She carried him on her hip as she walked up and down the village trails. 'Ganga, you should get married so you can have your own,' her relatives teased her. She'd laugh and give some friendly reply even though their remark didn't amuse her.

41

Like every year, Tikaram asked his nephew Saila to slaughter the sheep on Nawami, for neither he nor Chandrey liked to carry out the killing. Saila came with a squad of three or four eager young men. Tikaram dragged the unwilling sheep out to the front yard, threw some rice and petals over its head, and stepped back to let his nephew finish the job. A gaggle of kids gathered around the yard. One of the men held the sheep's legs while another held its chin firmly in place. Saila took a deep breath, raised the khukuri high above his head and severed the sheep's head with one fierce blow. Blood gushed from its neck. The children gazed awestruck. Saila turned on a transistor and placed it on top of the chicken coop before settling down to work. The Mangal Dhun music floated in the air while the boys skinned and disembowelled the sheep, cleaned the entrails and chopped the meat on the broad surface of a sturdy log. The women had no time to breathe. Apart from doing their daily chores, they had to assist the men, serve them raksi and cook a meal for the crowd gathered at the house. Tamule ji and Tikaram sat in the verandah and chatted.

'How come Rai kaka's house is so quiet?' Tamule ji said, looking across the yard to the two-storey house further up on the hill. The house had not been whitewashed. The thatch roof had thinned and faded to a dull brown. A few threadbare clothes hung in the empty yard.

'You don't know?' Tikaram said. 'They're not celebrating Dasain this year. They've decided it's not their festival.'

'Why?' said Tamule ji, surprised.

'Dammar's slogans have carried him away,' Tikaram said with a sigh.

'What slogans? Has he become a Maoist?'

'I think they're different from the Maoists. Khambuwan

Liberation something. They say Dasain is not our festival, Hindu kings forced it on us, so we should stop celebrating it.'

'Eh, I see.' Tamule ji thoughtfully nodded his head. 'I heard there was a bomb attack on the Sanskrit school in Dingla. Was Dammar involved?'

'He's part of the same gang, so I guess he must've been involved,' said Tikaram. 'God knows how he managed to convince his father. Even until a few months ago, Rai kaka was complaining about his politics. He just wanted him to finish college and find a job.'

The brothers kept quiet and looked around the yard. Saila sat on the ground piling chunks of meat with bloody hands. Ganga stood behind him holding her nephew. 'Babu, look,' she said in an excited tone, 'so much chi-chi. Mummy is cooking chi-chi. Babu will eat tasty chi-chi and rice today.' The child babbled with delight.

'That boy adores his aunt,' Tikaram said with a smile.

Tamule ji gazed absently at the child, his mind elsewhere. 'But dai, maybe it's not a bad thing altogether,' he said. 'The younger generation is not like us. They're not willing to accept the domination of Bahuns and Chhetris.'

Tikaram nodded. 'I don't disagree with everything they say,' he said. 'But how can we suddenly claim we're not Hindu? We've been celebrating Dasain-Tihar all our lives. It's our festival too.'

Tamule ji looked into the distance, trying to form his argument in his head. 'But one thing is for certain,' he said. 'Our ancestors weren't Hindus. I think they must have come from Tibet and settled in the west. Look at the Tamules in the west, they still use lamas instead of Bahun pandits. Many speak their own language. But we in the east are a confused lot, neither here nor there.'

'I wonder when our great-grandfathers decided to become Hindus,' Tikaram said with a faraway look in his eyes. 'Why do you think they did that?'

'Khai,' said Tamule ji. 'Maybe they had no choice. Or maybe

they thought that would be best for our people. Wasn't our father nicknamed Chimse Bahun?'

Both of them laughed.

~

On the last day of their trip, Ganga and her uncle went all around the village to receive tika from elders. Ganga took her nephew along. Their relatives crowded around them and inundated them with gossip. Ganga realized with a tinge of guilt that she had little patience left for their rambling provincial talk and their superstitions. So-and-so died because he didn't worship the clan deity on time. So-and-so used black magic spells to make her neighbour fall sick. This one was an excellent son, that one a terrible daughter-in-law. Her uncle listened and responded even though he clearly didn't believe much of what he heard.

Even their hospitality began to wear her out. Her aunts and grandaunts waited on her as she ate and kept dumping extra servings on her plate despite her protests. Seeing her nephew eat from her plate, they asked, for the umpteenth time, when she would get married and bear her own child. At one point she could take it no more. 'You think I'll follow in your footsteps?' she replied in a half-joking tone, 'I've seen what marriage and kids have done to you all.' Her uncle gave her a reproving glance. Ganga immediately regretted what she said and tried to make up by chatting with them for an extra hour. It was already dark when she left. She was tipsy from the countless bowls of raski and her stomach ached from overeating.

When she got home, she was startled to find an army of relatives sitting on the verandah, their foreheads covered with red tika. Children ran about the house laughing and crying. Some of her relatives had walked for three hours from Sintama, her mother's natal village. Her father and grandmother entertained them while Jamuna served them raksi and snacks. Malati bhauju, stationed in the smoke-filled kitchen, looked half dead from exhaustion. Ganga helped attend to the guests, serve food, and mind the children all evening. Some of the guests left soon after dinner, but the ones from Sintama stayed overnight. The children slept on mattresses spread in Ganga's room. The rest of them made their beds wherever they could find space around the house. The young men slept on the verandah, using their bags and jackets as pillows. Once everyone had settled in for the night, Ganga went to her room. It had been a long, hectic day. She stepped over the sleeping children, sat on her bed and blew out the lantern flame. As she was closing the window, she saw the silhouette of a woman squatting outside washing the dishes in the moonlight. It was Malati bhauju, scouring an enormous cooking pot with straw and ash. Piles of dirty dishes lay around her. Ganga slipped into bed and remembered, with a mixture of relief and pain, that she would be leaving the village early next morning.

42

Before the holidays began, Sumnima had borrowed Manisha's notes, photocopied them and prepared a strict study schedule for her twelfth grade mid-term exams. But her plans had fizzled out amid the whirl of festivities. She celebrated Dasain as she did each year, visiting relatives she liked, relatives she detested, and relatives whose existence she remembered only once a year. Throughout her childhood, everything associated with Dasain and Tihar had filled her with a dizzy delight. The lights and the marigolds, the feasting and gambling, the battle of kites in the sky, and the clean, crisp notes that her elders slipped into her hand after putting tika on her forehead. But the charm of the festivals had faded over time. The sight of the empty streets and closed shops and offices brought on a sense of stagnation. Excess of food and chatter dulled her brain.

Sagar did not call her during the festival. A day before Phulpati, she had had dinner with him at a restaurant in Thamel. Afterwards, as they stood caressing each other in a dark, empty lot, things had gone a little out of control. Before she realized it, Sagar had pulled down her pants, gripped her buttocks and brought his erect penis alarmingly close to her. 'Stop!' she had cried, pushing him away. Sagar had glanced at her terror-struck face, quietly zipped up his pants and tucked in his shirt. 'I'm running late,' he had said in an icy tone, and left without even offering her a ride to the taxi rank.

Now all kinds of questions plagued Sumnima as she sat trying to memorize a physics formula for her mid-term exams. Had she offended Sagar in some unpardonable manner? She had read in a magazine that rebuffing a man's advances could seriously damage his self-esteem. She opened her book again and tried to read. Maybe Sagar was just trying to take their relationship a step further. Had she pushed him away at a decisive moment? Could her prudish behaviour have turned him off? He was not a conventional Nepali man after all. A freethinking guy with an American education, he would presumably want a freethinking, Western-educated girl. Was that why he always said they were 'not lovers but more than friends'? Would they have become lovers had she allowed him to— Sumnima rose from her chair. No, of course not. She may be broadminded, but she had values she could not compromise on. Besides, why did she always have to place his desires above hers? Sumnima paced back and forth around the room. She could not remember him making a single effort to reciprocate her affection and generosity. After returning from Bangkok last month, he had spent a full hour gushing about 'those Thai babes', the beautiful resort in Chiang Mai, the variety of seafood he'd eaten and so on and so forth, but he had brought her nothing, not even a candy, as a souvenir. Her eighteenth birthday had come and gone without him noticing it. She stopped near the window. Rishiram, who sat on the terrace playing his guitar, looked up and smiled. She quickly drew the curtain. As for the philosophical flourish with which Sagar always passed her the restaurant bill, she sometimes doubted it was a gesture of respect towards women. Equally puzzling was how easily he asked her to run errands and bring him food at his office. Last month he had made her exchange a few cassettes at a store and pay the difference on her way home. Did his behaviour reflect their growing intimacy or—Sumnima heard the phone ringing downstairs. A moment later Ganga appeared at her door.

'Thuli, come fast, a call for you.'

'I knew he'd call!' Sumnima cried, leaping out of the door.

43

Although Sumnima's mid-term exams didn't go well, she was shocked when she saw her report card three weeks later. 'Failed'— the letters were printed in bold red ink at the bottom of the marksheet. She had flunked physics by just two marks. Mid-term exams were supposed to be graded leniently. How could Ramhari Sir be so cruel? Around her, her classmates were comparing their marks and calculating their percentage scores. Some whooped with joy, others grumbled and frowned. Yet none of them seemed to have received such a severe blow. Was she the only one who had flunked? Tears tingled in her eyes. She stole out of the hall and went into the lab, walking past the life-size skeleton and jars filled with bloated specimens. A faint chemical smell lingered in the room. She sat on a chair at the back of the room and examined her report card again. Only two marks short. She didn't know that Ramhari, named Ram Hairy, was such a callous marker. 'Sumnima, don't do the process of side talking,' he said if he found her chatting during class, 'otherwise the reduction of ten marks will take place.' She had never imagined that he would put his comical threat into action. What would she do now? Beg him for grace marks? It was too late. The only person who could possibly help her at this stage was the principal.

Once all the students had left and the building became quiet, Sumnima came out of the lab and went up to Balram Sir's office. Balram Sir seemed fond of her. Unlike Reshma and Tejaswi, she had kept her promise of enrolling in his college. Still, she must be careful not to appear too pushy. He did not like assertive women. He had recently fired Bandana Ma'am for being 'too proudy'.

~

Balram Sir sat at his desk reading a Nepali tabloid, basking in the late autumn sunshine that poured in through the windows.

'Excuse me, sir, may I come in?' Sumnima asked.

'Oho, Sumnima,' he said, surprised. 'Come in. How come you're still around?'

'Sir, I need a huge favour.'

'Take a seat.' He put the tabloid on his desk. It carried an image of watermelons that looked like an enormous pair of breasts at first glance. The caption read: 'Sundar swasthya ko lagi kharbhuja'.

Sumnima sat down and handed him the report card.

'Sir, see, I'm only two marks short,' she said. 'Please, sir, can this paper be re-evaluated?'

Balram Sir went through the report card. His cheeks gleamed with a new layer of fat. He handed back the report card and shook his head. Sorry, there was nothing he could do at this point.

'Sir, please, I beg you.' Sumnima burst into a sob. 'My parents will kill me if they find out. I've never failed a course...'

Balram Sir watched her intently as she pleaded with him.

'Sir, I need your help, or else I'm doomed,' she said, wiping her tears with a handkerchief.

Balram Sir got up from his chair, looked out of the window and walked towards her. 'Shh, don't cry.' He bent over and placed his hand on her shoulder. Sumnima winced. 'I'll talk to your physics ma'am,' he said.

'You mean Ramhari Sir?' Sumnima asked in a feeble voice.

'Eh, yes, yes, Ramhari,' he said, rubbing her back in slow, circular motions.

Sir, please take your hands off me, Sumnima wanted to say, but the words choked in her throat. She sat paralysed as his hand slithered down her back and rested on the curve of her waist. 'How pale you look,' he said. His face loomed close. She could see the beads of sweat glistening on his upper lip. 'It won't be easy,' he murmured, 'but two marks can be adjusted, come here...' His hand slid up towards her breast.

Sumnima's mind went blank. Her limbs froze.

Right at that moment they heard the sound of quick footsteps coming up the stairs. Sumnima jumped out of the chair. Balram Sir leapt to his feet, grabbed a folder from his desk and began flipping through it. It was the woman who worked at the canteen. She stopped at the door for a moment and entered hesitantly, her head bent and eyes fixed on the floor as though she feared witnessing something inappropriate. She mumbled a greeting to Balram Sir, picked up the dirty teacups and threw Sumnima a suspicious glance before leaving the room. Sumnima stood rooted to the spot, covered in a cold sweat. Balram Sir did not look up from the folder. Sunlight filtered through his broad, blushing ears, making him look extraterrestrial. A sparrow flew into the room. It dashed against the wall, against the cabinet, and against the windowpane before flying out into the open. 'Don't worry, I'll talk to Ramhari Sir,' Balram Sir said in an extremely dignified voice. 'He can give you grace marks. But you better work hard for the finals.'

~

Sumnima stood outside the college gate for a long time, dazed and disoriented. She could still feel the strange warm paw sliding down her back, the hot breath moistening her skin. Was it deliberate or accidental? She felt a desperate urge to scrub herself clean from head to toe, but did not feel like going home. Perhaps she could go visit Sagar? Often when she called him at this hour, he would ask her to drop by his office and 'grab me some munchies along the way.' She tried calling him from a nearby shop, hoping that the receptionist would not answer the phone. That pesky woman always made her sign into the logbook, demanded her ID card and asked her a stream of irrelevant questions.

'Hello, IPAF-Nepal.'

Sumnima grimaced; it was the receptionist.

'Could you please transfer me to Sagar ji?'

'He's in a meeting.'

Sumnima hung up. Fuming, she started dialling Manisha's number, but remembered that Manisha had passed in first division despite claiming to have done badly. She banged the phone down and turned to leave. 'Oi, don't you have to pay?' cried the shopkeeper, already annoyed at her rough handling of the phone. Sumnima sighed and tossed a five-rupee note over the counter. It seemed the whole world was conspiring against her. She meandered through the streets without a definite plan, the scene with Balram Sir playing in her mind. Was he really trying to—the very thought made her skin crawl. Or could it have been a simple fatherly gesture? He was trying to comfort her after all. He had assured her he would talk to Ramhari Sir. She had reached the entrance of the public zoo. Men, women and children were going in through the rusty revolving gate with packets of chips and juice drinks in their hands. The leafy treetops beyond the wall looked inviting. Sumnima bought a ticket on a whim and went in through the gate.

A dungy smell greeted her and instantly triggered a rush of memories. As a child she often visited the zoo with her father and village relatives, for whom it was an unmissable attraction of the capital city. One day she had joined the newlywed Parvati aunty and Gyan uncle for an elephant ride. During the ride, Gyan uncle had pressed close to his wife and whispered endearments, thinking their little niece would not notice. Parvati aunty, who knew better, had repeatedly slapped his roving hand. Sumnima smiled at the memory. How simple life seemed back then, less contrived, more innocent somehow. The zoo looked as sad and forsaken as she remembered it. Emaciated animals gazed vacantly out of their dank cages. In one enclosure, several crows sat pecking on a rhino's back, making tiny red gashes on its dry, leathery skin. A family sat picnicking on the grass, banana peels and food wrappers strewn about them. Some boys stood throwing pebbles at a hungry baboon and cackling with laughter. They clucked their tongues and made a pass at Sumnima. She did not turn around. This was by no means what she thought of as a 'good crowd'. Only in jokes and parodies did girls from Rhododendron go 'dating' in the public zoo. But at this moment she did not even know why she had come here. She sat on the steps in the shade of a giant tree and watched a flock of swans gliding across the algae-covered pond. The reddish film on the water formed swirling patterns. At a little distance, a young couple sat in a two-seater pedal boat, their backs turned to Sumnima. The boy had his arm wrapped around the girl. Sumnima wondered if she and Sagar looked as silly in their moments together. The girl dipped her fingers in the pond and sprinkled water at the boy, squealing with laughter.

Sumnima recognized the laughter. Her first instinct was to get up and run off, but she stopped and waited until the boat came around. Yes, it was Manlahari, in the little red cardigan she had handed down to her a few days ago. Beside her sat a boy, his face hidden under the hood of a cap, his hair tied into a small ponytail. They seemed so absorbed in each other their boat almost hit the swans. Manlahari turned and gave a cry of mock horror. They quickly pedalled away, laughing at the near encounter.

Sumnima felt a bolt of righteous anger. So that's how she spent her college hours? She stared at her cousin as she teetered out of the unsteady boat, giggling and clasping the hand held out to her.

44

There was a blackout in Bhaisichaur. Sumnima walked past the houses with candlelight glowing in the windows, preparing herself for the volley of questions that would rain down on her. Why so late? How were your results? Show us your report card. Oh please, she would say, if only you knew what a stressful time I had. The admin assistant mislaid my report card, can you believe it? They'll have to make another one. I was in school all day trying to sort it out, I'm exhausted.

Entering through the back door, she found the house cold, dark and quiet. With a sudden surge of relief, she remembered that her parents were not home tonight. Her father had gone to Gorkha on a field trip. Her mother was at a wedding reception hosted by some relatives who had thankfully crossed out 'sushri' on the invitation card and spared her the ordeal of attending what was bound to be a slovenly, ragtag affair. There would be a tent pitched on an empty field behind the wedding house, a buffet consisting of cold greasy pulao and meat curry, stacks of dirty plates under the chairs and children running amok holding plates overloaded with sweets.

There was no one in the kitchen. Boju's door was latched from outside. A lone sputtering candle lit the corridor, casting huge shadows on the wall. A shiver of fright ran through Sumnima. She hurried up the stairs, jumping two steps at a time, and stopped on the landing. A glimmer of pale light came from her cousins' room. 'Ganga didi, are you there?' she said, walking inside. She was taken aback to find Boju in the room, rummaging in the Godrej almirah. Ganga stood behind her, shining a torch into a compartment.

'What are you doing?' Sumnima asked.

'Come see for yourself,' Boju said. She held out a chain with a heart-shaped pendant. 'Where do you think she got this?' Sumnima let out a weary sigh. Boju picked up a pair of pearl-drop earrings. 'And these?' Ganga shone the torch on a small compartment filled with lipsticks, eye pencils, a few bottles of nail polish and a body spray. 'And all these makeup things?' she said.

'Surely someone's been plugging her hole,' Boju said.

'Boju, please,' Sumnima said with a grimace. 'Those are all fake jewellery. She probably bought them herself. I gave her those makeup items.' She noticed Ganga's face darken in the dim light. 'They're half used and not nice at all,' she added.

'But Thuli, it's not just Boju,' Ganga said. 'Everyone knows it. Devi didi said she saw her on New Road the other day, walking with a long-haired guy who looked like a tyape.'

Sumnima considered this for a moment. True, the guy on the boat did look like an addict. But it did not seem wise to give Boju and Ganga more ammunition to use against Manlahari. She would rather grill her separately.

'No wonder she's always on the phone,' Ganga said. 'I really think we should put a lock on the phone. You know those boxes with fixed locks—' there was a sound of footsteps on the stairs. 'Laa!' Ganga cried. Boju, half inside the cupboard, leapt up in a panic. Sumnima moved away from them.

Manlahari stopped at the door and stared at the three figures assembled in the room. The almirah was open and all its contents lay in disarray.

'Boju, what are you looking for?' she asked.

'I was just...' Boju stammered.

Manlahari marched into the room and shut the almirah, wiggling the broken handle up and down. She turned to Boju. 'You can't just come into my room and raid my cupboard.'

Boju hesitated for a moment, then gathered herself and said with sudden authority, 'First tell me where you were all day.' Ganga flashed the torch in Manlahari's face. Manlahari flinched.

Her gajal was smudged, making her eyes look smoky and more audacious than usual. Her lips glistened with a fresh coat of gloss. There were small twigs stuck in her hair.

'There was a programme in our college,' Manlahari said, evading Boju's eyes.

'Programme?' Boju said. 'Programme for roaming around with thugs?'

Manlahari clenched her jaw, her face incandescent with rage. Ganga waved off the insects hovering around the torch beam.

'Speak up,' said Boju, 'you think we don't know what you're up to?'

Manlahari looked at Sumnima, who stood wondering whether she should intervene. 'So what if I roam with boys?' she said defiantly. 'They're my friends. Sumnima didi also has guy friends. Don't you, didi?'

Sumnima felt slightly nervous. She couldn't tell whether Manlahari was making an appeal or a threat.

'Didi, tell them,' Manlahari persisted. 'Is it a crime to have friends?

'God knows,' said Sumnima. Clearly the girl knew something. She grabbed the torch from Ganga's hand and went upstairs, leaving them growling in the dark. She closed the door behind her and took a deep breath. What a rotten day it had been. She turned on the emergency lamp. An envelope with three postage stamps lay on her desk. 'Numa!' she cried, and tore it open.

Hi sis, how are you? I haven't heard from you in a long time. Maybe you're busy running after Sagar. Has he worked some tantra mantra on you? Frankly, I can't wait for the day you get over him.

Yesterday was our college fair. It was great fun. Music, games, food stalls, huge crowds of young people. Some came all the way from Delhi and Chandigarh. We set up a momo stall. They were a big hit, sold out within half an hour.

Guess what we did last week? The three of us ran off to Chandigarh to attend a party at a dance club! It was Pauline's idea. We made sleeping dummies on our beds before we left, and luckily the warden who came on rounds got no wind of it. We'd have been expelled otherwise. A sleazy-looking uncle ji offered us a lift outside the college. He said we looked like 'pretty Chinese dolls' and kept making innuendos as he drove down the winding road in the dark. We gave him fake names and hardly spoke throughout the three-hour journey. After getting off the car, Kesang told him in Hindi, 'Uncle ji, from next time look in the mirror before you try your pickup lines, achha?' Pauline and I nearly died laughing. When we reached the club, we told the manager we were broke, and he smiled and waived our cover charge. Once inside, hordes of young men wanted to dance with us and buy us drinks. The music was atrocious but we danced the night out. One guy fell head over heels for Pauline, so we made him drive us back to our college at four in the morning. We had the time of our lives without having to spend a single penny!

Time for a confession. I finally kissed someone two days ago. Don't panic, it's a girl! A friend. We were walking towards our dorm after dinner, chatting as usual. She said something that annoyed me, and then she started saying sorry, I didn't mean it, don't be angry, and suddenly, she held me and kissed me on the mouth. I was shocked. We fell silent for a while, and then burst out laughing. I don't know how it happened. It felt strange. She told me she had kissed other girls in her high school. All right, no point hiding: it's Pauline. Anyway, next morning we were back to normal. Write soon. Love, Numa

Sumnima felt amused and a little uncomfortable. She knew attraction between girls was not unusual in girls' schools. Many girls at Rhododendron were smitten with their schoolmates, especially the boyish and athletic ones. They'd follow them around during lunch break, give them greeting cards, chocolates and flowers, and scrawl their names on desks and bathroom walls. Silly as it may seem, such behaviour was accepted as normal within the walls of Rhododendron Girls High School. But kissing? That was taking it to another level. She hoped the episode Numa mentioned was just a one-time aberration, a passing fit of madness.

~

Although Premkala did not entirely believe the rumours, she decided to err on the side of caution: Manlahari wouldn't be allowed to leave the house for a week. The girl would stay home, do all the housework and take time out to study for her first-year exams. If she banged pots and pans, made secret phone calls, or tried to sneak out, she would be packed off to her parents in Assam without further questions.

Manlahari served her sentence in resolute silence, leaving little room for complaint. She released her pent-up anger by scrubbing the floors harder than usual and wringing wet laundry with demoniacal strength. She spent one whole afternoon beating the dust out of the carpets with a rod, a piece of cloth tied around her nose. Sumnima, afraid she might expose her in a fit of rage, offered help, but Manlahari emphatically turned her down. She no longer went to Sumnima's room to listen to *Bollywood Dhamaka*. She shunned Ganga and Boju, forsaking even her favourite Indian serials, and stopped talking to Devi didi, who still refused to admit that she had snitched on her. Every day she stayed up till late night and crammed *Guess Questions* booklets for her exams.

Boju and Ganga joined hands and stepped up their vigil. Manlahari's cold silences, the malevolence that blazed in her eyes, and the way she strutted past them with her nose in the air made them increasingly wary. Was she serving out her punishment or plotting revenge? Had she been spitting on their food like those disgruntled factory workers they had heard about? What if she put rat poison in their meals or brought that thug boyfriend of hers to attack them?

45

One morning Tamule ji received an excited phone call from Rajan. By an astounding stroke of luck, he had got a visa to go to America. He would be entering the country as a member of a troupe that was going to perform at a Nepali cultural event. He had a friend in Texas who would help him find a job and settle down. The fixer had charged him fifty thousand rupees for the paperwork. Tamule ji did not know how to respond to the news. A part of him felt ashamed that his brother-in-law had decided to 'sink' into America as an illegal immigrant. But another part felt relieved for him. At thirty-six, Rajan had no stable job or career prospects. His business ideas had flopped one after another. He lacked the skills for networking or extracting favours. Going abroad was probably his best bet.

Besides, the country was veering towards conflict. The Maoists hadn't stopped their attacks on police stations and government offices. In recent weeks they had robbed a bank, vandalized a distillery and hacked a village chairman to death. The government had dubbed them 'terrorists' and was trying to introduce draconian anti-terrorist laws. In the mid-western districts, the police had arrested and killed scores of men and women on suspicion of being Maoists. Two unarmed men had recently been pushed off a cliff after their arrest. A few had already been 'disappeared'. During his recent trip to Gorkha, Tamule ji had heard how the police had stormed the village school and fired at schoolchildren who were protesting against the arrest of their teacher. A fourteen-year-old Dalit boy had died in the incident.

Two days later, on a cold and gloomy afternoon, Rajan showed up unannounced at the Tamule house. The whole family except Manlahari sat huddled under blankets in the TV room. 'Get dressed everyone,' Rajan said. 'We're going out to eat.' He switched off the television, pulled off the blankets and hustled them out of the room. 'Hurry up, the taxi is waiting outside.' Ganga was the first to get ready. She wore a thick hooded jacket over her shiny mirrorwork kurta surwal. Tamule ji and Premkala, who preferred staying home on Saturdays, reluctantly got dressed and allowed themselves to be herded into a Maruti taxi van parked on the newly built road. Inside the van were two little boys, Rajan's neighbour's kids, whom he had decided to include in the excursion. They were bouncing on the seats and banging on the window while the driver shouted at them. Sumnima gave many excuses to stay home but Rajan would not hear of it. He even coaxed Boju into joining them; Boju, who never left the house and considered herself too old for such frivolous jaunts. Only Manlahari refused to go. 'Leave her alone,' Boju said to Rajan, 'she'll just spoil the fun. Her face has been like a puffed-up roti since last month.' Besides, the taxi was already packed and they needed someone to guard the house. Before boarding the taxi, Boju made Ganga lock the bedrooms, the telephone box and the TV cabinet. Boju sat in the front seat while the rest of the party crammed together in the back. Ganga was shoved into the last row with the kids.

It was their first family meal in a restaurant. They sat at a large table and ordered everything that caught their eye. Pork momo, mushroom pizza, chicken burger with French fries, and grilled-meat platters that sizzled and released clouds of steam as the waiters carried them to the table. The adults ordered chilled beer and drank a toast 'to America'. Sumnima sat in a corner facing the wall, not wanting to be seen with this motley group of people. Her little cousins scampered about and kept colliding with the busy waiters. Her mother stuck a fork in a momo and squirted its oily juice on the table. Boju tore the pizza with her fingers and rolled it before putting it in her mouth, as though she were eating a roti. When Sumnima gently tried to correct her, she fumed and made an obscene hand gesture that made the waiter blush. Ganga was assigned to mind the children. She spent the two hours chasing after them, escorting them to the bathroom, mediating their fights and wiping their hands and mouths. When Rajan paid up and announced it was time to go, she was the first to leap for the door.

A storm was brewing when the revellers left the restaurant. Clouds rumbled as though giant boulders were hurtling across the sky. Rajan flagged down two taxis, one for the Tamule family and the other for him and the kids. They clambered into their respective vehicles and parted ways. A deafening clap of thunder drowned their boisterous goodbyes.

When they arrived, they found the house in a state of disorder—window shutters swinging and banging in the wind, doors slamming shut one after another, paper and plastic bags from the garbage pit flying in the air, chickens running about the yard in panic, and the vegetable patch strewn with undergarments that had blown off the clothesline on Sumnima's verandah.

'What the hell is she doing?' Boju roared. 'Hunting lice in her bush?'

Ganga leapt into action. She shut the windows, picked up the underwear, and put the chickens inside the coop before running upstairs to look for Manlahari. The door to their room was closed. 'Oi, open the door,' she said. 'Can't you see there's a storm coming?'

There was no answer. A pot fell in the neighbour's kitchen with a ringing sound that lasted almost a full minute. Ganga furiously turned the handle and pushed the door. It was open after all. Only, Manlahari was not in the room. Her things lay scattered. A few old clothes, ball pens, plastic bags, back issues of Nepali tabloids, empty nail polish bottles, postcards of Indian film stars. Ganga stared at the clutter, dumbstruck. She heard voices outside and leapt to the window—just some schoolgirls laughing as a gust of wind lifted their skirts. She shut the window and opened the steel almirah. It was empty. She opened the inner cabinets lined with newspapers, then climbed onto a stool and looked over the top compartment. Nothing. She knelt down and peered into the bottom compartment, found a stuffed plastic bag and ripped it open— just some old panties and period rags. Where was she? With a flash of hindsight she recalled that Manlahari had spent the whole afternoon yesterday cleaning her cupboard, ironing her clothes and arranging her things with that smug expression on her face. Had she run away? A chill ran through Ganga. She rushed out of the room and began searching every room, corridor, verandah and terrace. Manlahari was nowhere in sight. She checked the bathroom: Manlahari's shampoo was missing from the shelf. She ransacked the shoe rack outside the main door: both pairs of Manlahari's shoes were gone.

A bewildering mixture of shock, anger and pain gripped Ganga. The wind shook the trees, stopped passersby in their tracks and turned their umbrellas inside out. Waves of dust rose up from the sand and gravel piles at the building site. The sky roared, and then it rained.

~

Tamule ji had never seen such heavy rain in winter. It drummed on the roofs like bullets, drowning out all other sounds. The traffic on the ring road slowed down. Pedestrians ran pell-mell, covering their heads with handkerchiefs and plastic bags. The fields, houses and trees blurred into one another behind the slanting sheets. Tamule ji gazed out of the window till the rain subsided to a drizzle. A faint glow of sunset appeared over the dark-grey horizon. The houses slowly came into view. The last raindrops bounced and burst on the roofs in quick succession. Tamule ji grabbed an umbrella, put on his jacket and gumboots and strode out into the neighbourhood with an air of determined purpose. First he would gather clues from as many people as possible. Next morning he would go meet her teachers and track down her friends at her college. If nothing came of it, he might have to approach the police.

But he had only reached as far as Fancy Mart when Bhairey solved the mystery.

'Namaste, Tamule dai, looking for your niece?' he said, leaning over the counter, his face framed in a monkey cap that only showed his eyes, nose and mouth. Tamule ji stopped and looked at him in surprise. 'I saw her earlier,' Bhairey said. 'She came here around two o'clock to make a phone call.'

'Really?'

'Yes, she was carrying two huge bags. I asked her where she was headed but she didn't answer.'

'Eh.'

'She seemed in a rush. I couldn't hear what she said on the phone, she was talking in whispers, but immediately after she hung up, a guy came on a motorcycle. Then she sat behind him and off they went God knows where.'

'Are you sure?' Tamule ji said, slightly irritated by Bhairey's eager tone.

'Absolutely. I saw with my own two eyes. I kept wondering who he was. Thin-thin, with longish red-red hair. Never seen him around.'

'Hm.'

'To be honest,' Bhairey said, lowering his voice, 'he looked like a tyape.'

Tamule ji turned around and walked back home. It was getting dark. Water drained away through roof outlets, flowed down the eaves and hammered into the cans and buckets lined below with an unsettling sound. Tamule ji slowly walked back home, his gumboots squelching as he waded through puddles. 'Shameless ingrate,' he said to himself. 'Wait till the romance turns to hunger pangs.'

46

News of Manlahari's elopement spread fast throughout the neighbourhood. Within days it was established that she had run away with a tyape who stole pots and pans from his own house to fulfill his craving for smack. There were conflicting speculations about his caste. One of Premkala's relatives said the boy was a Magar from the western hills, the degenerate son of a Gurkha lahure. Devi said he was a Newar boy whose family owned a house in Kathmandu. 'Ha, those Jyapus are so communal they'll never let her into their house,' Boju said gleefully. Tamule ji contained his rage and waited, hoping his niece might return and prove them all wrong, but when no word came from her even after two weeks, he took up a pen with a heavy heart and wrote to his brother in Assam, apprising him of his daughter's ignominious act. He also called his relatives in Lungla and dutifully gave them the news. Thulkaki clucked her tongue and said, 'Like mother, like daughter.' Tamule ji wished he could bury his head in shame. His conversations with the neighbours grew strained as they tried to avoid the subject that was foremost in their minds. 'Did you hear?' he imagined them saying afterward. 'Tamule's niece went poila with a tyape.'

Manlahari's absence seemed to have sucked all vitality out of Ganga. She seemed withdrawn and often sat brooding like a person in mourning. Her guardians began to worry she might follow in her cousin's footsteps and leave the family in the lurch. In Premkala's view, it was not homesickness or Manlahari's absence that had brought down Ganga's spirits but her cooped-up existence. She decided to engage her in some gainful activity outside the house. After exploring a range of options from a cooking course to counter sales work, Premkala finally found a job that seemed right for Ganga. The preschool down the road was looking for a part-time assistant. The school proprietor, reluctant at first, hired Ganga after realizing he could pay her peanuts. 'Thousand rupees a month is not bad for part-time work,' Tamule ji exhorted his niece. 'You know how much my first salary was?'

Ganga took the job. Every day after serving the morning meal, she would walk to the school and spend a few hours in its brightly painted classroom. She would put together teaching materials for the teacher, chaperone the kids during playtime, clap her hands when they chanted English rhymes, and help them with their snacks, tossing pieces into her mouth when no one was looking. She welcomed the change in her routine, even though her supervisor, a young woman her age, snapped at her for being slow, and some of the kids punched her and yanked her hair for fun. Each passing day lessened the shock of Manlahari's elopement, and after some time, it was as though she had never been there at all.

47

Balram Sir had kept his promise and Sumnima had scraped through her mid-term exams. She returned to school in a zestful mood, wearing a baggy sweater over her tight skirt and a new pair of woollen stockings. On her way to class one morning, she ran into Balram Sir on the stairs. She hadn't met him since the incident in his office. She looked down and tried to slink past him, to spare him the embarrassment of facing her, but he blocked her path and said, 'Oho, Sumnima, ke cha?' His tone was friendly but authoritative, as though he wanted to show that he had nothing to hide, that he remained every bit as respectable as his position demanded, that his attempt to grab her breast in his office had not diminished him. 'Your finals are coming soon, better study hard.' A group of students walked up the stairs and greeted him good morning. He waited for them to pass. 'Remember,' he said, 'I can't help you if you flunk this time. Last time it was a special favour.' Sumnima remembered the sensation of his hand and felt goosebumps all over her body. She felt a strong urge to send that round mass of flesh rolling down the stairs, but she merely shook her head and walked away.

~

Sagar had called Sumnima once during Tihar and disappeared again. After calling his office many times and receiving the same vague answer from the receptionist, she swallowed her pride and asked for his co-worker Roshan ji. 'He said he was going to India, but that's all I know, sorry,' Roshan ji said. His pitying tone suggested he was fully aware of her predicament. Beneath her shame and anger, Sumnima couldn't help wondering why Sagar might have gone to India. As far as she knew, he had no family, friends, or professional contacts in India. Couldn't he at least have called her before leaving and spared her embarrassment of having to ask his colleague? There was only one thing she ought to do now: cut him off from her life. The wound would not heal unless it was cauterized. Sumnima took up a pen and started writing a letter, knowing, even as she wrote it, that the letter would never see the light of day. Over the past months she had composed break-up letters of every variety—a brief note with a parting shot, an anguished letter meant to turn his heart, a scathing letter that exposed his worst traits, and a heartfelt essay written in the hope that someday in the distant future, a repentant Sagar would come back begging for her love, only to hear her say, 'Sorry, it's too late.' But one phone call from Sagar was enough to destroy her resolve and get her to tear all those scrupulously composed letters to shreds.

~

It was the final scene of the Saturday afternoon Hindi feature film. A mortal combat was taking place in a vast warehouse setting. Shots were being fired and the villains being pummelled amid loud punch-and-kick sound effects. 'Serves you right, saley,' said Ganga, who sat on the floor with a bowl of garlic pods before her.

'That one should get a few more kicks,' Boju chimed in, squinting behind her new glasses.

Sumnima sat slouched in a chair, scowling, her legs stretched on the tea table. Sagar had not called her for almost two months. She had been half-heartedly preparing for her final exams. Her undergarments had been soaking in detergent for days. A kind of creeping inertia had led her to spend a full hour on a film that she thought was beneath her taste. Predictable plot, soppy dialogues, melodramatic scenes. Yet the film seemed to wring Ganga's heart. Poor Ganga didi, Sumnima thought, she needs some distraction. The preschool had fired her a few days ago to make room for an SLC-passed candidate.

After dutifully handing the maimed, bloody-nosed villains over to the police, the hero embraced his loved ones and burst into a song, bringing a smile to Ganga's face. The film was over. The thickly curtained room suddenly felt bleak and stuffy. Sumnima stretched herself, half rose and sank back into the chair. Boju yawned, opening her mouth so wide Sumnima could see the yellowish coating at the back of her tongue. Ganga sat still, weighed down by the melancholy that washed over her every time a movie came to an end.

It was time for commercials. The three women watched one ad after another in a stupefied daze. Upbeat jingles about a skin-softening soap, a healthy cooking oil, and a tyre that would last a hundred years.

The sound of heels clicking up the stairs broke their trance.

All three heads turned towards the door. A sweet, cloying scent wafted across the room before the shapely figure appeared before their eyes.

'Namaste, Boju. Hi Sumnima didi!' Boju, Sumnima and Ganga stared with eyes wide open. The young woman standing poised on her heels was none other than Manlahari. Manlahari, who was supposed to be languishing in some godforsaken hole with an addict. Only last week Devi said she had bumped into her in a tempo, looking pale and malnourished, her clothes stained with grease and turmeric. All the way to Sundhara the poor wretch had looked away from her and covered her face with a hanky, so Boju was told. Could Devi have seen someone else? Boju thought, adjusting her glasses. Malnourished? Quite the opposite. She looked fitter and finer than ever, like a lady, in a flowing pink kurta surwal and a handbag in her arm, her face radiant with health and makeup, hair set into spiral curls. A married lady, Boju reckoned, noticing the gold tilhari on her neck. And it had hardly been three months since she left.

Manhalari took off her shoes and stood at the door for a moment, allowing them to collect themselves. Her bright, bemused eyes bore no trace of remorse. 'Ammai!' said Boju. 'I almost didn't recognize you.' Manlahari came in and handed her a bag of fruit.

'Bless you,' Boju said with a smile. 'Ganga, open the curtains.' Ganga rose stiffly and pulled the curtains apart. Light flooded the room. Boju picked up the remote control and turned off the television. Sumnima got up and offered Manlahari her chair, the only one left in the room.

'No, no, I'll sit on the floor,' Manlahari said.

'No, no, just sit here,' Sumnima insisted.

'No, no, you sit...'

Ganga smiled uneasily at this mutual display of politeness.

'Gangotri, stop gawping and go get a chair from the verandah,' said Boju, carefully stowing her fruit bag away. Ganga's face darkened. She left the room, stepping on the heeled shoes in the doorway. When she returned with a chair, she found the three of them deep in conversation.

'We got married at Guheswari Temple,' Manlahari was saying. 'Just a simple tika-talo. We only told his family afterwards. Of course they were angry, but they couldn't kick their son out, could they?'

'And his family? Are they okay?' Boju asked.

'He comes from a good family,' Manlahari hastily replied. 'They have a house in Ghattekulo. He's the youngest of three sons, and has two sisters, both married. His father held a permanent job at the government post office, poor man, died of a stroke last year. But his mother. A horrible woman, she called me a whore because I wore pants, imagine?'

'O God,' sighed Sumnima.

Ganga softly chuckled to herself.

'Well,' Manlahari said, 'I bore with her for two weeks, then finally I told him, 'Either we leave this house or I leave you.' So we moved into a small, dungeon-like room in Koteshwor. I'd rather live in a dungeon than with that evil woman.'

Sumnima and Boju supportively nodded their heads.

'She's been spreading vile rumours about me since we left. Still goes around saying, 'that beggarly girl ruined my home, cast black magic spells over my son, stole pots and pans from my kitchen,' and so on and so forth.'

Boju and Sumnima drew audible gasps of shock even though the story sounded a little overblown to their ears.

'That witch tried hard to separate us,' Manlahari fumed. 'She sent her older sons to poison his ears, but he didn't listen. So guess what they're planning to do? They're planning to eat all the property. The house, the land, the old furniture—his brothers want to take everything.'

'That's too much,' Boju cried.

'But then, just as I began to curse my fate, God answered my prayers,' Manlahari said, her face lighting up. It seemed she had reached the part of the story she was most keen to share. 'An old friend of his works in Japan, and with his help, he just got a Japanese visa.'

'Oho, sanchhai?' Boju exclaimed. 'He's going to Japan?'

'Yes, he's leaving next month.'

'Does he have a job?' Sumnima asked.

'Yes, he'll be working with his friend,' Manlahari said proudly, 'in a factory, they build auto parts. I'm so relieved. But we're not going to let his brothers get away so easily.'

'Of course not,' Boju said.

'I heard I can even file a court case against them. But I don't know how such things work. Actually, I really want to consult Kaka Kaki about it.' She paused for a moment. 'But I guess they're still mad at me, are they?'

'They'll be fine,' said Boju. 'What's past is past.'

'Really?'

'Of course,' said Sumnima. 'You've committed no crime.'

Manlahari smiled, shed a few tears and laughed out of embarrassment. Energized by this unusual atmosphere of goodwill and harmony, Sumnima clapped her hands and said, 'On that note, let's have a nice cup of tea, shall we?'

Everyone turned to Ganga, who sullenly picked up the bowl of garlic and headed towards the kitchen.

48

'Didi, I'm glad you've come to your senses. Life is short. No point wasting your time on people who don't value you…'

Sumnima smiled as she read the letter. Numa the fount of practical wisdom—if only she knew the truth. Not only had Sumnima trashed the breakup letter, she spent all her waking hours waiting for Sagar's phone call. Her horoscope forecast that morning had suggested her romantic troubles would end soon, and she felt positive and hopeful after a long time.

'You know why my friends and I enjoy life? None of us are caught up in boy issues. You'll be so much happier without—'

Sumnima heard the phone ringing. Her gut instinct told her it was Sagar. She jumped up and rushed downstairs, her anger fading fast, tender feelings coursing through her. It had been three months since she heard his voice. She made sure no one was within hearing range before answering the phone.

'Hi Sumnima. How are you?'

Hope died in her. The voice was of a young woman, familiar but not quite.

'Who's this?' Sumnima asked.

'What? You forgot me within two years?'

Sumnima cried in sudden recognition, 'Reshma!'

They spent a few moments blaming each other for losing touch before Reshma came to the point. It was Tejaswi's wedding the following weekend and she had left Sumnima's invitation card at Reshma's house. The wedding, initially scheduled for spring, had been postponed at the suggestion of their family astrologer.

'Do you want to come by and pick up your card?' Reshma asked.

Sumnima thought for a moment. A few weeks ago she had spotted Rajani aunty in a department store, reading a shampoo label in the toiletries aisle. Sumnima had slipped past her without greeting her, unsure whether Rajani aunty, now a prominent gender expert, would recognize her.

'Never mind,' said Sumnima. 'I'll come directly to the reception.'

'OK, it's at 6 p.m., at their residence. I heard the King and Queen have also been invited. What will you wear? Tejaswi said I should wear a sari. Great, let's both wear saris. See you there. Bye!'

Sumnima hung up with a sigh. She felt a strange weariness at the prospect of meeting her old friends. They already seemed to belong to a closed chapter of her life. She wondered what might have held them together for so long. The shared laughter and secrets and those fervid promises of lasting friendship seemed hollow in retrospect. There was nothing solid to cling to.

~

The wedding house looked magnificent under the night sky. Hundreds of string lights were draped over the windows, verandah railings and trees. A military band stood near the gate and played one tune after another. The drumbeat and the shrill pipe music echoed throughout the neighbourhood. The guests stood in small groups under a massive tent pitched in the garden, chatting and sipping their drinks. Young women in glittering saris and short-sleeved blouses clustered shivering around the kerosene heaters. The bride and groom sat in gilded chairs on a lavishly decorated dais, greeting a continuous stream of guests.

Sumnima, dressed in a sari for the first time, felt exceedingly self-conscious as she walked up to the dais. She congratulated the wedded pair, barely registering the face of the groom, and offered Tejaswi a gift-wrapped pashmina shawl that had cost her a fortune even at a wholesale store. Tejaswi thanked her with a wan smile. She looked a little tired and overwhelmed by the enormous garland hanging from her neck. Several women milled about her, touching up her makeup, arranging her gifts, whispering instructions in her ear. It took Sumnima a moment to realize that the skinny woman adjusting the bride's veil was Anushka dijju, Tejaswi's older sister. She hadn't seen her since she got married eight years ago. Although decked out in a sequined sari and abundant jewellery, Anushka dijju looked like a ghost of her former self. Her cheeks were sunken and there were dark circles around her eyes. Her hair, artfully puffed up and held with a crescent-shaped gold clip, did not hide her balding pate. Sumnima ventured a tentative smile at her. Anushka nodded in faint recognition.

Sumnima had barely exchanged a few words with Tejaswi when one of the aunties darted forward and told her to make way for other guests. She stepped down from the dais and wandered around for some time, carefully holding her sari pleats, searching for a familiar face in the crowd. Suddenly a pair of cold hands grabbed her shoulders from behind. She shrieked and turned around to find Reshma laughing at her. 'Scared you, didn't I?' she said. Sumnima watched her in surprise. Not only had Reshma lost a lot of weight, she also looked very stylish in an electric blue sari and a silver blouse, an ensemble that stood out among the throng of women dressed in red and gold. Her face looked fresh with subtle shimmery makeup, and her short, bouncy haircut added vibrancy to her bearing. There was also a certain coyness in her manner that Sumnima had not noticed before, in the way she cocked her head and flashed a half smile as she spoke. A few minutes into their conversation, Reshma revealed what Sumnima had been guessing all along: she had a boyfriend. 'We met at a party just last month,' she said. 'So I don't know him that well.' She paused, as if measuring how much to give away, and added, 'But our parents have known each other for a long time. His family owns Alpine Brewery and the Greenside Resort.'

'Eh, I see.' Sumnima looked suitably impressed.

'We are both applying to colleges in America,' Reshma said. 'I really hope we'll end up in the same college, or at least the same town.'

Sumnima felt a twinge of envy. The medical colleges her father was exploring were all in Nepal. A few of them were in districts outside Kathmandu.

'And you?' Reshma said. 'Do you have a boyfriend?'

Sumnima still didn't know how to answer this question. Sagar had grown more elusive than ever. He hadn't even called her before leaving for India. She had no idea if he was back in town.

'No, I enjoy being single,' she replied somewhat loftily.

~

Sumnima and Reshma walked around the tent guessing who was who in the crowd. It seemed all the movers and shakers of Kathmandu had congregated at Manjari Niwas that evening. Royal Nepal Army officers, top politicians, foreign diplomats, media house owners, prominent businessmen, bankers, and so on. Reshma knew some of the guests through her parents and reluctantly went over to greet them, while Sumnima stood near a heater and waited for her. Although she felt distant from Reshma, she appreciated her company at the moment. She felt cushioned by Reshma's energy and confidence, the ease with which she moved in that exclusive circle. Reshma spent a while talking to a tall, dignified, middle-aged man in a dark suit and glasses. The minute he turned around to greet someone, she hurried back to Sumnima, sighing over the prolonged exchange of banalities. 'That's Dr Pandey,' she said. 'His daughter Prerana was in our class till sixth grade, remember?' Sumnima nodded and glanced at him again. Many years ago her father had returned from Dr Pandey's clinic seething with powerless rage. 'I'll never visit him again, never!' he had cried like a petulant child, as if his absence would make a scratch on Dr Pandey's flourishing practice. Sumnima was wondering how that suave-looking gentleman could have offended her father when a hum of excitement ran through the crowd. 'Their Majesties have arrived!'

Everyone rose and straightened their postures. The band started playing the national anthem. Uniformed army personnel paced the driveway speaking into their walkie-talkies. A gleaming black Mercedes drove in through the open gate and stopped near the portico at the entrance. The crowd watched in silence. An aide held the door as the King and Queen disembarked from the car. The hosts led them towards the bridal dais, flanked by bodyguards, followed by cameramen. Sumnima and Reshma waited near the dais with a group of women in red saris and buffed hairstyles. 'I've never seen raja-rani in real life,' Sumnima said to Reshma in a breathless whisper. A woman who stood behind them tapped Sumnima's shoulder. 'Tch, tch,' she said in a low voice, 'don't say raja-rani, say sarkar.' Sumnima nodded and gave her a guilty smile.

Sumnima felt her heart pounding as the royal pair approached them. Taking a cue from the aunties, she bowed her head, touched her nose and said in a trembling voice, 'Darshan, sarkar.' For a fleeting instant she thought she saw the King look directly at her and smile, bringing her senses to a standstill. It was the first time she had come face to face with him. Until then she had experienced his glory only through pictures, anthems, textbooks and Nepal Television footage. She felt ennobled by his grace. Their Majesties greeted the newlyweds and were promptly led inside to be entertained among other dignitaries behind closed doors. Sumnima could not catch another glimpse of the royal couple.

As Sumnima and Reshma sat down for dinner, Tejaswi's cousin Samriddhi came and joined them at the table. She too was now married to a military officer, but her husband had recently been posted to a remote district in west Nepal.

'I can't even visit him,' she said, putting a spoonful of pulao into her mouth. 'He says the place is infested with Maoist terrorists.'

'That's scary,' Sumnima said. 'Can't he return to Kathmandu?'

'No, he's posted there till the end of the year,' Samriddhi said with a frown. 'But he'll be in town next week, for an anti-terrorism seminar.'

'One of Daddy's party members got beaten by the Maoists last week,' said Reshma. 'He's in Kathmandu for treatment. He said those hooligans hate people with land and money.'

'Bloody terrorists,' Samriddhi said. 'I hear there are women Maoists too.'

'Daddy said there's nothing to fear,' Reshma said. 'The police have been sent across the country, they are crushing those terrorists like insects.'

'They better,' Samriddhi said.

Sumnima had gathered, in bits and pieces, that some kind of conflict was brewing in the countryside. She often heard her father lamenting the death and destruction reported in the newspapers. She remembered Sagar saying the government should 'grow some balls' and mobilize the army to control the situation. But she could not fully grasp the situation. The turmoil seemed too distant to have any bearing on her life. 'By the way,' she said, changing the topic, 'Anushka dijju looks so different. Is she okay?'

Samriddhi laid down her spoon, bent forward and said in a hushed undertone, 'Poor dijju, she's been through rough times. Only between us, but her prince turned out to be a monster. Last month he got sloshed and tried to strangle her.'

'Really?'

'Yes. It's been going on for years. Now she wants a divorce, but her father is against the idea.'

'Why?' Sumnima and Reshma asked in unison.

'He thinks divorce will bring shame upon the family. And he doesn't want to cut off ties with her in-laws, they're Indian royalty.' Samridhi paused and looked around. 'I heard he used to beat Manjari aunty when he got drunk.'

Sumnima and Reshma gasped in shock.

'A half-bred scoundrel,' Samriddhi said, wiping her mouth.

49

The long-awaited call finally came one spring morning. But the timing was far from perfect. As Sumnima picked up the phone, she saw her mother grading papers on the verandah outside the landing door.

'Hey, how are you?' Sagar said in a cheerful voice.

'Hi! Can I call you later?' Sumnima said, her thoughts all in a muddle.

'I just wanted to ask,' Sagar said, 'can you come by my office? Say around one?'

'But it's Holi, they'll throw balloons,' Sumnima said, one eye fixed on her mother, who was shaking her head as if she'd spotted a silly error.

'They're balloons, not bullets,' Sagar chuckled. 'Can't you take a cab?'

Sumnima couldn't think clearly. She saw her mother close the pen, bundle up the papers and get up from her chair.

'All right, see you at one, bye!' She hung up the instant her mother came in.

'Baba?' she asked.

'No, a classmate,' Sumnima said without batting an eyelid. 'One of our teachers was rushed to emergency last night. We have to go see her today.'

'I thought it was your Baba. He's coming back today. Maoists have attacked a police post in the area, so they can't travel further.'

'Oh no.' Sumnima made a worried expression.

'What happened to your teacher?' her mother asked.

'I'm not sure, I'll go find out,' said Sumnima, and ran up to her room.

It was only after she closed the door behind her that the reality of her brief exchange with Sagar sank in. Sagar had reached out after four months of silence. He seemed impatient to see her. Had he had some kind of epiphany during their long separation?

It was eleven o'clock. Sumnima jumped into the shower, not even bothering to ask Ganga for a bucket of hot water. She crooned, laughed and shivered as she soaped and rinsed herself, thrilled by the sensation of the ice-cold water. She dried herself off and rubbed lotion all over her body, massaging her legs and arms and belly and breasts, luxuriating in the feel of her smooth, naked skin. It was a public holiday. Sagar would be alone in the office. She took out her black lacy lingerie, removed the price tags and slipped them on. Anything might happen with just the two of them in that huge empty building. What if—no, she wouldn't go that far, not today. She smiled at the slender and seductive figure in the mirror. After trying on at least three outfits, she settled on a pair of jeans and a red camisole that showed her cleavage if she bent a little. She sat on a sunny patch near the window and combed her damp hair and plucked her eyebrows and painted her nails. Shouts of laughter rose from the houses and made her giddy with happiness.

~

The entire neighbourhood was celebrating Holi. Men, women and children ran around their yards throwing colours and water at each other. On Devi didi's terrace, Rishiram and his friends hid behind the water tank and threw water balloons at passersby. A balloon hit a target; the boys slapped each other's backs and doubled up with laughter.

Ganga had gathered some neighbourhood kids to play Holi. They sat near the drum filling water balloons, their sleeves rolled up above their elbows, trousers folded up to their knees. 'O Gangeshwari, stop wasting water!' Boju yelled from somewhere. Ganga tittered and bit her tongue. She opened the tap and let the water stream into the balloon until it swelled and turned translucent. She tied its end into a knot and put it in a tub filled with colourful water balloons. 'Old hen, shame on you playing with those children,' Boju cried. 'Why don't you go play with your own balloons?' The kids looked at Ganga and giggled.

Ganga had not found another job yet. A few weeks ago her aunt had enrolled her in a dhaka-weaving workshop run by a relative from Tehrathum. At first Ganga was unenthusiastic. She had grown up seeing Rai and Limbu women in the hills ply the traditional loom in their homes. She saw it as a dying, backward trade. But after joining the workshop, she realized she didn't entirely detest it. There was a soothing quality to the thump and clatter of the loom, and the repetitive rhythm of her hands moving in sync with her feet. Although she didn't dream of ever mastering the craft, she liked to watch the fabric come into being thread by thread, and the colourful patterns emerging before her eyes. Her fellow weavers were mostly young women from outside Kathmandu. They would walk home together after the training, stopping to drink tea or buy vegetables. 'My training is so much fun,' Ganga would boast aloud when Manlahari visited the Tamule house. 'How nice,' Manlahari would say with an offhand smile. Ganga felt she no longer had any power to incite her envy, if she ever did at all. It hurt her how easily her uncle and aunt had accepted Manlahari back into their lives. Even Boju seemed to have forgiven her now that she had a life of her own, independent of the Tamule household. 'Ganga, bring Manlahari a nice cup of tea.' Every time she heard these words, Ganga felt like smashing something.

~

Sumnima threw a black pashmina shawl over her camisole, picked up her bag and ran down the stairs. 'Don't be late,' her mother shouted from her room. 'Which hospital by the way?' Sumnima ignored her. She opened the main door to find a little boy aiming a balloon at her. 'You want a slap?' she warned. The kid backed away and let her pass. As she went out through the gate, she heard whispers and giggles coming from Devi didi's terrace. The boys seemed poised for action. She tightened her grip on her shawl and quickened her pace as she passed the house. Just you try, you idiots, she muttered under her breath. To her great relief, they didn't throw any balloons at her. Had they run out of their stock? 'Miss, don't be afraid,' one of them shouted. 'Rishi won't let us hit you.' There was a wave of laughter. Rishiram pounced on his friend and covered his mouth, but the boy wrestled free. 'Miss, why did you break our Romeo's hurt?' Sumnima kept walking with a resolute gait, chuckling softly over his pronunciation. 'Our Romeo is still waiting for your reply!' Sumnima strode fast, embarrassed and a little sorry for that luckless admirer of hers. According to Ganga, Rishiram had failed his first-year exams and Devi didi was trying to send him to Korea for employment. Poor guy, she thought, walking past the houses at various stages of completion, and forgot about him by time she reached the ring road. The road was empty. The jacaranda trees were in flower. Blooming creepers covered the mass of tangled up wires that hung between the poles. Sumnima found an autorickshaw just in time to escape a group of bare-chested, helmet-less, colour-smeared men on speeding motorbikes.

Sagar's office was housed in a large residential building with a front garden. Sumnima had never seen the place so quiet. No murmur of voices, no hum of machines, no generator noise. Although she knew the receptionist wouldn't be there, she felt a palpable sense of relief on seeing the desk near the entrance empty. She removed her shawl to flaunt her arms and deep collarbones. She stopped in front of the glass door and touched up her lipstick before climbing the wide marble stairs. It was so quiet she could hear the thud of her own heartbeat. She had visited the office many times before but never properly looked into the rooms. Usually she would run up the stairs as soon as the receptionist allowed her in and head straight for Sagar's cubicle without looking left or right. She worried about the impression she made on his colleagues, those tame and respectable office-goers. They knew she was not exactly a friend of Sagar's, nor a girlfriend, nor a professional contact.

Sagar was alone in the room he normally shared with Roshan ji. He sat with his back to the door, staring at the image of a grimy little boy on his computer screen. She stopped at the door and waited for him to greet her, but he seemed not to have heard her footsteps.

'Hello, busy bee,' she said.

'Hey,' he said, turning around. 'Come sit down. Can you give me a minute?'

Sumnima placed her shawl on the back of the chair. Although his preoccupied air rankled her, she felt a spasm of longing for him when she sat beside him. He looked pleasant and casual in his t-shirt, track pants and hiking sandals. His hair was damp from a recent shower and his face freshly shaven. He looked leaner than she remembered. Had he lost weight or was it just his loose clothing? She also noticed for the first time that he had nice feet with well-shaped toes and clean, clipped toenails. She waited quietly while he touched up the face on the screen using various Photoshop tools. 'I have to send this brochure by tonight,' he said, leaning back to examine the zoomed-out image. Then he closed the computer window, turned to her and said with a relieved sigh, 'Done.'

Sumnima smiled and waited. She wished he would move closer, embrace her, quench the desire that had been tormenting her for months. But he glanced at his watch and said in a distracted manner, 'So how have you been?'

Sumnima felt a stab of pain. Why did he seem so distant even in such an exquisitely private moment?

'So you were in India all last month?' she asked.

'Yes,' he said. 'I went to visit a friend in Banaras.'

Sumnima looked surprised and amused. Banaras sounded so antiquated coming from his mouth. That was where her grandfather had wished to die. He had wanted his earthly body to be laid on a sandalwood pyre on the banks of the Ganga before it turned to ashes. The poor old man had had no such luck. He was doubled up inside a doko on a porter's back, being rushed to a doctorless health post when he breathed his last.

'She's interested in death rites,' Sagar explained. 'She wanted to see the ghats.'

The feminine pronoun cut through her like a knife. She had a sudden premonition of an impending disaster and wanted to forestall it anyhow.

'So have you fixed a date for your photo exhibit?' Sumnima said in an unnaturally bubbly voice.

'Not yet,' Sagar said, and added with a weak smile, 'but I do have to tell you something.'

The smile gave her a strange, queasy feeling in the pit of her stomach.

'I hope you'll be happy for me,' he said, with an almost shy expression that seemed eerily out of character. 'You've been such an awesome friend to me.'

Sumnima kept quiet and braced herself.

'I think I mentioned her to you a few times,' he said in a calm, measured tone. 'We came to Kathmandu together three years ago.'

Sumnima could only stare. The American ex-girlfriend?

'We had lost touch after we broke up. But last month, out of the blue, I got an email from her. She was going to Banaras and asked me to join her there. Life is so unpredictable,' he said with a wistful sigh. 'We had a great time in Banaras. It's such a cool place.'

'Where is she now?'

'She's in town actually, staying at a lodge in Thamel.' He paused as if to gauge her reaction. Then, seeing her smile in a strained but unthreatening manner, he went on, 'She says she wants to live in Nepal for a few years, work here, be with me.'

Sumnima's head was reeling. Her throat tightened and tears stung her eyes.

'Such is destiny,' Sagar said airily. 'I had no such plans, but I guess there's no harm settling down. I'm getting old anyway.' He tilted his head and gazed at her for a long minute, as if trying to store her face in his memory. 'Unlike you, so young and beautiful, with the world at your feet. I'm so glad we got to know each other.'

Sumnima looked at him in mute terror, unable to grasp the reality of what was happening. Her nostrils tingled; the tears were about to fall. She pulled herself together and rose decisively from the chair.

'I must go now,' she said.

'Really? So soon?'

'Yes, I'm getting late.'

'OK, if you insist,' Sagar said with a rueful sigh.

Sumnima glared at him in utter disbelief. He hesitated, his lips stretched into an odd grin. 'If you want,' he said in a feeble voice, 'I can drop you off to a taxi round the corner.'

Sumnima made a sharp turn and walked out of the door, hot tears streaming down her cheeks. Sagar did not come chasing after her. It was only when she exited the building and marched out through the gate that she realized with a pang: Sagar had dumped her, abruptly and unceremoniously. She turned into a lane strewn with burst balloons, stopped and looked back at the office, now partly hidden behind an unfinished multistorey building. She pulled a handkerchief from her bag, wiped her eyes and blew her nose. She walked slowly, clinging to a last thread of hope that he might come after her on his motorcycle and console her with words he'd left unsaid. Did she make a mistake leaving so impetuously?

She had almost reached the main street junction when an object came flying at great velocity and smashed against her left cheek. The pain numbed her for an instant. A ringing sound came from somewhere deep inside her ear. Threads of water coursed down her neck towards her bare chest and trickled down the gap between her breasts. She rubbed her smarting cheek and glared at the house from where the ambush had been launched. A faded two-storey concrete building with a dirty towel hanging from the verandah railing. Its narrow front yard was cluttered with steel pipes, bricks and empty tin cans. A chained dog was sleeping on the floor, morsels of stale rice strewn around its grimy bowl. The house looked hushed and still, except for the swinging shutter on a top-floor window. Sumnima waited. A head popped above the windowsill and disappeared. She heard a chuckle, then smothered voices. Without another thought she picked up a stone from the path and hurled it full force at the window. It hit the glass pane, shattering it. The dog rose and started barking. Frantic voices came from inside the house. A baby squalled. A middle-aged woman came rushing out to the verandah, her unbound breasts jiggling under her cotton maxi gown.

'Oi, pay for our window or I'll call the police!' she yelled, using the impolite form of 'you'.

'Go call them!' Sumnima shot back, using the same discourteous pronoun. 'They'll throw your kids in jail.'

Faces appeared in the neighbouring windows. A girl about Sumnima's age came outside to join forces with the woman. Her head was wrapped in a plastic bag that leaked dark trails of henna on her forehead. She gripped the railing with her orange hands and screamed above the barking and the wailing, 'What do you think you are? Should I set the dog on you?'

'I'm not scared of your mangy little stray!' Sumnima yelled, defiantly thrusting out her chin. She felt capable of knocking anyone down at that moment.

'First you break our window, then you bark at us?' the girl roared, wagging her finger at Sumnima. 'You should be dumped in a madhouse!' She inclined her head to stop the flow of henna. 'Don't you know it's Holi? Who told you to go tramping about looking like a slut? Look at you, one might as well go naked.'

Sumnima took a deep breath and cast a withering look at the two women. 'Ha!' she said. 'What can one expect from such ill-bred, uneducated, *pakhe* people? Cast a stone at a lump of shit and you only soil yourself.'

'You...you...you...' the woman in the maxi stuttered, her face swollen red.

'Ill-bred?' The girl snorted a laugh. 'Says the one who looks like she just got banged behind a bush.' The woman in the maxi glanced at the grinning faces next door. She nudged the girl, but the girl kept shouting, 'Why should I be afraid? I'll say it like it is. What can that bitch do to us?'

'O just shut up and go to hell!' Sumnima bellowed, and turned to leave.

'*Set up and go to hell,*' the girl parodied her words in a high-pitched voice. 'You think your English rant will scare us? Go show your angrezi to someone else!'

She carried on in this vein for a while until the older woman calmed her down and dragged her inside the house. The onlookers retreated into their homes. Sumnima hurried towards the junction, stopped a Vikram tempo and hopped on board. A few minutes into the ride, she noticed a middle-aged man sitting across from her staring at her breasts. She hunched over and pressed her handbag to her chest. Only then did she remember that she had left her shawl in Sagar's office.

50

Sumnima was crushed. She spent many days brooding in her room, assailed by hurt, anger and shame. She prayed that the worst of disasters would befall Sagar, and derived fleeting comfort from dramatic fantasies of revenge. What if she barged into his office, like the jilted lover in a Hindi movie, and slapped him in front of his colleagues? Or exposed him as a two-timer before his American girlfriend? In calmer moments, her outrage seemed entirely groundless. After all, he had made no promises and owed her nothing. If she dared confront him, he would set the record straight with a cool smile. He seemed invulnerable, capable of emerging from every situation unscathed. Any attempt to spite him and drag him down would only blow up in her own face.

Her final exams were a few weeks away. Balram, that lecherous swine, reminded her of his 'special favour' every time he met her. Sumnima couldn't bear the thought of having to beg him for grace marks again. She gritted her teeth, buckled down and began studying as if she were preparing for battle. She told herself she had found a purpose higher than Sagar, though at the back of her mind she kept hoping he would change his mind, or at least call her under the pretext of returning her shawl. Sometimes she felt like throwing prudence to the winds and calling him to ask if he still cared for her. At other times, the very idea seemed outrageously stupid.

Days turned to weeks. At the beginning of summer, Sumnima took her final exams and bid goodbye to her friends at Galileo International Academy.

Sagar did not call.

~

Numa passed her first-year exam and came home for the summer, bringing fresh energy and laughter into the house. She exuded the confidence of a person who has seen new places and learned new things. Sumnima set everything aside and took refuge in her company. The summer was warmer than the previous one. As the top-floor was unbearably hot during the day, the girls spent most of their afternoons in the yard, under the shade of the gourd vines. Numa sent Sumnima into fits of laughter with her animated impersonations of her classmates. Once in a while Boju would scream from somewhere, 'Laugh softly, it sounds like a whorehouse!' This made the girls howl even louder. Their noise sometimes brought Rishiram out on the terrace. He would sit in the sweltering heat strumming his guitar as long as the girls stayed in the yard. 'Your Shah Rukh Khan is roasting himself alive,' Numa would say. But Sumnima did not feel like making fun of him anymore. His small act of decency—of refusing to throw balloons at her—had transformed him from an object of ridicule into a person worthy of sympathy. In her heartbroken and humiliated state, she even saw him as a fellow sufferer. She wished him well and hoped he would soon get a job in Korea.

One evening the sisters sat on the verandah after dinner and talked deep into the night.

'I wonder what she looks like,' Sumnima said.

'Ugly I'm sure,' said Numa.

Sumnima smiled, pleased to hear this. She looked around at the houses where people lay asleep and dreaming. She looked at the sky. Big stars and small stars, twinkling stars and dull stars, lonely stars and grouped stars, stars arranged like a question mark, stars arranged like a polygon—the sky above Bhaisichaur had never looked starrier.

'I feel sorry for that woman,' Numa said, 'Apparently all her tapasya failed to open her eyes.'

Her hushed voice echoed in the midnight's silence.

'Maybe she's the right person for him,' Sumnima said. 'Maybe I just wasn't good enough.'

'And you think he was good enough?' Numa said. 'Give nothing, only take take take. A small-hearted, stingy little man, he'd never make you happy. '

~

The month flew by and it was time for Numa to return to India. She went out with her friends, ate momos at her favourite restaurants and made courtesy visits to her relatives. She made multiple trips to Bishal Bazaar and bought foreign-made clothes and toiletries to impress her roommates. Sumnima accompanied her everywhere. She sometimes went all day without thinking of Sagar, and when she did, she felt no rancour, only subdued pain. As they cruised around the city in a taxi, looking out at the shops, temples and passersby, Numa would rhapsodize about Kathmandu, a city grown dear to her while away, and Sumnima felt she too had come home after a long spell of gloom.

Sumnima's final exam results came out at the end of summer. To her great surprise, she had passed in first division. A celebratory mood prevailed in the house. Tamule ji, who had been steeling himself for the worst, lit lamps and offered a prayer of gratitude at a temple. They distributed sweets in the neighbourhood and hosted a dinner for close relatives. Everyone heaped congratulations on Sumnima and called her 'our Doctor Saab', reminding her that if a Matwali doctor was rare as gold, a Matwali woman doctor was rarer than a diamond. Her parents began to explore medical colleges across the country and took stock of their property. Sumnima basked in their praise and attention. First division, that too without having to grovel before Balram Sir. Her battered self-confidence began to reassert itself. She felt ready for the long journey ahead; her future, brilliant and worthy, seemed almost within her grasp.

Epilogue

Sumnima entered a residential medical college on the outskirts of Kathmandu. During her second year, when she was home on a weekend break, she came across Sagar again. She sat in her room flipping through a newspaper when his face leapt out at her from one of its pages. The weekly section showcased a wide range of local celebrities—philanthropic businessmen, rich and gifted housewives, writers and artists, empowered women bankers, successful Nepalis from the diaspora, and fresh graduates of American colleges eager to 'do something' for their homeland. The picture showed him sitting at a restaurant table with an open laptop, a mobile phone and a tall iced drink garnished with a lemon wedge. Despite his summery appearance, his face looked solemn, as though burdened with a great, unresolved question. The article described him as a 'conflict expert, writer and filmmaker' who divided his time between the United States and Nepal. At this time he was in Nepal to make a documentary film about the Maoist insurgency raging across the country. 'I want to capture the plight of innocent citizens caught between the army and the Maoists.' Even to a politically naïve person like Sumnima, this sounded a little stale. She read the article again, her heart pounding with a strange mixture of emotions. It seemed almost absurd that the man in the picture, with his big round knowing eyes, once had such absolute hold over her. She wondered how his life might have unfolded over the years. Had he married and become a family man? Or was he still a self-described 'vagabond'? Staring at his picture she realized how completely his magic had worn off. Her heart felt so empty now, so bereft of passion that she could not help remembering their doomed affair with a wistful yearning. Those days of feverish joy and pain, those moments of reckless intensity. Her present world seemed drab and insipid in comparison. She had no boyfriend or close friends in Kathmandu. Her classmates at the medical college were utterly sparkless—too compliant towards authority, too doggedly studious, or too competitive to offer any possibility of adventure or romance. Numa was in Australia, attending college in the daytime and working evening shifts at a restaurant. Kathmandu may have been bursting with people, cars, restaurants and malls, but to Sumnima the city felt desolate. Bhaisichaur, despite its cyber hubs and shopping marts, felt like a pathetic little backwater.

Only one thought energized Sumnima. As soon as she completed her MBBS, she would apply for a residency programme in America, the country that had become her new reference point. She could describe its universities, shopping malls, famed landmarks and fast-food outlets as though she'd already been there. Once in a while she received a call from Rajan mama. He was in Texas, working at a petrol pump (or 'gas station' as they called it) owned by some Pakistanis. 'They're better than Indians,' he'd said with conviction. He seemed proud, but also a little concerned, that his children now spoke and behaved 'exactly like Americans.' Like everyone else, he warned Sumnima against remaining stuck in poor, unstable, war-torn Nepal.

The situation in the country was going downhill. In one of the most dramatic events in decades, the entire royal family had been massacred earlier that year. Sumnima and her friends had watched the news at their hostel, all of them in a state of petrified shock, tears streaming from their eyes. Some of the boys in her class had shaved their heads to mourn the dead. According to the official narrative, the crown prince had machine-gunned his family members in a drunken rage before turning the gun on himself. But most people did not believe it, and several books of conspiracy theory had already hit the market. Violence had increased since the new king came to power. The Maoists now controlled large parts of the countryside. The Royal Nepal Army had been unleashed across the villages, and reports of killings, torture and disappearances had become widespread. Although the war was being fought in the countryside, Sumnima was not entirely shielded from its impact. The strikes and shutdowns often resulted in the surprise cancellation of classes, and spared her the ordeal of travelling to the outlying villages to practice community diagnosis. But the roadblocks also caused a shortage of essentials and disrupted daily life. The armed checkpoints around the valley and the sight of armed guards patrolling the city made Sumnima uneasy. At home, the flow of relatives from Lungla had increased. Many of them, especially young men, had been fleeing the village since the Maoists began their recruitment drive. Whenever she came home from college, she saw at least one or two of them camping in Numa's room, their pitiful bags and bundles arranged neatly against the wall covered with posters of American rock stars.

The relatives came in large groups and slept on old mattresses in the TV room. Even Ganga, who liked having guests from Lungla, found the recent arrivals a nuisance. She was glad her ageing parents were not among them. A year ago, soon after Grandmother died, her family had left the village and moved to a small town in the district centre. They lived in a two-storey brick house with a corrugated tin roof. Her older brother Chandrey now worked in a factory in Malaysia and sent money home regularly. Ganga sometimes thought of leaving Kathmandu and moving in with her parents, but was afraid of breaking the accustomed rhythm of life at her uncle's home. Besides, as long as one lived in Nepal, one progressed forward by moving into, not away from Kathmandu. If only she could find a job and stand on her own two feet. What jobs hadn't she tried over the past few years. She had packed soil in a local nursery, stood at the counter of a women handicraft shop, made pickles that were put on sale at Fancy Mart, and even opened a momo stall outside Oxford Academy. But whether she was ill starred or lacked some essential life skill, all of her ventures had fizzled out one after another. Marriage seemed like a viable option, but the potential match her relatives had found—a Gurkha lahure based in Brunei—had politely turned her down after learning she hadn't even passed the SLC.

In contrast, Manlahari had been propelling herself forward by dint of sheer will and good fortune. Her husband was in the process of obtaining legal status in Japan. The court case she had filed two years ago had been decided in her favour, bringing her a small plot of land where she planned to build a storefront unit for commercial lease. She had passed her intermediate-level exam and enrolled in a bachelor's program. She visited the Tamule family every month with sugar-free biscuits and vegetable juices for Boju. During meals she discussed real estate and foreign work permits with her uncle, while Ganga shuffled back and forth between the table and stove, ladling extra helpings on their plates in deferential silence. Her resentment towards Manlahari had gradually disappeared into the widening gulf between their destinies. She had become quieter and more religious in recent months. Her dead desires and unspoken grudges seemed to find an outlet in the prayers and bhajans she chanted aloud every morning.

Ganga had taken over Boju's cherished duty because Boju could no longer kneel down before her gods. Her body had become a storehouse of ailments. Diabetes, arthritis, high blood pressure, poor eyesight. As she couldn't climb the stairs, Premkala had installed a separate television in her room. Boju spent her days in front of the television, amid piles of junk that accumulated around her like geological deposits. Curiously, her eroding physical and mental capacity had only intensified her desire to grasp and hoard, and her failing eyesight doubled her appetite for television. She consumed everything that appeared on screen, from movies, documentaries and cooking shows to wrestling matches and fashion parades. Her favourite was an Indian drama serial where a virtuous young woman kept falling victim to the conspiracies of her sisters-in-law. The instant she heard footsteps outside her door, Boju would stop the passerby and make them watch TV with her, providing a running commentary on the show. Everyone in the house, including Ganga, had fallen into the habit of walking on tiptoes around Boju. The television was now her most loyal companion, a window into the world that was slipping from her grasp. If power went out in the middle of a show, she would twist her face and yell, 'Bastards, where do they send all the electricity? Into their mother's hole?'

Premkala would hear her upstairs and wearily shake her head. She was tired of her mother's obscenities and infirmities, tired of her husband's people landing in her house every so often, tired of the blockades and price hikes. The headlines about the killings and abductions in the villages disturbed her peace every morning. A week ago, the headmistress had turned down her request for a raise, saying the war had hampered business. Meanwhile the new hire, a girl her daughter's age, earned double her salary because of her 'good English'. Premkala could not suppress her glee every time the Maoist student union forced private schools to close down. The headmistress had now joined a club of wealthy school proprietors in their campaign to declare schools a 'zone of peace'. Premkala wished she could quit teaching altogether, but having learned no other trade, felt permanently stuck in her career. Some days she imagined moving to a clean and prosperous country on the other side of the world, a place without civil unrest and daily hardship, a place free from the demands of extended family and community, where one could live a guilt-free life simply by looking after one's home and garden. But moving to such a place would also mean having to suffer all kinds of indignities. She did not envy her brother. He spent his days pumping fuel into strangers' cars while his wife fed and carried and picked up after entitled

American kids. If only she could get another job...

'Budi, no matter where you go, a job is a job, not a carnival,' Tamule ji would say. He had recently won a small trophy for completing ten years of service at GIDC. He was grateful for the recognition although the job may have sapped his energy and clogged his brain with aid jargon—poverty reduction, capacity building, awareness raising, gender mainstreaming, social mobilization, and of late, conflict resolution and peacebuilding. GIDC had closed its offices in most of the districts for security reasons, and the staff rarely travelled outside Kathmandu. Tamule ji sat at his desk all day, mostly reading newspapers or playing Solitaire, and yet arrived home drained and beaten down. With so many relatives around, he could not even soothe his nerves with imported scotch. If he shared it, his stock would dry up in no time, whereas drinking alone would make him guilty, compounding the feelings of guilt already weighing him down—his old guilt over marrying a non-Tamule woman, his chronic guilt over the hard and destitute lives of his kinfolk, his occasional guilt over lacking a son who would carry on his lineage, and his fresh guilt over failing his final duty to his mother.

His mother's picture now hung on his bedroom wall beside his father's. She had died at a time when the entire village was reeling from the shock of Dammar's death. Rai kaka insisted his son was innocent, that he'd never been a Maoist. He was only a minor ethnic activist fighting for the long-denied rights of his people, the Matwali ethnic groups who now defined themselves as the Adivasi Janajati, indigenous nationalities of Nepal. But according to Birkha Sir, the old headmaster, Dammar had joined the Maoists like hundreds of other Janajati men and women, for the Maoists too were fighting for the oppressed caste and ethnic groups. Whatever the reason, the police had murdered the boy in cold blood. The night before Tamule ji's mother passed away, they had dragged Dammar out of his house, taken him to the nearby forest and shot him dead. No one knew who tipped off the police. Fear and suspicion had gripped the village in the wake of the incident. Tamule ji had heard the news only three days later as the Maoists had destroyed the telecommunications tower in the district. In such an atmosphere he could not travel to Lungla to perform his mother's last rites. Yet again, the great responsibility had fallen on his brother's shoulders. But once the situation became normal, he would go back and build something as a tribute to her memory. A resting shed by the trail along Gurase Danda, or a water tap, or perhaps a small community hall for public events...

Such were the thoughts drifting through Tamule ji's mind as he sat on his verandah drinking tea on a restful Saturday morning. All around him he could see houses piled upon houses, an expanding jumble of concrete blocks. Rooftop water tanks, half-built pillars and parapets, dish antennas, a Buddhist prayer flag fluttering on a terrace, clothes hung out to dry in the sun, an iron cross on a residential building that housed a new church. At Oxford Academy they were adding a fifth storey that would block the last beam of sunlight that entered his house. Devi and her husband had sent both their sons to Korea and rented their ground floor out to a sekuwa joint frequented by drunks. The grazing pasture and the open field had been wiped out. The neighbourhood children played on the side road, grudgingly giving way to oncoming cars. The peepal tree near the Mahadev temple had been cut down. In its place stood a massive hoarding board that advertised a new housing colony in town. Identical white buildings that stood in symmetrical rows. The large complex included a swimming pool, a gym, twenty-four-hour water and electricity supply, and twenty-four-hour security. A cluster of images offered glimpses of family life guaranteed at the complex. The mother stood smiling in a fully equipped kitchen, her face pasty with makeup; the father, all suited and booted, relaxed on a leather couch, his briefcase on the floor; and the children paddled in the pool with white, blond-haired playmates. *'Beverly Hills Apartments, classy living for classy people, the blissful abode of your dreams.'*

Acknowledgments

I owe an immense debt of gratitude to Manjushree Thapa, who read an earlier draft of the manuscript and provided incredibly thoughtful and useful feedback.

My sister Subha has been a constant and indispensable source of ideas and inspiration, and kept me going when my energy seemed to flag.

Sepideh Bajracharya, Sandhya Banskota, Juliet Case and Sristi Bhattarai read an initial draft of the manuscript many years ago. I'm grateful to each of them for their advice and friendship.

My editors Anurag Basnet and Aruna Ghose at Speaking Tiger for their valuable support and encouragement.

Prawin Adhikari, Jemima Sherpa, Prashant Jha and Bhaskar Gautam have each helped in one way or another in bringing this book to fruition.

Sharareh Bajracharya and my sisters Prashanti and Nubha for their advice on various aspects of the book and for all the love and laughter.

Aditya Adhikari for reading the manuscript at different stages, for our daily conversations and for being a perfect companion overall.

Lastly, I'm grateful to my parents and all other family members (the Ghales, the Rais & the Adhikaris) for their love and support and to all my friends old and new, near and far, for enriching my world.